# BLOOD ON THE BONES

*Geraldine Evans titles available from*
*Severn House Large Print*

Absolute Poison
Bad Blood
Dying for You
Up in Flames

# BLOOD ON THE BONES

**Geraldine Evans**

**Severn House Large Print**

London & New York

This first large print edition published 2008
in Great Britain and the USA by
SEVERN HOUSE PUBLISHERS of
9-15 High Street, Sutton, Surrey, SM1 1DF.
First world regular print edition published 2006 by
Severn House Publishers, London and New York.

British Library Cataloguing in Publication Data

Evans, Geraldine
  Blood on the bones. - Large print ed. - (The Rafferty and
  Llewellyn series)
  1. Rafferty, Joseph (Fictitious character) - Fiction
  2. Llewellyn, Sergeant (Fictitious character) - Fiction
  3. Police - Great Britain - Fiction 4. Detective and
  mystery stories 5. Large type books
  I. Title
  823.9'14[F]

  ISBN-13: 978-0-7278-7663-8

Printed and bound in Great Britain by
MPG Books Ltd, Bodmin, Cornwall.

For George,
who's always been there for me

# One

'*Nuns?*'

As Detective Inspector Joseph Rafferty considered what his DS, Dafyd Llewellyn, had said, he was filled with so many emotions he was momentarily incapable of voicing any further words. Which was probably just as well.

But while he waited for one emotion to gain ascendancy, he surreptitiously palmed and pocketed the letter he had received in that morning's post. Even though he had read and re-read it a dozen times, its contents still made him go cold all over. He had been worrying about it all day and had yet to decide on a response.

Now, after the news which Llewellyn had so calmly delivered, he knew he had to put the letter out of his mind. His sergeant was still standing in front of him, presumably expecting some further response and eyeing him as if he was an exhibit in one of the museums he and his new wife Maureen preferred instead of having a good laugh in the pub like the rest of the team. Rafferty

7

didn't know which of the morning's two messages was the worst: the paper one the postman had delivered or the verbal one Dafyd had just presented to him. For the moment he was forced to put on a brave face about the latter one at least, and be thankful that neither Llewellyn nor anyone else knew anything about what the postman had brought. So, although dismayed at Llewellyn's news, and not feeling much like it, Rafferty forced the disbelieving grin that he knew was expected, gazed at Llewellyn's serious, thinly handsome face, and asked, with little expectation of an affirmative reply, 'You're having a laugh. Right?'

But when Llewellyn – never one of the Essex station's jokers at the best of times – simply stood impassively, his intelligent brown gaze patient as he waited for Rafferty to face up to this latest dilemma, Rafferty added on a plaintive note, 'Aren't you?'

Llewellyn shook his head and, with the merest hint of empathy visible in his eyes, added, 'The Mother Superior of the Carmelite Monastery of the Immaculate Conception rang the emergency services to report that one of the sisters had found a body buried in a shallow grave in their grounds. PCs Green and Smales were despatched. They've just radioed through to confirm that there *is* a body at the location. One that's been partially disinterred.'

He paused, clearly awaiting some further

8

response. And when Rafferty remained silent, he added quietly, 'It's the Roman Catholic convent out past Tiffey Reach and Northway.'

Unwillingly, as though to do so would confirm that which he would rather not have confirmed, Rafferty nodded a gloomy acknowledgement. 'I know where it is.'

But even as he made this despondent reply, a far more likely explanation for the body's presence in the convent's grounds occurred to him and he brightened considerably. Maybe he would, after all, be able to escape heading up an investigation into the nuns' just-discovered cadaver. The thought was a cheering one. 'Most likely the body of one of the nuns from way-back-when, who died from natural causes,' he told Llewellyn, unable to hide the relief his deductions had brought him. 'Seems to me that such holy ladies, what with their vows of poverty and all, would be likely to have given their dear departed only simple interments years ago. Such burials would certainly save them plenty of the old moolah.'

Llewellyn let him down gently. 'I think not, sir. For one thing, Constable Lizzie Green said the corpse was wearing a man's watch, and one that looked expensive. And for another, from what they were able to see of the skull, she said it looked as if it had sustained damage consistent with a blow of some sort. And then, there was no coffin.

The body was just laid naked in the earth. I don't think a group of holy and modest nuns would give one of their number such a casual burial, do you?'

Rafferty didn't. But unwilling to be so quickly deprived of his escape clause, he muttered, 'Maybe he just genuflected too low in a bout of over-enthusiastic religious fervour and bashed his brains out on a stone floor.' But even as he uttered the thought, he accepted that he was just clutching at straws like some desperate yokel. Llewellyn's next words confirmed this suspicion.

'The damage was to the back of the skull, not the front, according to Constable Green, and was inflicted with sufficient force for the victim to suffer severe trauma.'

He's not the only one, thought Rafferty morosely, after Llewellyn had revealed the latest details of what, as he had said, sounded horribly like a suspicious death. One, moreover, that was after all destined to turn into *his* investigatory baby.

'Lizzie Green said they've secured the scene and will await our arrival and that of the Scene of Crime team and the pathologist.'

Rafferty nodded absently, but said nothing. He was miles – years – away. Back in the south London boyhood that had not been improved by religion's harsh, unforgiving hand. Some of those old Catholic teachers certainly knew how to administer a caning.

And he should know, having been on the receiving end more times than he could count. Strange that all that praying didn't manage to make them kinder human beings, he thought. Why, he remembered ... But Llewellyn's voice dragged him back from his unpleasant memories.

'Sir?'

The addition of the question mark to Llewellyn's address wasn't lost on Rafferty. He put his reverie behind him for long enough to go, 'Mm?'

'Would you like me to contact Dr Dally and the Scene of Crime team, or will you do it?'

Rafferty waved a hand. 'You do it.' No way did he want to give Sam Dally a chance to laugh at his predicament. Certainly not until he'd figured out how he was going to handle it. He gazed into space as Llewellyn turned his back and picked up a phone. 'Nuns,' he muttered again, under his breath this time. What were a bunch of penguin-dressers doing getting mixed up in a suspicious death?

And what had *he* done to deserve getting dumped with a case in a Roman Catholic convent? he asked himself self-pityingly. Of all the locations for their latest corpse to turn up, this really was Divine punishment at its most inspired. Any location that held even a sniff of Catholicism was normally a place to be given a wide berth by the long since and

11

gladly-lapsed Rafferty. It was grim to think he'd now have to *voluntarily* return to his religious roots.

Then he gave a fatalistic shrug. One thing at least: the nuns' cadaver would help take his mind off his unwelcome letter, if only insofar as a second trauma lessens the pain of the first.

It was some minutes later, after several low and discreet exchanges, when Llewellyn put the phone down and turned round.

'I managed to contact Dr Dally,' he reported. 'He's confirmed he'll shortly make his way to the scene.'

Rafferty nodded grimly. 'I bet he can't wait. I could hear him laughing from here.'

Llewellyn refrained from making any comment on Dally or his amusement and just continued. 'The SOCOs are also on their way.' Quietly, he added, 'As I suppose we ought to be.'

As his sergeant walked to the door and held it open, Rafferty's fatalism wore off. Now his mouth drooped downward as if he'd suffered a mini stroke. But the only stroke he'd suffered was another one from a supposedly loving God. Morosely, he thought: Oh, let joy be unconfined. Because, between his unwelcome letter and the news of the suspicious death at the local RC convent, Rafferty knew deep down to his lapsed Catholic soul, that Sam Dally wasn't the man not to make the most of his opportunity. Purgatory awaited. Several sources of Purgatory, in fact.

And as Llewellyn said 'Shall we go?', Rafferty knew that these several Purgatories were impatient for his arrival.

He shrugged heroically, like a man with an urgent appointment with the hangman, and said, 'Why not?' Even though he could think of a round dozen reasons 'why not', he mentioned none of them.

Instead, slowly, as though doom really did dog his heels, he rose from his chair, grabbed his jacket against the lowering October skies, and followed Llewellyn from the office to meet his fate, muttering *'Nuns!'* in tones of growing horror as he went, and fingering the letter in his pocket that seemed so hot with threat that he imagined he could feel it burning its way through the material of his jacket to singe his flesh.

Certainly, that morning's letter had already made his day far from pleasant. The suspicious death in the Catholic convent seemed likely to complete the job the letter had started. He only hoped he'd enjoyed whatever murky sins he'd indulged in a previous life. Because whatever sins he had committed in that incarnation, he suspected he was shortly to pay for them in *this* one.

# Two

The rich black soil had been disturbed, by a fox or some other scavenging animal, Rafferty assumed. Its scavenging had exposed the left arm of the corpse in its shallow grave. It was over this limb that one of the nuns had stumbled as she walked in the convent's grounds, head presumably bent over some devotional book.

The fast-fading light of the mild early October evening would have provided a gentler, more welcome illumination. Denied such gentleness by the powerful police lighting that left nothing to the imagination, Rafferty stared at the grave and the stark and gruesome remains of the partially disinterred corpse. Its pared-to-the-bone white forearm protruded from the earth and pointed accusingly to the sky, as if blaming the Almighty.

But even Rafferty couldn't blame the Almighty for the fact of the man's death or its location. It had been a human hand, not that of God, which had struck the killing blow and then set about concealing the body.

The bite marks left by the snacking fox were clearly visible on the bones of the forearm above the heavy, man's watch with its cracked glass. Even after its immersion in the damp soil, it was still possible to see that the watch had been an expensive one, as PC Lizzie Green had said. Maybe it had been a gift and would have an inscription on the back marking some birthday or wedding anniversary?

Rafferty supposed he could hope that the latter proved to be true. But he wasn't about to bank on it.

The hands of the watch had stopped at twelve o'clock, he noted. Twelve noon? Or twelve midnight? he wondered. Had the man been killed at the witching hour, when handsome princes once again became frogs and smart carriages metamorphosed back to pumpkins? This man would be returning to nothing but the soil, and oblivion. Ashes to ashes, dust to dust. A tiny shiver passed through Rafferty at the thought. Unless, that was, Paradise existed and he was one of the Chosen, in which case the immortals had already claimed him as their own and left his soul's shell for them.

But the religious incantations for this man's death would certainly have to wait, even if some god or devil had already whisked his soul off to eternal reward or punishment. And as his fingers thrust into his jacket pocket and he touched that morning's letter, Rafferty was unwillingly reminded of its existence. The discovery of the convent's cadaver had brought only a temporary amnesia and again his fingers drew back as if they, perhaps like the deceased, felt the flames of Lucifer's hellish pit. The letter and the threats inherent in the writer's taunting words would also have to wait, he reminded himself. Because before he was again likely to find the solitude necessary to consider a possible course of action, he had another investigatory show to get on the road. And before religious rites, eternal dust, *or* his letter could demand attention, Rafferty knew that their well-murdered cadaver wasn't the only body likely to be subjected to indignities at the hands of Sam Dally.

Rafferty jerked his head at Llewellyn. They walked away from the shallow grave, leaving more room for the scene of crime team and Lance Edwards, the photographer, to do their work. They followed the tape-marked path already set up by Lizzie Green and Tim Smales in order to keep the trampling and contamination of the gravesite to a minimum. Ducking under the outer tape, Rafferty nodded a 'well done' to young Smales as he marked them down on his clipboard as leaving the scene. He and Lizzie Green had made a good job of securing the grave site. Timothy Smales was finally growing into the job, Rafferty realized. He no longer sulked if given a task he didn't fancy. He just gritted

16

his teeth and got on with it. But then he'd had a good teacher. The best, most experienced teeth-gritter in the station, was Rafferty's thought, and his teeth ground together even harder as his several-stranded future opened itself uninvitingly before him. Once again he forced himself to put one of these strands out of his mind and concentrate on the latest problem; at least, he thought, unlike the other, murder was within his compass and might therefore be open to a reasonably speedy resolution.

Lizzie Green, as the more experienced officer, had, after getting Smales organized into securing the scene, also ensured that Sister Rita, the nun who had found the body, was kept isolated so she couldn't confide anything more about the corpse than she might have already revealed to the rest of the religious community. As Smales had confirmed on their arrival, the nun was being kept suitably cloistered by Lizzie until Rafferty and Llewellyn were ready to speak to her.

Rafferty gazed around him, studying the scene. All round the eight-foot-high walls surrounding the convent's grounds clung the evergreen pyracantha, a climber with sharp thorns currently wearing the brilliant scarlet berries of autumn. He had been careless and had already experienced the sharpness of the thorns for himself. He had a gash across the back of his hand to prove it and to remind

17

him to be more wary in future.

If the vicious talons of the firethorn weren't enough of a barrier to intruders, in front of the climbers were grouped the equally thorny berberis. The rich red and maroon of its leaves concealed many little stiletto-sharp barbs. Together, these two razor-edged plants could usually be expected to deter even the most determined would-be burglar.

Rafferty wondered how many of the local villains appreciated that the high walls and all that thorny security were indicative, not of the rich plunder awaiting the more daring thief, but only of the nuns' desire to be shut away from the world.

Because, of course, there weren't any riches. Or at least none of the sort likely to be appreciated by Elmhurst's more light-fingered residents. Unlike so much of the rest of the Catholic Church, with its fabulous Vatican, bishops' palaces and extravagant, priceless and glorious art, the sisters lived simply. As Rafferty had noticed on his arrival and passage through the community's home, their lives were austere in the extreme. They truly embraced their poverty instead of applying mere lip service to it. He found it quite humbling. But as he knew that such an emotion was unlikely to be helpful at the start of the inquiry, he glanced at Llewellyn and asked, 'First thoughts, Daff?'

Llewellyn hesitated and Rafferty instead

18

supplied his own first thoughts. 'Under other circumstances, I'd have strong suspicions that this was an inside job, given the height of the walls and the other deterrents. But—'

'But even you find it hard to conceive of holy nuns being guilty of murder?'

Rafferty shrugged. 'Something like that, I suppose.' But it wasn't even that, not really. He knew the religious had over the years gone in for plenty of violent acts against people who disagreed with them; they were still at it in the twenty-first century. He supposed the current lot of Catholic Holy Joes and Josephines were as capable of violence as their counterparts in other religions.

No, he thought, it was more a case that man needed *something* to believe in, something to hold on to in a world where change tended to be too rapid and way too ugly. He smiled. 'We'd better start from the basic fact that the sisters are all human beings first and nuns second, and proceed from there.'

Llewellyn nodded, presumably pleased by the rare logic encompassed in his inspector's pronouncement.

Rafferty sank into contemplation. From where he stood, he could see the entirety of the convent's extensive rear grounds. But if the detached house with its large garden was the sisters' one extravagance, it was a necessary one, because the building was home to a community of women, although he was not

19

yet certain of the precise numbers. The spacious grounds, too, were essential for a group of women who were almost entirely self-sufficient.

The body and its shallow grave had been found by the right-hand side wall, close to what Rafferty had taken to be a shed, but which Llewellyn had discovered was one of the convent's two hermitages, where the sisters could pray in solitude. Small and without any form of heating that Rafferty had been able to discern, they must be as cold as charity in the depths of winter. He could only suppose God kept the sisters warm, in spirit at least, if not in body.

The convent's small apple and pear orchard, heavy with ripe fruit, was between the right-hand side wall and the wall facing the back of the house. A large glasshouse, shed and soft fruit plot were near the centre of the grounds. The vegetable plot, at the back of which was to be found the second hermitage, took up almost the whole of the left-hand side of the grounds.

Next, Rafferty directed his attention fifty yards away, towards the main building of the Carmelite Monastery of the Immaculate Conception, just in front of which a little gaggle of brown-habited, black-veiled nuns, were observing with horrified fascination the scene of crime team at work.

The SOCOs moved slowly, deferentially almost, as if they were observing some religious rite of their own, one that required an attention as rapt as a nun's devotions. Which it did, of course, if they were to miss no possible clue as to who had placed their cadaver in the soil.

As Rafferty watched, Mother Catherine, the Prioress or, as he thought of her, the Mother Superior, to whom he had spoken briefly on his arrival, made her brisk way across the grass from the main building to where the other nuns were standing. As the sun fought its way briefly through the increasingly dark clouds, it glinted on her tinted spectacles and seemed to galvanize her into action. She clapped her pitifully scarred hands and, with a flapping motion, as if encouraging a flock of unruly chickens to take roost for the evening, tried to persuade the gaping nuns back to their duties. But such was the sisters' goggle-eyed fascination with this dramatic departure from their normal routine that her silent entreaties met with only a limited response.

The dead man could count himself a lucky corpse in one way, Rafferty reflected in the brief moments before the lapsed nature of his Catholicism caught up with him once more. Since the body had been found in the grounds of the RC convent, whether he had been a sinner or not, whether he wanted them or not, whether he was a believer or not, he would have prayers in plenty for his soul's passing.

21

Rafferty didn't feel quite so blessed. He disliked being forced to face his Catholic demons – if such they could be called. Neither did he like being obliged to call the community's matriarch 'Mother'. He had assumed he had long since put all that religious mumbo jumbo behind him. He never even called his own mother 'Mother'. Well, apart, that was, from when he was trying to display his disapproval for some behaviour of hers and ma was being stroppy – which, come to think of it, was most of the time.

Another thing to be regretted was the fact that, although this was an enclosed order of nuns, which he hoped would limit the potential suspects, they were also a silent, contemplative order; their days, and a fair chunk of their nights too, he presumed, were given over to prayer. How on earth could he encourage the usual tittle-tattle that was so invaluable to a police investigation if none of the usual tittle-tattling gender indulged?

However, the Prioress, Mother Catherine, seemed to consider that the current unique circumstances warranted a breach of the rule of silence, for when the sisters, being as full of curiosity as the rest of humanity, failed to obey her flapping commands, she supported her arm signals with orders of the vocal kind. Rafferty heard her voice carry clearly as she admonished her charges.

'A little Christian charity, if you please,

sisters. A man – a child of Christ – is dead. He is entitled to some dignity in death, not to be stared at in his nakedness by women who should know better. Come. We must pray for his immortal soul.'

'Amen to that,' Rafferty muttered, thankful she was taking her flock off before he was obliged to order her to do so. He always hated to have an audience at a scene of crime. Though it amused him that she had just assumed the dead man was a follower of Christ. For all she or any of them knew, in life he might have prayed to Buddha or some other deity. Or no one at all, of course, which, in an increasingly irreligious Britain, was probably the most likely option.

Beside him, he felt Llewellyn stir as if in disapproval of his flippant remark and he glanced at him. But, although Llewellyn didn't say anything, he didn't have to. Apart from his ma, Rafferty had never met anyone who could convey disapproval or irritation with just a few almost imperceptible shifts of facial muscles. But while Llewellyn's subtlety was a natural part of him, Rafferty's ma's was not. As a mother of six, she had discovered the hard way that shouting was mostly counter-productive, and along the way she had learned to conserve her energy.

Llewellyn had never possessed Kitty Rafferty's original, primitive, urge to shout and holler. Sometimes, Rafferty regretted it. He knew where he was with shouting and bawling. It was what he had been used to for so long. He found these subtle manifestations of disapproval harder to counter or defend against.

Rafferty scowled – a far from subtle muscle shift. It was all right for Llewellyn. *His* present location was unlikely to make him feel as off-kilter as it made Rafferty. Flippancy would, he suspected, as he watched the nuns' departure and thought again of the letter in his pocket, be his only crutch in the days and weeks that loomed ahead.

Already – even without the letter and the anxiety it engendered – he was experiencing a sinking feeling in the pit of his stomach. Even here, out in the open, with a fresh breeze scattering the first fallen leaves of autumn, he imagined he could smell the overpowering scent of incense. It was making him feel nauseous. Suffocated, even. And the investigation hadn't even properly begun yet. Of course, that smell was linked in his mind with the Catholic ritual he had so loathed as a child and a youth: the breast-beating of confession; the expectation, no, the *demand*, that one believe without question; the authoritative nature of it all. None of these had appealed even then to the rebellious youthful Rafferty. In his maturity they held even less appeal.

But soon he would need to begin questioning the sisters themselves. And although he was conscious that it wasn't a duty he could shirk indefinitely, it wasn't one he was looking forward to. He had always thought nuns an unnatural species, set apart from the rest of humanity, with whom he suspected he would not find communication easy. Why, he questioned, would any woman voluntarily agree to being shut away from the world, as this enclosed Carmelite order were? He had never understood it, doubted if he ever would, in spite of the fact that he had aunts on both sides of his family who had become Brides of Christ.

How many such Brides did one God need? he wondered. And what on earth did he do with them all?

Briefly, a smile flickered around his lips as humour came to his aid, and he thought that God must by now be finding Heaven a veritable Hell, and must also regret his growing harem, assuming all his Brides, the silent ones and the rest, were allowed to speak once in Heaven. Poor old God must get nagged 24/7.

'Is there something about our latest unfortunate cadaver that amuses you, Rafferty?'

Rafferty emerged from his uneasy musings to find that Dr Sam Dally, the pathologist, had arrived and was struggling to enclose his rotund body in its protective gear. Rafferty's smile faded immediately at the thought that some of his previous blasphemy might have earned him his current reward. 'No,' he replied feelingly. 'Nothing at all is amusing me.' Not *now*, anyway, he added silently to himself.

By now, Lance Edwards, the police photographer, had taken all the shots he needed. The SOCOs had carefully sifted and bagged most of the soil surrounding the body, along with the shucked-off casings of insects with their telling life cycles. And as Rafferty, again acknowledged by Smales, returned to the scene accompanied by Dally and Llewellyn, he saw that the cadaver now lay open to their unhindered scrutiny.

Apart from the indentations made by the animal's bite marks on the skeleton's forearm, even after the usual cycle of insect activity the body still retained a fair amount of flesh, which, Rafferty supposed, indicated that their corpse had not been in the soil for any great length of time.

Whoever had killed and buried him had removed all his clothes, presumably to make identification more difficult if his body should one day be disinterred.

He hadn't been buried too deeply, either, which made the latter event more likely. As the day's events had proved. Strange that the killer had neglected to remove the watch which, although damaged by autumnal damp and the attentions of scavengers, as Rafferty had already noted, still retained sufficient of its original elegance to make clear it had been a costly timepiece.

Perhaps the watch had just been overlooked? Killers invariably made some error in their haste to cover up their crime. And given the number of women in the community and their presumed self-sufficient busyness about the house and grounds, the killer couldn't have had much time to murder his victim, strip and then bury him.

Maybe the watch had been a gift, as an earlier brief burst of optimism had allowed him to hope? Maybe, Rafferty allowed himself another small glimmer of confident expectation, maybe they would get lucky and the watch *would* have an inscription on the back?

Get real, he told himself, as Sam bent his plump body with difficulty over his latest patient and began his examination. Such a nice juicy piece of luck was not likely to fall into *his* lap; certainly not on this case, which was already beginning to feel like some deliberate punishment doled out by the Almighty.

If such it was, the deity was unlikely to make the investigation one easily solved, as Rafferty acknowledged with a sigh.

Beside him, hearing the sigh, and undoubtedly sensing some of Rafferty's lapsed Catholic angst, Llewellyn murmured tentatively, 'I could do the preliminary interviews, if you'd prefer?'

For a moment, for several moments, Rafferty was tempted by the offer. But something, maybe some stray tenet of his lapsed faith, wouldn't permit him to be led into the temptation of the easy option. Not now. And certainly not *here*.

He straightened his back and strengthened his resolve in order to force out the 'No' he wished could be a 'Yes'. He glued on a false smile as he replied, 'Grist for the mill, Dafyd. Grist for the mill for a lapsed lily like me.'

'Maybe,' Llewellyn murmured. 'Or maybe not. I suppose it depends on whether or not one believes one can truly escape one's upbringing.' He paused, then added, 'I believe it was the Jesuits who said: *Give me a child till the age of seven—*'

'*And I will give you the man,*' Rafferty finished for him. 'Yes. I'm familiar with the quotation. And, much as I hate to admit it, those boys knew what they were talking about.'

He rather wished they hadn't. But he was damned if he was going to let himself be spooked by a few nuns' habits and the smell of incense. 'Are we not all brothers and sisters under the skin?' He nodded towards the convent door through which the sisters had disappeared in response to the Mother Superior's admonishments. 'It should be interesting to take a peek under *theirs*.' And at least, this time, unlike his previous unwilling interaction with the Catholic Church, this time *he* would be doing the interrogating.

But, in his current unwelcome situation, Rafferty found this small consolation.

# Three

Trying to encourage within himself some enthusiasm for the task ahead, Rafferty permitted himself no more prevarications. Pausing only to tell Sam Dally to send a uniformed officer to find them when he had finished examining the body, he strode with a brisk step towards the back entrance of the Carmelite Monastery through which the sisters had disappeared, conscious of Llewellyn, like a determined whipper-in, following on behind.

Momentarily forgetting his whipper-in, he muttered the question that had been puzzling him since his arrival at the scene: 'Wonder why it's called a monastery rather than a convent?'

But, of course, the oracle that was the university-educated Llewellyn had heard, and as he moved up to Rafferty's side, he proceeded to enlighten him.

'I believe it's connected to the fact that the Carmelites were originally just a masculine order and—'

Annoyed with himself that he'd carelessly invited a lecture on top of the day's other torments, Rafferty tuned Llewellyn out and studied the building. It was a relatively modern one; Edwardian rather than medieval, from the outside it looked more like a pleasant country home than a house of prayer. The convent that had originally stood on the site had been torn down by Henry VIII in his sixteenth-century wrecking spree of England's religious buildings. Elmhurst's Priory, another casualty of the times, although not razed to the ground like the earlier convent, instead to this day remained an enormous impressive ruin. It provided a stark, rather eerie, welcome to visitors approaching the town from the west.

Rafferty entered the large, echoing rear lobby, its lighting as frugal as only the whole-hearted embrace of poverty could make it. Dimly, through the gloom, he made out three corridors leading off the high-ceilinged hall which was decorated with a statue of the Virgin and Child and three grim pictures of saints suffering assorted martyrdoms. They provided an even less welcoming ambience than did the blackened ruin of the priory.

'Cheerful little gaff,' Rafferty commented, with a gloom that was a perfect match for the hall. 'Don't I just love Catholicism?'

If the rest of the convent was as coffin-dark as the rear lobby, he suspected his wearing of spectacles, adopted for convenience during a previous case, would turn into an adoption of necessity before this case reached its conclusion.

He followed his nose and the dim illumination and, to get his bearings, found again the front entrance with its Latin display of the Carmelite motto beside the no-longer-used 'Turn Room' with its little turntable which had enabled gifts and mail to be accepted while the 'turn sister' remained unseen.

'*Zelo zelatus sum pro domino deo exercituum,*' Llewellyn had read the motto to him on their arrival, and, as expected, had gone on to provide the non-Latin-reader Rafferty with its translation and the explanation: 'It's from the Vulgate or Latin Bible and means: *With zeal have I been zealous for the Lord God of Hosts.*'

'Very nice, I'm sure,' had been Rafferty's response. He had felt an urge to make some sarcastic comment suggesting they ought to produce some zeal themselves, but he had swallowed it.

Now that he'd seen the body buried in the grounds of this house of contemplatives he felt it might be appropriate if he allowed *himself* a few moments for contemplation. And, although aware that he found the life of an enclosed religious community incomprehensible – alien, *surreal*, even – he was aware that he would need to *try* to understand such a vocation if he was to get to grips with this case. Particularly if one of the nuns should turn out to have embraced the violence of some of the Catholic faith's earlier blood-letting adherents and had committed the ultimate sin.

So he read again the Carmel motto, studied again the Shield of Carmel with its groups of three stars which Llewellyn, his personal shedder of light where before had existed only darkness, had already explained, stood for Carmel in its Greek, Latin and Western eras. There was a hand with a torch, which Llewellyn had told him was supposed to remind the community of God's fiery intervention on Mount Carmel at the behest of Elijah.

The twelve surrounding stars symbolized the twelve points of the Rule by which the community lived: obedience, chastity, poverty, recollection, mental prayer, Divine Office, chapter, abstinence, manual labour, silence, humility and works of supererogation – Rafferty hadn't even bothered to seek enlightenment on the latter, words with six syllables being way beyond his desired vocabulary, particularly when they were religious ones.

But now, thinking again of the zeal of which the motto spoke, Rafferty swept past the statue of Saint Teresa of Avila, the sixteenth-century Carmelite reformer, who held the book and pen which, again according to his personal Oracle, symbolized her power as a writer while the arrow-clutching angel at her shoulder depicted God's love.

By now, with all this religious symbolism, Rafferty was getting a serious case of the willies. He hurried down another gloomy corridor, Llewellyn at his heels, and finally found the Mother Superior's office. As he discovered as he flicked on the overhead light, like the rear lobby and the front entrance hall, her office was drab and badly-lit, and lacked physical comfort of any sort. It was simply furnished, with just a basic desk, hard wooden chairs and a battered, presumably second-hand, filing cabinet. Another smaller statue of the Virgin stood in a recess behind the desk. The sparsely furnished room was also empty of any human presence and Rafferty recalled that Mother Catherine had said she and the other nuns must pray for the immortal soul of their now-disinterred cadaver. Presumably, she – and they – was in the community's chapel.

Feeling as if he was on his very own magical mystery tour, every twist and turn of which brought fresh unwanted discoveries, Rafferty flicked the light off and headed back down the corridor to the hall. He tried the second corridor off it as he searched for the chapel. Prayers could wait, he thought. The dead man had, after all, done without them for however long he had lain in that hole in the convent's grounds. And, considering the vastness of eternity, his soul could wait a while longer.

Concerned he was in danger of allowing

the nuns, the oppressive religious aura of the building, and Catholicism's age-old rituals, to intimidate him, Rafferty was keen to stamp his authority on the community from the start. Consequently he stifled any remaining qualms at interrupting the nuns' prayers. And as soon as he found what he thought must be the chapel, he opened the door with an accompanying loud creak.

In an automatic, unthinking reflex action, he found his fingers dipping towards the basin of holy water at the entrance. Alarmed to discover how insidiously lingering was the Catholic indoctrination of his boyhood, he pulled his hand sharply back, aware that Llewellyn was close behind him and could not have failed to notice the jerky movement.

Not without an uneasy sense of guilt, he skirted the basin with its holy water lure, and marched up the central aisle of the surprisingly spacious and airy chapel, his shoes, on the bare wooden flooring that gleamed a warm golden colour from copious quantities of beeswax and elbow grease, sounding like those of the vanguard of an advancing invasion force.

Once he reached the small table that he presumed served as an altar when their priest administered Mass, and fighting the reluctance to use the religious address, he said, 'Sisters,' in as firm a voice as he could muster, one intended to convey that he would brook no challenge to his authority. 'May I please have your attention?'

Slowly, to his left, to his right, ten – no, eleven – heads, in the single pews aligned along the outer walls, were raised from their silent prayers for the dead man. Eleven pairs of eyes studied him. He was grateful the stares weren't accompanied by noisy questions as was usual at the beginning of an investigation.

But his gratitude for the sound of silence faded a few seconds later. Instead, its un-naturalness began to unnerve him. It was a silence so strange in the circumstances in which the community – and he – found themselves, that he continued in a rush.

'I apologize for interrupting your devotions,' he began. 'But as your Prioress observed a short while ago, a man is dead. It was unlikely to have been a natural death.' Anxious and feeling out of his depth, he added acerbically, 'And as it is equally unlikely that he managed to bury himself, this is officially now a murder inquiry.'

Rafferty paused to let this sink in while he scanned the faces. Apart from two young women, one in ordinary clothes and one in the pale veil which told him she must be a novice, the rest were all either middle-aged or elderly and had, according to the Mother Superior to whom he had spoken on his arrival, lived in the Carmelite monastery for two, three or more decades each.

Although the presumably normal calm serenity on the faces of most of the older nuns was marred by nothing more than a mild anxiety conjoined, in a few cases, by an unholy tinge of excitement, the two young women, by contrast, looked scared half to death.

Unsure of the strength of their love for God, Rafferty assumed. Or of His for them. And given God's latest unlovely behaviour towards *me*, he thought, he believed the two young women, would-be nuns or not, would be wise to be unsure of such an unreliable and fickle thing.

He again addressed his little congregation in order to introduce himself and Llewellyn. 'My colleague Sergeant Llewellyn and I will be conducting the investigation. Perhaps, Reverend Mother –' again he forced a religious title past unwilling lips as he turned towards the Prioress, trying not to recoil from the features that had been dreadfully altered by burns – 'you could manage to find a room that could be put at our disposal?'

He waited for her nodded confirmation, then added, 'We will need to question each member of the community to see if any of them are able to shed light on why a man came to be buried in your grounds.'

Slowly, with an immense dignity, Mother Catherine rose from her knees and smoothed her immaculate brown habit. Even through the burns that transformed her face into a grotesque mask of puckered red skin overlaid in parts with an unnatural shade of white, she exuded an astonishing serenity as she prepared to respond to Rafferty's remarks. So unnatural did such serenity seem to Rafferty, that he wondered whether her calm demeanour might not owe more to the numbness of shock than to religious quietude.

'I'm sure, Inspector Rafferty, that if any one of the sisters knew anything about this poor man's death they would have already confided such knowledge to me. They have not done so. Clearly—'

Rafferty interrupted with a smoothness he was far from feeling. 'I'm sure you're right, Reverend Mother,' he told her, again finding the maternal salutation slip unwillingly past his lips. 'But it is surprising how often questioning by experienced police officers uncovers vital evidence, the significance of which has perhaps not previously been appreciated.'

He again glanced over the assembled faces before him: pleasant or severe, rosy or pallid, chubby, emaciated, and every style in between. 'Sisters. Please hold yourselves in readiness for interview. I would prefer it if you all remained here in the chapel until you are called individually for questioning.

'Mother,' he again addressed the Prioress. 'Perhaps we could start with you? If you would accompany me back to your office...?'

Rafferty abandoned his position in front of the simple altar, a position selected for its imbuement of what he had hoped would be a priest-like authority, told Llewellyn to find a female officer to guard the door of the chapel so the remaining nuns didn't wander, and followed the now not-quite-so-serene Mother Superior through the high arched double doors and back down the corridor till they reached her office.

They had barely settled themselves on either side of the plain desk on the wooden chairs that were every bit as uncomfortable as they looked, before Llewellyn arrived. He nodded to confirm that Rafferty's instructions had been carried out, before he sat down quietly and brought out his notebook.

Rafferty smiled uneasily to himself as his glance took in the comfortless room. *Isn't this cosy?* he thought with a determinedly irreligious sacrilege. 'Perhaps, Reverend Mother,' he suggested as he turned back to the Prioress, 'you can let me have a list of the sisters' religious names, along with their original names, dates of birth, last known addresses and family details? I shall also need to know the identity of anyone who had easy access to the con – monastery.'

Mother Catherine's previous serenity was certainly beginning to fray and was clearly tested by his first request. Rafferty became aware that Mother Catherine's gaze, fixed on him from behind the tinted lenses, was now troubled, as if recent events were finally sinking in. And she commented, in a voice in which, although still firm, he could now detect the tiniest tremor of strain, 'Surely, Inspector, you can't suspect a member of our community of being responsible for what happened to that unfortunate man?'

Rafferty shrugged. 'At the moment, Mother, I don't know what I suspect. But as his body was buried here, it seems a possibility that the dead man, his killer, or both, must have had *some* connection with your community, however tenuous that connection might turn out to be.'

She inclined her head in unwilling acquiescence. He didn't add further explanations as he judged, from what little of her expression he could gauge through the dreadful scar tissue, that she had taken his point.

'Very well, Inspector.' She rose and seemed to glide over to the filing cabinet, removing a bunch of keys from a pocket concealed in the depths of her dark robes as she went. After selecting the required key, she unlocked the filing cabinet and removed a number of buff folders. 'These files are, as I'm sure I don't need to tell you, confidential.'

'And will be treated as such,' Rafferty was quick to assure her as she handed them over.

As she resumed her seat, she said, 'As to your other request – this is, as I believe I explained to you earlier, an enclosed order.

As such, no one has easy access. Anyone who wishes to gain admittance must ring the bell at the entrance door, which is always kept locked. Generally, the only visitors permitted are the priest who ministers to us, our GP, nuns from a sister convent, women here on retreat and contemplating the life of a religious and, more rarely, members of the sisters' families.'

Rafferty had taken particular note of the double doors that gave access to the Carmelite monastery and its extensive and quiet grounds. Eight feet high, they were similar to those that opened on to the chapel. Like those doors, the ones guarding the entrance were solid, apart from a nine-inch-square barred grille let into one of them, through which the sisters were able to screen their visitors.

The double doors looked sturdy, capable of repulsing a small army if necessary. The huge lock was equally sturdy and supplemented by some serious-looking bolts, as well as a heavy metal bar that slotted into iron brackets either side of the doors. The entire monastery and its extensive grounds were, as he had already noted, surrounded by an eight-foot-high wall front and back. With its thorny hedging, the Carmelite Monastery struck him as being as enclosed and private as one of Her Majesty's prisons. Without access to the keys getting out would be far from easy, but then, so would getting *in*.

It was a realization that made him uneasy. Because unless one of the holy sisters *had* killed and buried the man, someone else must have managed to get through all their impressive security and gain access to the grounds in order to conceal the victim in his shallow grave, all the while dragging the weighty cadaver of his victim behind him.

A pretty unlikely scenario, was the conclusion Rafferty had already come to and which was contributing to his unease.

'I presume your priest visits regularly?'

The Prioress nodded.

'And what about your GP? I suppose, even nowadays, your doctor makes the occasional home visit? Or does the surgery use a locum service?'

'No, our doctor is very good and still makes home visits.'

'What about other visitors? For instance, have any of the sisters' families or women on retreat visited in – say – the last two months?' he questioned.

She shook her head.

'I'll need to speak to your priest and your GP. Can you please let me have their names?'

'Of course. Our regular priest is Father Kelly of St Boniface, and our GP is Dr Peterson. He's with the group practice in Orchard Street.'

Rafferty barely managed to restrain his

41

astonishment at the discovery that the sisters' human provider of spiritual succour should come in the person of that old reprobate Father Roberto Kelly. Surely, he marvelled, even cloistered as they were, they must have heard something of the priest's reputation as 'the greatest sinner in the parish'?

Father Kelly was scarcely the most appropriate priest to minister to a house of celibate women, even if most of them were by virtue of age beyond being tempted by the sins of the flesh. Not that Rafferty had ever understood how any woman could be tempted by the more-than-discreet charms of the ageing priest.

But, he thought, as he recalled the tinge of excitement he had detected on a few of the sisters' faces at their unaccustomed presence at a murder scene, perhaps even nuns enjoyed having a bit of vicarious spice in their humdrum lives?

For certain it was that Father Kelly came with spice as plentiful and colourful as the entire Indian sub-continent – if Rafferty's ma, who was more than capable of embellishing her stories for effect – could be believed.

But now, with the second part of her information, Mother Catherine surprised him again. And this time, his reaction must have managed to penetrate his 'investigation face', as he liked to call the expressionless poker-faced look he tried, and mostly failed, to adopt during a case.

'Of course, we used to have a female GP, but our old doctor left the practice.' The Mother Superior's scarred face was softened slightly by a faint ironic smile, as she added, 'And, much as it might surprise you to learn, Inspector, even a clutch of mostly ageing nuns is capable of moving with the times. Dr Peterson suits us very well. He is quiet and respects our ways and the times and duration of our daily offices.'

Rafferty nodded and directed his attention to the files in his lap. Quickly he counted them. There were only ten. So where was the eleventh? Was it that of the Mother Superior herself that was missing?

She must have understood his questioning look because she immediately responded to it.

'My file is not kept here, Inspector. It is held at the main diocesan offices. But I can, of course, myself provide you with whatever basic information you might for the moment require.'

She proceeded to do so. Llewellyn took notes. She was born in 1940, which made her sixty-six now, and had first embraced the spiritual life at the age of twenty, taking her life vows seven years later.

Rafferty did a swift calculation and was astonished at the discovery that Mother Catherine had committed herself for life to her vocation in 1967. An incongruous time to find God, he thought, especially as it had coincided with the musical revolution and the era of free love that most of the rest of the country's youth had so enthusiastically embraced.

He supposed this discovery revealed just how strong her vocation must have been. To stand aloof and embrace God when your peers were embracing one another with as much enthusiasm as they embraced cannabis resin and Indian gurus was indicative of a resolve far more sturdy than most.

'And what of your family?' he asked, once he had got over his mathematical surprise. 'After over forty years as a nun, I imagine any contact must be minimal?'

'It's not even that, I'm afraid, Inspector. I have no living relatives remaining to me. My parents were quite old when they had me and I was an only child. Some of the other members of our community are more fortunate, though of course what with house moves, marriage break-ups and the sequestered nature of the life of a nun in an enclosed contemplative order, over the years contact tends to diminish. Especially as friends and family can only visit infrequently. In some ways, I suppose, nuns of our order are lost to their families, some of whom, particularly those not inclined to religion, find it easier to lose their religious relatives in return.'

44

'I see.' He tapped the topmost file. 'So I won't find many family details in these?'

'You will, of course, find a few that are up to date, particularly those of the two youngest members of the community, our novice Sister Cecile and our postulant Teresa Tattersall.'

'A postulant?' Rafferty queried. 'I must admit, I've never understood the difference between the two, though I noticed that one of the young women in the chapel was wearing her own clothes.'

'Postulancy is a way for a woman to test her vocation before making any kind of commitment,' Mother Catherine explained. 'Most who wish to take the veil will spend six to twelve months as postulants, after which, if they and the rest of the community feel this life is right for them, they are dressed as novices. Becoming a fully fledged nun is a far longer process than most people imagine, Inspector. We don't grab naive young girls off the street and bundle them into a habit. In fact, we turn many young girls away and advise them to experience something of the world outside before they consider embracing the life of a nun. It is impossible to decide to make such a commitment without experiencing life and knowing oneself.

'But you were asking about who else's family details are up to date. Of our older sisters, fortunately, not all of their families prefer to put a distance between themselves and a professed family member. For others of our community, we have only the families' names and last known addresses. We do, of course, try to track down next of kin when one of our community dies, but we're not always successful. As I said, beyond our novice and postulant, a few of our sisters have families that have managed to keep in contact over the years. But generally, once one's parents and siblings pass away, cousins, nephews and nieces generally find they are too busy living their lives to think much about the woman who chose to shut herself away from the world.

'Occasionally, I'm sure, the parts of the families that remain do think of their loved ones. But when they realize just how long it is since they last made contact, embarrassment tends to ensure the severing of contact is final. It's probably better that way, as some of the families who do try to keep in contact seem to have difficulty in finding anything to say on their rare visits.'

Rafferty nodded. That he could understand. What could their families talk about after all? Football? The latest episodes of one of the soaps? Hardly. The sisters embraced poverty, chastity and obedience, not the latest tedious doings on *EastEnders*. No wonder the relatives at one remove, such as nieces and cousins, gradually cried off on the visiting. Though even he, who had some-

46

times had cause to wish for a severing with his own family, found it sad, cruel even, that families should be split asunder by the God who had put them together in the first place.

His too-expressive face must have betrayed some of his thoughts, for the Prioress said, 'I suspect, Inspector, that you, like so many people, share the belief that to enter the cloister is to waste one's life. To run away from it, even. Am I right?'

Rafferty didn't attempt to deny it. It *was* what he had always thought.

The Prioress didn't appear offended by his antagonism to their lifestyle. On the contrary, she admitted, it was a common response.

'Common, but misconceived. I've always felt that the general public's conception of nuns as "running away" from life is a strange notion in many ways. Especially when you think that, unlike in the world, a nun has no chance to avoid facing up to her own weaknesses and problems.' She paused briefly, as though seeking examples.

But Rafferty thought it likely she had outlined such examples many times to sceptics such as himself and would have little need to think about them. Certainly, once she began, she appeared to require no pause for reflection.

'In the outside world, if you don't want to face up to something, there are always distractions. For instance, one can go to the cinema for some Hollywood escapism. Or to a concert and let the music drown your thoughts. Or, for a different kind of drowning, you can turn to alcohol or drugs. In the world, you can drown out an inability to cope with life by filling your every waking moment with non-stop clamour.'

Rafferty stirred uncomfortably as he recognized himself in her words. He had often used the clamour of life to ignore things he didn't want to face up to. Alcohol had often featured prominently, too.

'Imagine a world, if you can, Inspector, with your busy life, where silence mostly prevails. A world where, after nine thirty or ten o'clock every evening, you will not communicate with another soul but God and your conscience till after breakfast the next day. A world where you can't pop out to the cinema or the pub to distract yourself from disturbing thoughts. No, in a nun's world, there really is no "running away", so one must learn to face up to things if one is to be at peace with oneself.'

She faltered for a moment, as if she had forgotten the script, but then continued with the admission, 'It's not a calling that many can survive. The discipline of such a life is what causes most novices to give up. Some have to be encouraged to see that they are not suited to the life and are asked to leave. That's why the time spent in preparation for taking one's life vows is such a long and demanding one: seven years or longer, mostly.

'But for those who can take the life, a convent is a joyful place to be because each person has chosen to be there. Not only chosen the life, but been forced to consider their choice, not once, but many times. A nun is asked to question her choice and then to choose it again.'

A smile flickered briefly across her poor scarred face. 'I often think that marriages in the world would be better, happier and of longer duration, if all would-be marital partners were required to question their choice as rigorously. But most of the time, young married couples really have little idea of what they're getting into. Little understanding of what they've "chosen".

'We *do* understand our choice. We have taken our free will and made a positive choice, fully aware of all the pros and cons. By the time a nun is ready to take her life vows she has been encouraged to question her commitment time and time again until all uncertainty is gone. Committed nuns have found what they are meant to do with their lives. And even if we can rarely see our families, we have God and each other. It is enough. Such certainty is glorious.'

Her description of her life and that of the other professed sisters, made Rafferty feel envious of such certainty. He was so full of uncertainties about so many things that he found it impossible to grasp a life that held such a total lack of doubt.

His only certainty – with regard to work, at least – was that if he failed to find some answers to all *his* questions during the course of this investigation, Superintendent Bradley or 'God', Rafferty's personal all-powerful super being, would cast a very large dark shadow over his life. The thought reminded him he had much yet to do. It seemed it was a thought the Prioress had discerned for herself.

'But I apologize. I didn't mean to give you a lecture.' She became brisk. 'Now, per-haps we should get on?' Mother Catherine returned to the dictation of her personal details for Llewellyn, quickly supplying her original name and that of her family, along with the last address she had for them. She removed a cheap A4 lined pad from the desk drawer and quickly wrote a few lines.

'I have put down the address and tele-phone number of the diocesan office which holds my records as well as the name of the person responsible for them.'

Mother Catherine had been called Erica Jardine, Rafferty noted, and her now de-ceased family had come from the north of England, near York. But in the intervening years any trace of a Yorkshire accent had vanished as surely as had her previous life.

Rafferty nodded acknowledgement of this information and turned to other matters.

'What about keys to the convent?' he now asked. 'How many are there and where are they kept?'

Mother Catherine responded by raising the large key ring that he had already noted and which she carried about with her. 'We have two sets. This is one of them.'

'You always carry it on your person?'

She nodded. 'Except when I'm in bed. Then it hangs from the inside doorknob of my cell.'

'You said there was another set. Where is it kept?'

'In the key cupboard in the back lobby.'

'This key cupboard – I take it it's kept locked?'

Mother Catherine looked surprised at his question. 'No. Of course it's not kept locked. We only keep them all together in the cupboard so we know where to find them and where to replace them. We are all devout people here, Inspector. We see no need to lock things away.'

She paused and gave a faint smile as if she appreciated the irony of what she had just said and corrected herself. 'Or perhaps, I should say, that the only things we lock away are ourselves and files containing information of a confidential nature. Why would anyone want to take the spare keys?'

So they could gain access to the convent, he could have said. Such as when they needed a convenient time, when the sisters were otherwise occupied in the chapel, to bury a body. But the Mother Superior was an intelligent woman. She could work out the answer to her question herself once she had got past the difficulty of realizing that not everyone with legitimate, regular and knowledgeable access to the convent was necessarily as trustworthy as they might appear.

'I'd like to see this key cupboard, Mother,' he said. It must be kept in an unobtrusive place, he thought. He hadn't noticed it in the back lobby as they had returned from the rear grounds and the scene of the crime.

'Very well.' She rose from her seat. 'If you will follow me. Though I'm sure your implication is groundless. The spare keys will still be where they are meant to be.'

They weren't. They all peered into the dark key cabinet in the little cubby-hole round the corner from the main part of the back lobby. The hook with the label above it saying Spare Keys, was empty.

'But—' Mother Catherine frowned as she stared at the empty key hook. 'But how can this be? Where can the spare set have gone?'

Where indeed? Rafferty was surprised that the key was missing. Or rather, he supposed, he was surprised that it was *still* missing. Given that the victim had certainly died some weeks earlier, whoever had taken it – presuming they were also the murderer – had had ample time to get a copy and replace the spare. So why hadn't the murderer done so as soon as he'd accomplished the interment of his victim?

Rafferty noticed he was using the masculine pronoun. For the first time, he began to believe he might be right to do so. Before, he had believed that Father Kelly and Dr Peterson, although being regularly admitted to the convent because of their callings, had lacked easy access and had still to gain permission for entry, the same as any other would-be visitor. But if one of these two gentlemen had taken the spare keys, which both would have had ample opportunity to do, they could now be said to have made a significant rise up the suspect list.

Rafferty, Llewellyn and Mother Catherine all trooped silently back to her office, each appearing deep in thought.

'Perhaps now you would prefer that I left you to look through the sisters' files before you speak to each of them?'

Rafferty nodded and thanked her. 'And about an office for us?'

She nodded and slipped a key off her ring. 'You can use the office next to mine. It's seldom used.' She handed him the key. 'Should you need me for any reason, I will be in the chapel with my sisters, communing with our Heavenly Father and praying that in His divine mercy he will forgive the sins of His children.'

Only the swish of her habit and the tiny click of the door closing behind him told

Rafferty that she had gone. He breathed out on a sigh of relief. He couldn't help it. In spite of Mother Catherine's ready explanation of their calling, nuns still spooked him. The whole place did.

'Right,' he said. 'Let's shift ourselves next door and make a start.' He handed half the files to Llewellyn. Once they had unlocked and settled themselves in the next-door office, he said, 'I don't suppose this place runs to a photocopier, so just jot down the salient details: Date and place of birth, religious name, previous name and last family address. We should, from that, be able to track down anyone we might need to speak to.'

Llewellyn interrupted to correct another assumption. 'Actually, I think you'll find you're behind the times when it comes to the religious life. The sisters have embraced modern technology. They have a photocopier and a fax machine in their general office. According to Constable Green, they even have their own website. But,' Llewellyn picked up his pen and began to note down the information from the files. 'I don't suppose it would be right for us to presume to help ourselves to the sisters' paper and equipment.'

This was a sentiment with which Rafferty was in wholehearted agreement; not being willing for the Catholic Church to think his embrace of their equipment meant he was

54

ready or willing to embrace anything else.

They had barely made a start when the head of Constable Timothy Smales appeared round the door, with the information that Dr Dally was ready to leave.

Rafferty, rather than leave confidential files lying about when the spare keys were missing, stashed his files under one arm.

Llewellyn did the same with his own pile, and they both followed the young constable out of the room.

Dr Sam Dally, who normally never rushed anywhere, for whatever reason now chose to champ at the bit.

'About time,' he complained when Rafferty and Llewellyn reappeared. 'I can't hang around here all evening, you know. I do have other bodies urgently awaiting my expertise.'

It crossed Rafferty's mind to wonder if he wasn't the only one to be spooked by nuns and religion. Maybe Sam also felt uncomfortable around them and their medieval robes. It was a pleasing thought.

'Keep your hair on, Sam,' he advised the balding doctor. 'I don't suppose your bodies are going anywhere. Much like mine and Llewellyn's here.' He paused, then enquired, 'So, what's the verdict?'

Sam nodded down at the body, now fully disinterred and lying in an open body bag, preparatory to being removed to the mortuary. 'My early inclination, given the normal cycle of insect infestation and the clemency of the recent weather, is that chummy here has been dead for a period of between six and eight weeks. I imagine the forensic entomologist's input will confirm that and should be able to tell you more accurately the likely timescale. And as to the cause of death, I would think that even you, Rafferty, can surely not have failed to notice the fact that his skull has a large dent in it.'

Funny man.

Sam picked up his bag. 'Obviously, until we get him and his little creeping creatures back to either the morgue or the lab, there's little else I can tell you, so I'll bid you good day.'

Rafferty held up a detaining hand. 'Before you go, Sam. Can I take it that one of the bodies you'll be giving your expert attention to later on this evening will be chummy here?'

'Certainly.'

Rafferty was taken aback by Dally's unusual ready agreement to be accommodating. He had taken Sam's eagerness to get away as a pointer that he shared an aversion to nuns. But now, as the doctor's next remarks revealed his true feelings, Rafferty realized how wrong his conclusion had been.

'I don't want to make this case any more difficult for you than it's likely to prove, Rafferty,' was Sam's unusually thoughtful-sounding explanation for his obliging behaviour.

Rafferty's gaze narrowed. Sam's ready accommodation told him that, far from empathizing with him and wanting to be helpful, the pathologist was preparing to bait him. And so it proved.

Sam gave him a huge smile, shook his head, and muttered, 'Nuns! Better not keep them waiting, Rafferty. If you do, you might find that God gives you an even greater penance to contend with than the one you've already got.'

Rafferty refused to give Sam the pleasure of a response, though he swore he heard Sam give a muffled snigger as he walked away.

He grimaced, then turned to Llewellyn and commented, 'Sam's right. We mustn't keep the good sisters waiting. Come on.'

# Four

Sister Rita, the nun who had found the body by literally stumbling over the exposed forearm of the cadaver in its shallow grave, was the first member of the community whom Rafferty wished to question. He sent Llewellyn to fetch her from her cell where she had been sequestered, incommunicado, with Lizzie Green.

While he awaited her arrival, Rafferty studied the information the Mother Superior had supplied, both on the origins and rituals of the community and on its other members.

Along with the files and the other information she had provided, she had given them some of the literature about the community here in Elmhurst, the Carmelite order as a whole, its origins and its history, which they sold from their website as a supplement to the other income they made from making crafts, communion wafers, priestly vestments and so on.

He picked up one of the community's brochures and read that: *'the Carmelite emblem depicts the Holy Land's Mount Carmel with a cross on top of it, and three stars.*

*'Mount Carmel was where the first hermits, mostly former crusaders and pilgrims, calling themselves the Brothers of the Blessed Virgin Mary, gathered in imitation of the prophet, Elijah, in a life of solitude and prayer. The cross on it is a reminder of the central importance of the death of Christ. The one star below represents Mary, mother of God, first among the redeemed, who stood at the foot of the cross. On either side are two other stars, to represent the prophets most associated with the Carmelite origins and ideals, Elijah and John the Baptist.*

*'It is thought by some,'* Rafferty determinedly continued with this unappealing tract, *'that the central star was representative of the opening of a cave, not a star, a cave wherein Elijah sheltered when the Lord appeared to him as the still, small wind. This alternative possibility suited the life of Carmel, silent and separated, away from the busyness of ordinary life.'*

Rafferty grunted, dumped the brochure to one side and picked up another.

*'Until the fifteenth century,'* he read, *'the Order consisted just of priests, friars and lay brothers, although, even then, several groups of pious women lived according to the Carmelite spirit. Following the 1452 founding of the Second Order of nuns, by Blessed John Soreth, Prior General of the Order, the 16th century Reformation saw the initiation of a reform movement by the Spanish Carmelite, Teresa of*

59

*Avila and after her death reformed monasteries were established in France and Belgium, with later communities settled in Britain and thence across the world.*

'*The two branches of the Order are those of the Ancient Observance and the Reformed, or Discalced Carmelites.*'

'Ouch,' said Rafferty, as he read that the word 'discalced' meant *without shoes*, which as far as Rafferty was concerned, would certainly have been a reform too far.

In spite of his earlier determination to get a grip on 'this religion thing', as he was wont to call it, and not let it get a grip on *him*, Rafferty decided he'd read enough religious tracts; he'd hand them over to Llewellyn to wade through. His holier-than-thou Welsh sergeant might even enjoy it. *He* certainly didn't.

Besides, he thought, as a sly grin found its way to his lips, what were sergeants for but to do the heavy work? Instead, he turned back to the study of the sisters' files, which the arrival of Timothy Smales had disturbed.

Sister Rita, the nun who had made the shocking discovery, was aged fifty-five and had been a member of Elmhurst's small Carmel community for twenty years, since several years after the untimely death of her husband. Although most of her working hours were spent looking after the convent's grounds, vegetable plots, fruit orchard and greenhouses, which supplied the community's kitchen, she also acted as the Novice Mistress and the community's stand-in for the Mother Superior when the latter attended religious conferences. It sounded a busy, demanding life.

Along with the other information, Mother Catherine had also given them a list of the convent's daily rituals and Rafferty, prodded by the early indoctrination which still powered a conscience inclined to guilt, had promised to do his best, as far as possible, to work his investigation around them.

Certainly, he thought, the first part of their day would be safe from his interruptions: why did the religious keep such *un*godly hours? he wondered as he broke off from reading through Sister Rita's file to study their routines.

The sisters rose at five thirty and Lauds, the first office of the day, so-called because it was 'praising God for a new day', was at six, which was followed by breakfast at six fifteen and an hour's silent personal prayer at quarter to seven. Then came Mass at eight, followed by Terce.

The general domestic and gardening work began at nine and was broken off at eleven fifteen for Sext. Dinner at eleven thirty was followed by half an hour's recreation and an hour when the nuns were free to either work or pursue personal interests.

A spiritual reading followed at one forty-five, with work resuming at three in the afternoon. At four thirty, work was again halted for Vespers and an hour's silent prayer. They had supper at six and then three-quarters of an hour's recreation until the seven thirty Office of Readings. It had been during this evening recreation that Sister Rita had made her unfortunate discovery. Then at eight came the Great Silence, followed at nine fifteen by Compline. They retired to bed at ten o'clock.

Rafferty's knees were beginning to creak in sympathy at the thought of all that praying. He returned to reading Sister Rita's file, but was interrupted before he had time to finish it by Llewellyn's knock on the door of the office. Rafferty closed the file, shouted, 'Come in,' and looked up as Llewellyn ushered the nun in.

Sister Rita greeted him with a simple nod, and without any sign that she was about to indulge in any of the histrionics which he had, in the past, experienced from women who stumbled over dead bodies. Instead, she calmly sat down in front of the table to await his questions, her work-worn hands lying still in her lap.

Perhaps there was something to be said for the disciplined life of the religious after all, was Rafferty's first thought. At least it saved him from the hysteria he had occasionally encountered in other, supposedly more worldly, women.

The nun, although not over-tall – around

five foot six – was well built, and her clear blue eyes and weather-beaten cheeks gave an appearance of rude health. Even under her long-sleeved brown habit and black veil, he could discern the firm muscles on her upper arms. Her name prior to her admission to the community had been Mary Robins.

Her work in the garden would keep her fitter than most of the other sisters appeared, he thought. All that physical labour must go a long way to counteracting the sedentary nature of the regular daily offices.

He smiled at the nun as she sat in front of the table and began by thanking her for her time. She merely inclined her head once more, but said nothing.

Rafferty experienced a momentary panic that all he was going to get from any of the sisters was a shake of the head for 'No' and a nod for 'Yes'. But surely, he thought, Mother Catherine had understood and explained to them that he required more than nodding dolls for interview and that their rule of silence was to be suspended during police interviews?

Perhaps Sister Rita, sitting so quietly and reposefully, had sensed some of his disquiet, because she immediately quashed it with the observation, 'My time is yours, Inspector, until you find the person responsible for this poor man's death. Mother Catherine has reminded us all of our duties and of what God will require of us, and we shall of course assist you in this matter to the best of our abilities. Naturally, we are anxious to do all that we can, so please ask whatever questions you need to.'

Relieved, Rafferty nodded and said, 'Thank you, Sister.'

Her file revealed that Sister Rita's family had come from a small village some miles outside Birmingham. Rafferty could still trace a hint of working class Brummie in her voice. Perhaps it was her ordinary background, along with the hard physical labour of looking after the community's grounds and produce, which made her seem so down to earth and uncomplicated.

'I can understand how upsetting it must be to you and the other sisters, firstly to find a dead man buried in your grounds, and then to have your peace invaded by a bunch of clod-hopping policemen.'

Sister Rita didn't seem noticeably upset by either event. But then she exuded the rude physicality and earthy practicality of a person born to work the land. She would, Rafferty thought, take nature in all its splendour and tragedy in her stride.

She gave him a broad smile that was more warm Earth Mother than chaste nun, and observed, 'Our Heavenly Father never asks more of any of us than we can bear, Inspector.'

This wasn't a sentiment with which Rafferty was in agreement, but he made no comment.

The sun-lined wrinkles around Sister Rita's brown eyes wrinkled some more as she added in as blunt a manner as an investigative policeman could wish, 'Besides, sorry as we all are for that poor man, I gather from something I heard one of your officers say that he has been dead for some weeks. And while we might be nuns, we *are* still alive. I hope it doesn't sound too shocking to you, Inspector, but this is the most excitement any of us have had in years. Even Sister Ursula, old as she is, has a twinkle in her eye at the sight of so many brawny policemen.'

Rafferty laughed, surprised to find that a nun should have an earthy humour to go with the Earth Mother smile. It wasn't how he remembered those religious who had dominated his youth.

Half afraid that the surface humour was merely a mask to conceal a desire to drag him back into the fold from which he had, or so he had thought, so long ago escaped, Rafferty was quick to say, 'Still, if it's all the same to you, Sister, we'll do our best to keep the excitement down to a dull roar. I'm not sure that *we* can stand any more than that.' His comment brought another twinkle.

'I understand, Sister, that apart from giving religious instruction to your young novice and postulant, you work mostly in the grounds and that you found the body sometime after six thirty this evening during your recreation break?'

She nodded.

Llewellyn put in a question. 'Clearly, because of your work, Sister, you must know every outside inch of the place. That's why I'm surprised you didn't notice before that the ground behind the shrubbery had been disturbed.'

It was a question that had occurred to Rafferty too. He awaited the nun's response with interest.

'I understand your surprise, sergeant,' Sister Rita quietly replied. 'And, if it had been earlier in the year, I would certainly have noticed. But at this time, we're always so busy with gathering in the last of the harvest, picking and storing the fruit from our orchard and planting the winter root vegetables, not to mention spreading the muck and compost on the soil, that the rest of the grounds tend to be neglected. But as it happens, that part of the garden has been given over to God and Mother Nature to do with it what They will. All I did was plant some wildflower bulbs and seeds.'

Rafferty's interest sparked at this admission. 'Could you tell us, precisely, when you last walked there and might reasonably have noticed that the ground had been disturbed?'

Sister Rita's sun-warmed face looked thoughtful. 'I believe, yes, I'm pretty sure, before today, it was somewhere in the middle of August. And I certainly would have noticed if someone had disturbed the ground sufficiently to inter a body.'

'Yet you didn't notice the man's forearm sticking up before you stumbled over it,' Llewellyn pointed out.

Sister Rita bent her head in acknowledgement. 'True. But I was reading the Psalms and examining my conscience rather than the ground. It is necessary to be wholehearted in such examinations, much as it is required to give oneself wholeheartedly to whatever duty one is performing, whether it is spreading muck or digging up the potatoes. An offering to God, sergeant.

'Of course, particularly in springtime, that part of the grounds is so beautiful, first with the snowdrops and then the wild daffodils and bluebells, that I like to walk amongst them for the pure pleasure of it. Though I ration my time there, too much of such self-indulgence not being good for the soul.'

Rafferty, something of a martyr to self-indulgence himself, smiled at this. 'Can you tell us the sequence of events once you found the man's body?'

'Of course. Firstly, I offered up a prayer for his soul. Then I went in search of Mother Catherine. As I told your female officer, Constable Green, I found the body during our usual recreation period, just after supper, so I knew I would most likely find Mother Catherine and most of the rest of my sisters still in the refectory. I broke the news quietly to Mother and she, after an understandable initial shock at the news, quickly took charge. She herself broke the news to the other sisters and instructed Sister Perpetua to return with me to the grave to confirm my discovery.'

'Mother Catherine didn't go with you herself?'

Sister Rita shook her head. 'No. I'm afraid our young novice, Sister Cecile, became somewhat hysterical at the news. I imagine Mother Catherine thought her authority would be put to better use calming her down. Besides, Sister Perpetua is a most reliable woman. Calm and as solid as what she terms her "too solid flesh" in a crisis.'

Rafferty nodded, glad to get the sequence of events clear in his mind. He had noticed the one really chubby sister in the chapel. He presumed this nun, who had a round jolly face, was the Sister Perpetua who would be the perfect partner for such a morbid enterprise.

'I know this is difficult, but was there anything about the body or what you could see of it – I'm thinking of the noticeably expensive-looking watch, in particular – that could cause you or Sister Perpetua to think you might have seen the dead man before?'

The nun shook her head. 'I certainly can't recall seeing such a watch before. And as Sister Perpetua made no such comment in my presence, I doubt she had either.'

Sister Rita answered their other questions as well as she was able, but although appearing anxious to be helpful, she was able to tell them nothing more than the Prioress herself had already told them.

Next, they questioned Sister Perpetua, whose nature was as jolly as her rounded appearance and smiling countenance had earlier suggested. A year older than Sister Rita, she had been in the convent for nearly thirty years, having joined as a young woman. Her previous name had been Annette Enderby and her family were from Devon.

But, although as pleasant and open as could be, apart from agreeing that she was currently on the community's rota to work in the kitchen and confirming all that Sister Rita had said, she could tell them nothing further, so Rafferty let her go.

Next they questioned Sister Benedicta who, at sixty-two, was another long-term member of the community. Her former name had been Daisy Hodgson and she was originally from Sussex. Another matter-of-fact country girl, she worked alongside Sister Rita in the gardens and was as tanned of face and as muscular as her garden labourer colleague. Though, again like Sister Rita, she told them she had no knowledge of the dead man or how he came to be buried in the community's grounds.

Sister Ursula, Edith Grey as was, originally from London, was a tiny wizened woman of seventy-nine. But while her back might be bent from osteoporosis and her hands folded into the curl typical of arthritis, she waved away Llewellyn's proffered arm with the air of one not yet ready to accept either that she might need assistance or that the yawning grave was her next likely destination.

She reminded ex-Londoner Rafferty of a London sparrow, all bright eyes and inquisitiveness. Her body might have let her down and have scarcely more strength than the sprightly little bird, but her gaze showed the alertness of someone still interested in life. And while she certainly studied the two policemen with every sign of appreciation, she admitted quite cheerfully that she had few duties nowadays beyond tottering about the place and showing willing.

However, although she might be willing to do whatever chores her ailing body would allow, Rafferty doubted it would allow her to swat a fly, let alone a grown man. Mentally, as soon as she had begun her slow stick-aided walk towards the chair, Rafferty had dismissed her as a possible suspect. Apart from any other considerations, their corpse was around the six foot mark, and she was so tiny that she would have needed to stand on a chair to hit him on the back of the head with any force. Nor, for that matter, was she able to claim any knowledge of their cadaver.

After Sister Ursula had left them, Rafferty decreed that they took a short break. He wanted to assimilate what they had learned so far, before he tried to force any more details into his head.

He sent Llewellyn off to the refectory in search of tea and on his return, he said, 'You're a deep sort, Dafyd – did you ever fancy the religious life?'

Llewellyn shook his dark head, placed the plain workmanlike mugs of tea on the table, for once not worrying about marking the already well-scarred surface, and added as he sat down, 'But I can see its appeal. Especially that of the contemplatives. Set against a modern world that is becoming increasingly complicated and with values ever more trivial, shallow and hedonistic, such a life has an attractive order about it.'

Rafferty, frequently baffled and frustrated by the modern world and its endlessly up-dated technology, was surprised to find himself nodding in agreement with Llewellyn's words. 'And then, I suppose, there's the added incentive of having no worries about paying the bills,' he commented, warming to the theme even though he felt slightly shocked that he should do so. 'All that stuff which grinds people down in the real world is taken care of for you.'

'True. But you'd have no money – or very little – to spend, either.'

Rafferty, denied the financial incentive for

such a life, again to his surprise found another attraction. 'At least you'd be guaranteed people to look after you in your old age. That's got to be a draw.'

But then he thought again. 'What am I saying? Let old age take care of itself. What's the point in worrying about that if you haven't lived the life you were given? Imagine turning senile and dying after spending your best years on your knees? I think I'd rather live my life with all its ups and downs, its difficulties and problems, than have a *non*-existence doing little more than have endless monologue conversations with the Big Bloke in the sky, who probably doesn't even exist.'

He took another slurp of tea. 'I always thought being a contemplative religious was a terrible waste of life. OK, if you must sign up for the cloister, at least join one of those communities who do something useful, such as caring for those no one else wants to care for, like the world's lepers, Aids orphans, and so on.'

Having got that off his chest, Rafferty began to consider other drawbacks. 'And apart from all the time you'd spend on your knees, praying, there's the no-sex rule to contend with as well.'

'Even the Garden of Eden had its snake,' Llewellyn murmured.

'Good old Hissing Sid?' Rafferty took another deep gulp of his tea. It was piping hot, strong and well-sugared, just as he liked it. He studied Llewellyn's face through the steam, as ascetic and serious-looking as that of any religious. He commented, 'I know you said a religious life held no appeal, but I can still see you as a monk.'

Llewellyn didn't even slop his tea at this remark, but just said, 'Easier than you could see yourself as one, I imagine?'

'True. I could never be a Holy Joe, me.' Rafferty raked his hand through his unruly auburn hair. 'The tonsure would be bad enough, but those *sandals* would finish me. Well, that and the lack of se—'

'Yes, I think we've already established that particular drawback.' Llewellyn straightened his already immaculate jacket and observed, 'For me, it would be the clothes. I understand that monastic orders that don't wear the habit buy their clothes from charity shops.' The elegantly attired Welshman gave a faint shudder.

Rafferty laughed. 'Perhaps you'd suit being a Catholic *priest* better. They're done up like the Christmas fairy for much of the year.'

'Possibly. If I was of the appropriate religious conviction. But as we've already discovered, neither of us has the requisite vocation. And apart from any other consideration, in my case, there's my wife to bring into the equation, and in your case there's my cousin Abra, and Mrs Rafferty.'

Rafferty fixed on the second person whom

73

Llewellyn had named. 'Ah, yes. Ma,' he said, before he paused reflectively. 'I wonder what she'd have to say if I renounced the world and the grandchildren she's still waiting for me to produce?'

'It's probably as well that you're unlikely to find out.'

Rafferty nodded, finished his tea and observed, 'Time to get back to work, I think. Back to the real world and its complications. Let's have the next sister in, Dafyd. The sooner we get these interviews finished, the sooner we might be able to get on with solving this murder.'

Sisters Agnes and Anne were next. Like the round and rosy Sister Perpetua, both were currently on kitchen duties. Though with such a small household to cater for, three sisters to do the cooking struck Rafferty as over-egging the pudding, especially as the well-rounded Perpetua was surely sufficiently enthusiastic about her food to be able to prepare and cook three simple meals a day without assistance.

Sister Agnes, formerly Cynthia Mayhew, was tall and thin, with a long nose that, to Rafferty, indicated that the woman would be naturally inquisitive. However, it must be a trait she did her best to subdue because she neither asked nor volunteered anything until nearly the end of their session.

And although Sister Rita had claimed that each of her fellow nuns was anxious to help all they could, it seemed that Sister Agnes, at least, didn't enjoy her colleague's robustness at the disturbance of her normal routines. Rather than showing a desire to be helpful, she seemed on edge, even a little resentful of their presence.

Her voice, unlike the warm tones of Sister Rita and the jolly chirrups of Sister Perpetua, was thin, with a tendency to high-pitched cut glass, which set Rafferty's teeth on edge. And when she finally allowed herself to give in to the aristocrat's natural inclination to take control, her first question was one that common sense should have told her was impossible for him to answer.

'How long is your investigation likely to last, Inspector? I understand that you have your duty to do, of course, but this man's death and the presence of so many worldly people is upsetting some of the older sisters. Most have been here so long, our daily routine is all they are used to, you see.'

Whether it was, as she claimed, really upsetting the older nuns – although Sister Ursula, clearly the oldest member of the community had shown little sign of any such discombobulation – certainly it was upsetting Sister Agnes, whose hands clutched anxiously at the folds of her habit.

'I understand that,' Rafferty told her quietly. 'Mother Catherine has already provided me with a list of your routines, and I promised her I'd do my best to work round them. But, as to how long our investigation will take, I'm afraid it's in the lap of the gods.'

Sister Agnes's long nose dipped in acknowledgement of this. 'Then I shall, of course, pray to the one *true* God, to aid your endeavours.'

Rafferty wondered whether he was meant to shout 'Hallelujah' at this. He felt like telling her not to bother praying on his account, as God had in the past generally shown a singular disinclination to aid him in anything. Instead, he thanked her for her promised prayers. Maybe God might more readily respond to the prayers of a religious nun than of a backsliding sinner? he thought as he showed her out, she having, like the other sisters, denied all knowledge of the convent's cadaver or how it had ended up in its temporary resting place.

The second of her two co-workers in the kitchens, Sister Anne, the former Margaret Andrews, was for all her sixty-five years meek, mild, very shy and apparently unwilling to say boo to a goose or indeed much else at all. She couldn't have been a greater contrast to the tall, thin and aristocratically nervy Sister Agnes or the short round Sister Perpetua with her rosy benevolence.

Two of the other nuns, Sisters Bernadette and Elizabeth, had been visiting a sister convent in the north of England for the past two months and had only returned a couple

76

of days ago, so if Sam Dally was correct in his estimated time of death both were unlikely to have had anything to do with their man's death.

Rafferty wasn't surprised to hear, as nun followed nun into the office which Mother Catherine had provided for them, each holy sister professed ignorance of how the dead man had come to end up buried in their grounds. Most of them appeared to be genuinely troubled at the discovery of his body and that he had presumably been interred without religious ceremony. And who could blame them for that? They had chosen the contemplatives' life above other, more worldly orders, seeking only to dedicate their lives to prayer. But now the wickedness of the world outside their isolating walls had intruded. Perhaps, in the process, it would destroy their serenity for ever?

It certainly would, if – a possibility that Rafferty already had reason to consider – one of the holy nuns turned out to be their murderer.

The last two of the community to be interviewed were the novice, Cecile, formerly Chrissie Hall, and the postulant, Teresa Tattersall.

Cecile's duties included keeping the chapel pristine and fit for the glorification of God as well as maintaining the community's website which she had set up some months previously. Teresa Tattersall the twenty-nine-year-old postulant, was variously employed in the infirmary and doing the craft work that helped to fill the community's coffers. Both had also been unable to shed any light on the man's death or burial.

Strangely, given the requirement that they love their fellow man, only the young novice Cecile, a pretty twenty-six-year-old – and, from the clue of her eyebrows beneath the all-concealing pale veil – a natural blonde, shed any tears over the man's sudden, violent end.

'Please forgive me.' She wiped her eyes after she had followed the last of her colleagues into the temporary interview room they had been allocated. 'I don't know why I'm so upset. It's not as if I can have known the dead man. Reverend Mother is always telling me I must master my emotions or they will master me.'

Cecile gave Rafferty a wobbly smile as she mopped the tears from her creamy skin. 'I'm afraid I'm still striving for serenity, but it's proving elusive. Clearly, I'm a long way from being ready to take my final vows.'

Rafferty, still appalled, in spite of Mother Catherine's attempts to convince him otherwise, that such a pretty girl should choose to 'waste' her youth and beauty by shutting them away behind convent walls, was similarly inclined to be over-emotional.

He smiled sympathetically, and told her, 'You're young yet. I imagine this is your first contact with death?'

She gave him an uncertain nod.

'I don't suppose even your Prioress, admirable as I'm sure she is now, was quite so in control of her emotions when she was your age.'

'Do you really think so?' she asked, clearly finding difficulty with the idea, but equally clearly rather taken by the suggestion.

'Sure of it,' Rafferty affirmed. Though he admitted to a certain thankfulness that the Mother Superior wasn't around to hear him say it. To have attained her current rank indicated a truly awesome mastery of ordinary human weakness.

But after ten minutes of questioning, it was clear that the young novice, like the rest, was unable to tell them anything much. Whether they were all really unable or simply *unwilling* and involved in a conspiracy of silence for reasons of their own, Rafferty was as yet unable to discern.

When the young novice had glided through the door, rather less smoothly than the Mother Superior, and back to her duties at the computer, Rafferty, who sympathized with the elusiveness of her serenity, sat back and remarked to Llewellyn, 'Looks like we've got the religious version of the three wise monkeys here, Daff. Shame they've multiplied.'

Llewellyn's lips twitched. 'Indeed. And though they still, it seems, see no evil, hear no evil, and speak no evil, I can't believe that they don't *sense* the presence of evil and have a pretty good idea from whence it springs.'

The nuns, perhaps because they were unused to inconsequential chatter, had mostly shown themselves to be sparing with words.

Rafferty could only hope this propensity altered the next time he questioned them. Maybe, if he was to get more revealing chatter, he'd have to liberate the communion wine and encourage the sisters to make free with it.

'Let's just hope that between them, Sam Dally, the forensic anthropologist, and the forensic entomologist, can pin down a shorter timescale for the man's likely death. Hope, too, that we're able to quickly identify him. One thing I find hard to believe is the sisters' denial that our cadaver could possibly have any connection to the convent or any of its inhabitants.'

Llewellyn nodded his agreement. 'And if it wasn't for the fact that the spare keys to the building are missing, it would not be easy for some outsider to gain access without the assistance of at least one of the community. If the murderer wasn't admitted via the normal route, he would have had to scale the walls—'

'Dragging a corpse behind him for good measure,' Rafferty interrupted, to add the thought that had already occurred to him.

'Quite.' Llewellyn's tightly drawn lips

expressed his displeasure at this description.

Rafferty chose to ignore his sergeant's silent reproof. 'Though why would an outsider choose to bury his victim here at all when he – or she, which would be even more unlikely if we *are* talking about an outsider – has miles of countryside, not to mention the North Sea close at hand?

'No.' Rafferty shook his head. 'The outsider-as-murderer scenario is too bizarre for words. And it's a damn shame those spare keys to the convent *are* missing, as it confuses the issue. But I think – unless either the doctor or Father Kelly turn out to be the culprit, having helped themselves to the spare keys – that we may well have already met our murderer.'

But the thought that their killer might turn out to be a contemplative nun was bizarre and really rather chilling. It meant that this case looked set to become the very devil.

# Five

By the time they had conducted all the preliminary interviews, it was nearly nine o'clock at night, but before he left the convent, Rafferty instructed Llewellyn to go and see Dr Peterson, the community's general practitioner, and take a statement.

He started to add that they would go to see Father Kelly together afterwards – he knew, from previous acquaintance, that the old priest was something of a late bird – when, just in time, it struck him just how many mutual memories he and Father Kelly shared; more recent ones as well as ones stretching back to his youth and boyhood, memories that he would prefer the mischievous priest not to share with Llewellyn. So, after voicing one word of this latter idea, he carefully bit his lip on the rest.

'You were about to say something,' Llewellyn noted.

'Was I?' Rafferty queried with what he hoped was a suitably vacant expression, before he added, 'Well, if I was, it's gone to where those three wise monkeys keep their nuts. And I don't much fancy going *there*.

But you feel free.'

Llewellyn wisely decided he didn't much fancy going there, either. Instead, after accepting his inspector's statement with the equanimity with which he greeted most of the mercurial Rafferty's pronouncements he asked quietly, 'And what will you be doing?'

It was a question put so quietly, that Rafferty, who fully intended to skive off for purposes of his own before he did anything else, wondered if his astute sergeant suspected something of the sort. The suspicion made him defensive.

'Me? I'm going to visit Father Kelly, the convent's priest. See if he can shed any light on this business. If he's got any sins he wants to get off his chest, he might more readily confess them to a fellow Catholic, even if it is to one of the lapsed variety. You can contact me on my mobile if there are any developments.'

He didn't reveal that before he went to see the priest, he intended heading back to the station for purposes of an entirely personal nature.

As Llewellyn had said, the RC convent was situated on the north-western edge of the old Essex market town of Elmhurst. To reach the police station, Rafferty had to cross the River Tiffey at Tiffey Reach and pass the ancient, ruined Priory.

After his recent experiences, he shuddered

as he passed its night-cloaked and starkly broken stones, with their reminder of religion's inclination for violent retribution. And, before he turned left into Cymbeline Way and the back doubles' approach to the police station, he was, for once, relieved to see the bright lights of Mammon in the form of the shopping centre illuminate the sky

Inclined, now he was free from observation, to fret and brood about his morning's post, he inevitably found that fretting and brooding achieved nothing but a thumping headache.

Once parked up in the police station car park, Rafferty scurried up to his second floor office and swallowed a couple of pain killers. Then he removed from his pocket the letter he had received that morning, and read it again.

Got yourself into a fine mess back in April, didn't you, Nigel? Fortunate for you that your boss never found out about that alter ego business. It's my hope that he never learns of your duplicity during the Made in Heaven murder case. You must share this hope, I'm sure. Perhaps I can help resolve your difficulties and ensure your secret remains just that? I'll be in touch, Inspector.

Appalled all over again at the letter's implied threat, Rafferty sat back and did some more useless brooding as yet another chill sweat slicked over his face and neck.

Who could have sent such a letter? he wondered again, as possibility after possibility Schumacher-ed its way across his mind and were as speedily rejected. It took, he thought, a person with a particular mindset to write blackmail letters. A person, for instance, with a liking for power over others. A person with a certain arrogance.

He didn't, of course, need to ask *why* his unwelcome correspondent had sent the letter. His guilty conscience provided reason enough. Two beautiful young women were dead, after all. And even though he hadn't killed them, their fate still troubled him. But what troubled him even more, was why his correspondent had waited till *now* to write to him, as the business to which the letter referred had happened months ago.

What did the blackmailer want? The usual money? At first Rafferty thought that this was unlikely. Because, after racking his brains, off and on, since he had received the letter, considering and discarding possible suspects, he had, just before he had arrived at the convent, come to the inescapable conclusion that his blackmailer was most likely to be found amongst his one-time fellow members of the Made in Heaven dating agency. Which one, though? That was the question.

All were well educated professionals with incomes to match, so why would they think it worthwhile, not only to risk damaging their high flying careers, but also to risk a prison sentence, in order to blackmail him and extract part of his strictly limited police income?

At first he had thought his conclusion made sense. But later, during their mostly fruitless questioning of the nuns, it had struck him that the saying 'the rich get richer while the poor get poorer', had been coined for a very good reason.

With their frequently extravagant lifestyles, the rich proved every day just how much they liked money. And the more of it they managed to pile up, the more they wanted, even if the means of acquiring it were morally reprehensible. Shady businessmen with their backhanders proliferated. Shady politicians, ditto. Greedy insurance and pension salesmen more interested in increasing their commissions and bonuses than in ensuring their clients were sold the most appropriate policies for their needs, had all, in recent years, featured frequently in the news.

The country was full of the financial and other scandals of the monied-classes. He thought it possible that some amongst them wouldn't turn their noses up if the opportunity for a lucrative spot of blackmail presented itself.

It was his firm belief that the worst elements of such classes had a preference for

keeping the mass of the population un-
educated and ignorant, particularly about
financial matters. Feed them a steady diet of
mind-rotting swill such as soaps and TV
reality shows and they were likely to lose any
discernment they started out with.

The proles as milch cows, in fact. Always
there to have more squeezed out of them.
The proof for this was certainly there: the
mass of people were more appallingly educated than ever before, the same applied to
their equal lack of financial education.

It all went to prove that wealthy people
were often greedy people, uncaring of how
many poorer folk they robbed of their
futures. They were mean, too, as many
charity collectors would confirm.

OK, a chunk of the rest of the population
shared such traits. But Rafferty had always
thought the monied-classes were a breed
apart when it came to ruthless self-interest.
You only had to look at the scandals attach-
ing to government ministers of whatever
political colour to realize there was little to
which they wouldn't stoop.

Which meant he couldn't discount the
possibility that any one of his ex fellow Made
in Heaven members might be the blackmailer.

It had to be one of them, surely? he reasoned. One of those who had met him both as
Nigel Blythe, the alter ego he had, at the
time of the Made in Heaven investigation,

felt it essential to adopt before signing up as a fellow lonely heart and Made in Heaven member, *and* as Inspector Joseph Rafferty, the policeman who found himself at the same time both the chief suspect and the officer charged with investigating the violent murders of two lady members.

It wasn't beyond the bounds of possibility that one of his fellow members had seen through the disguise he had been forced to adopt in order to conduct the investigation and avoid anyone recognizing him and months down the line had decided to have some fun and financial gain at his expense.

Rafferty forced himself to think back over a period of his life he would really prefer *not* to dwell on, as he studied the letter again.

Its words remained the same and were every bit as threatening as on all the previous readings. In his earlier anxiety, he had been unable to recall all the names of the Made In Heaven dating agency's members amongst whom he had adjudged himself most likely to find the culprit responsible for the blackmailing letter. And even now, back in the quiet seclusion of his office, he was still able to recall the names of only one or two, those of the rest still eluded him.

But he was wasting time. At the thought that Llewellyn might well, by now, have finished questioning Dr Peterson and be on his way back to the station, Rafferty abandoned the hunt through memory and instead began what he had returned to the office to do: which was to find the list of other members. He invariably threw into his desk drawers any discarded scribbles from a concluded investigation. He had intended to clear the entire shebang out as it was becoming difficult to close the drawers. But now, he thanked God that such good intentions had gone the same way as previous ones. And as he smoothed out screwed up piece of paper after screwed up piece of paper, only to see that each successive missive didn't contain the information he sought, he pleaded with his neglected God to help him.

Christ, some of these names went back *years*, he realized, aghast.

Please God, he pleaded again. Let their names be here or I'm sunk before I've even begun to try to find out who sent me the blackmail letter.

His desk was littered with paper scraps before he finally found what he was looking for. He sat back with a sigh of relief as he scrutinized the names on the list.

There had been Dr Lancelot Bliss, the flamboyant TV doctor and his producer friend, Rory Gifford, with his careful and cynical adoption of a rakish, bohemian image. And then there had been Ralph Dryden, the on-his-uppers property developer, and Adam Ardley, the website designer and the barrister, Toby Rufford-Lyle: not that he looked short of money from what Rafferty had seen of his house and motor. But, as he had already concluded, that didn't necessary remove the desire for more of the folding stuff.

And then there were the partners and staff. Such as Caroline and Guy Cranston and the other partner, Simon Farnell. And though Rafferty thought it less likely that Caroline could have had anything to do with the blackmail letter, it wasn't impossible. And on the staff side, there was Isobel Goddard and the efficient part timer, Emma Hartley.

Isobel, at least, as he had learned during the case, was capable of selling her soul for money, so would hardly be likely to hesitate if the opportunity for a little blackmail came her way.

In view of his current desperate situation, it was fortunate that he hadn't done that much mingling on either of the nights he had attended the agency's parties, which lessened the number of potential black-mailers. He could surely cross off the names of those members who hadn't had the opportunity to view his features at close quarters?

Actually, he thought he would *have* to discount them. He was barely at the beginning of another murder inquiry and would never have the time to check them all out as potential blackmailers. So that left how many?

Rafferty had a quick count up as he studied his list of names. There were ten of them. He thought it most likely that he would find his blackmailer from amongst the ranks of those ten people. The realization caused him to sag in the middle.

Because he had no idea how he could possibly make an approach to *one* of their number, never mind ten. He wasn't even sure he should. Did he really want to rattle the blackmailer's cage? And what the hell was he supposed to ask them, anyway?

'*So when did you realize that the inspector in charge of the Lonely Hearts' murders and Nigel Blythe, the original suspect, were one and the same?*' didn't strike him as the most discreet question he could pose.

But he had to do something. And to think, with the passing of the months, he had begun to hope that that time and all the trouble it had caused him was firmly behind him and he was free of it.

But the past, he was discovering, like life itself, had a nasty habit of creeping up on you and biting you in the bum. Mostly, when you least expected it.

When he'd joined the agency under the name borrowed from his cousin, Nigel Blythe, he'd adopted the alter ego touch, amongst other understandable reasons, simply to stop his ma from finding out that he'd joined a dating agency. He knew that if she had found out she would have enthusiastically re-launched her own matchmaking campaign. It was because he had been heartily sick of her efforts to galvanize his love life that he had joined the dating agency under an assumed name in the first place.

At the time, he'd considered the alter ego adoption a masterly touch and that, should he find that special woman, he could confess all and they'd have a laugh about it. He'd found the special woman. In fact, he'd found *two* of them, but neither had done much laughing. Nor had he once the Made in Heaven nightmare began.

He slouched in his chair, sighed again, and stared with the brooding countenance of a latter day Heathcliff at the untidy pile of unscrewed discards while he pondered a possible course of action.

Trouble was, of course, that now he'd found the list he wasn't sure what he could do with it. As he'd already realized, the last thing he should do was go and see each person on the list and ask them pertinent questions. But what else could he do? Hope for Divine intervention? Fat hope *that* was.

Stumped, Rafferty threw his head back and closed his eyes. When he opened them again a few seconds later, it was to find his DS, Dafyd Llewellyn had returned from seeing Dr Peterson and stood, gazing in wide-eyed astonishment at Rafferty and his paper mountain.

Llewellyn stared for a few more moments, apparently speechless at the apparition before him. Then he protested, 'But it was only this morning that I filed all the accumulated paperwork that had gathered on top of your desk.'

For once, Llewellyn's thinly handsome face betrayed some emotion and it wasn't pleasure. 'Where on earth has that pile appeared from?'

'My desk drawers,' Rafferty told him as he gazed, with even more emotion than Llewellyn had displayed, at the paper he had piled in front of him. Frantically, trying not to betray his anxiety, he tried to locate the blackmail letter. The last thing he wanted was for Llewellyn to see it. Even though his sergeant knew all about his uncomfortable secret, he would prefer he didn't also learn that his secret had now grown horns.

But thankfully, he realized that the blackmail letter was buried out of sight beneath the other scraps of paper and he sat back as he wondered how he could possibly retrieve it without piquing Llewellyn's curiosity even further.

'Are you going to tell me the reason for the mess?'

'Are you going to tell me the reason for the mess, *Sir*,' Rafferty corrected, resorting to what, even to his ears, sounded uncomfortably like priggish pedantry while he sought a believable explanation.

Unsurprisingly in the circumstances, Llewellyn didn't grace this particular piece of rank-pulling with any more attention than it deserved.

Rafferty acknowledged that his rank-pulling was pathetic. It hadn't done any good, either, because Llewellyn continued to complain as if he recognized that Rafferty's attempts to make him 'sir' him had merely been done for distraction purposes.

But perhaps that wasn't so surprising. As Rafferty admitted, he *had* tried repeatedly to get Llewellyn to put aside such formality, but, at least while they were at work, Llewellyn was still invariably punctilious in his address. Even stranger, given that they were now related, since Llewellyn had been married to Rafferty's cousin, Maureen, for the last six months.

'But—' Llewellyn was still seeking an answer when Rafferty interrupted him.

'I thought I'd have a clear out,' Rafferty now confided, aware that his obsessively tidy sergeant would certainly feel entitled to an explanation of his litter-bugging. It quickly became apparent that this explanation was not one of his finest.

'A clear out? You?' With the faintest tinge of the sarcasm which he usually considered the lowest form of wit, Llewellyn added, '*Sir*,' reached out a hand to the visitor's chair in front of the desk and sat down with exaggerated care as if concerned the shock of Rafferty's revelation might cause his legs to give way.

'OK, sarky, you can cut that out,' Rafferty

advised him. 'I might not tidy too often, but when I do, I'm thoroughness itself.'

'So I see. Would you like me to order a skip?'

'My, aren't we the comedian today? What's Maureen been feeding you on? The contents of Christmas crackers? Because that's about the level of your wit.'

Llewellyn sighed and climbed back to his feet. He reached out a hand again, as though to pick up handfuls of the desk detritus. But Rafferty grabbed his wrist before he could do so. Hastily, he snatched up the list of names. 'I want that,' he said as he stuffed it in his pocket out of sight, conscious that although he might as yet have no idea what he was going to do with it, if he did eventually hit on a cunning plan to discover the identity of the blackmailer, he'd be stymied without the list of names and their contact details. It wasn't as if he relished leaving *his* name with either computer or filing clerk in such a connection. Discretion being the better part of valour and not being found out.

'And I said *I'm* doing the clear out,' he insisted. 'No assistance required.'

'Yes, but will you?' Llewellyn questioned, his expression indicating more than a little doubt at this claim. 'Or will it still all be piled there in the morning when I come in? Along with all the usual duties that seem to be my responsibility at the beginning of another murder inquiry?'

'Oh ye of little faith. Just watch.' With that, Rafferty picked up the litter basket he kept for papers requiring shredding and swept the pile off the desk and into the small container. The overflow landed on the floor to the accompaniment of another sigh from Llewellyn. Then Rafferty sat back. Sweeping an arm over the now paper-free desk with the flourish of a conjurer, he joked, 'See? It's almost like magic, isn't it?' Though he didn't feel much like laughing.

Certainly any such inclination vanished altogether when Llewellyn's next words revealed that not only had he succeeded in incurring his sergeant's curiosity, but that his Welsh colleague was as sharp eyed as ever.

'The Lonely Hearts' case?' he commented as he nodded at Rafferty's jacket pocket wherein he had speedily secreted the list of names. 'Why on earth do you want to retain that particular scrap of paper? Sir. The case was solved.'

'I know that.' Rafferty urged his brain to hurry up and provide him with a believable excuse for its retention. Then he hit on one. 'It's got sentimental value for me.'

Llewellyn's normally poker face was getting more than its usual workout. His elegant dark eyebrows rose over matching dark eyes. 'I would have thought that would be the one case you'd prefer to forget. Especially—'

'Well you'd be wrong. I had my heart broken during that case. Twice over, in fact,' Rafferty reminded Llewellyn, hoping the sympathy vote would do it for him. He wasn't lying, either. The memory of the love he had briefly felt for the two victims was only now beginning to fade.

But the relentlessly logical Llewellyn didn't do sentimentality. Nor did he believe that one should hold a torch for other women when one was in a relationship, as he wasn't slow to tell Rafferty.

'But you're with Abra now, sir. Memories of old loves that came to nothing are surely better put through the shredder with the rest of life's sad past events? It doesn't do to start wallowing.'

Abra, Rafferty's live-in girlfriend, was Llewellyn's first cousin, so it was natural that he was concerned that Rafferty should appear to be dwelling a little too heavily on past lady loves, even if both romances had been of extremely short duration and both the ladies were dead.

'I'm not wallowing, as you call it,' Rafferty retorted sharply. Eager to get away from this Welsh inquisition, he grabbed his jacket and coat, for a glance out of the window at the trees opposite the station told him the October evening had turned blustery. 'I'm going to question Father Kelly,' he said. 'I only stopped off here for a spare notebook and got sidetracked. Knowing what a garrulous man he is, he's sure to run through my current one. You can tell me what Dr Peterson had to say when I get back.' He made his escape before Llewellyn began to dig deeper.

He was halfway down the stairs when he froze. Christ, he realized, Llewellyn's nagging had made him forget all about the blackmail letter. Originally at the bottom of the paper pile on his desk it was, presumably, now perched somewhere near the top of the rubbish basket and open to Llewellyn's scrutiny. That was the last thing he wanted.

He raced back to his office and grabbed the litter basket, much to Llewellyn's further astonishment. But his hasty snatching caused him to knock the basket over. Half of its contents ended on the floor.

Rafferty scrabbled inelegantly on his knees until he found the blackmail letter. He stuffed it in his jacket pocket, aware of his sergeant's growing astonishment as he did so.

Carelessly, he thrust most of the rest of the discarded paper back in the bin and hurried out of the office for the second time, before Llewellyn's surely increased curiosity could find further voice.

# Six

Father Roberto Kelly lived, with two other priests, in the Priests' House beside the parish church of St Boniface. The two buildings were situated in the ancient High Street, with its mishmash of building styles, from the sizeable, detached, Victorian property on three floors that the priests shared, to the smaller, timber-framed, Tudor houses and others, older still, their small bricks pillaged from Roman remains.

Rafferty remembered his ma telling him that as well as sharing a home, the priests also shared the services of a housekeeper, though he had gained the impression that Father Kelly made rather more use of the housekeeper's services than did his brother priests.

The door was opened to Rafferty's knock by the latest in a long line of these housekeepers; a pretty, curly haired young woman wearing a frilly white apron and a short black dress. A creature from male fantasyland, he thought. Lucky old Father Kelly.

The frilly apparition told him that Father Roberto Kelly was at home working on his

Sunday sermon and couldn't be disturbed. But Rafferty asked her to tell the priest of his arrival anyway, thinking it likely that he would welcome any interruption from such a task.

She returned with the news that Father Kelly would see him and as he followed her down the hall, Rafferty mused that, with a mixed Italian and Irish parentage, perhaps it wasn't so surprising that the ageing priest should have turned out to be a not-so-secret mix of Lothario and reprobate.

'Ah, Inspector. Come away in,' Father Kelly jovially invited when the pert house-keeper ushered Rafferty into the priest's stuffy study.

After Father Kelly had patted her equally pert behind, she told him he was a naughty priest and should learn to keep his hands to himself. But this rebuke was spoken in tones more flirtatious than offended. With a twitch of her bottom, she went out, shutting the door behind her.

'Come to confess your sins, have you?' the priest asked Rafferty with a broad grin. With a dramatic flourish, he consulted his watch. 'Sure and I've got a few hours to spare before my bedtime cocoa.' He nodded at a chair and invited, 'Clear my junk from that and take a load off,' before he threw down his pen and turned his face away from his sermon with, as Rafferty had so rightly anticipated, all the glee of a schoolboy abandoning his maths homework.

Rafferty sneaked a glance at the sermon's title as he removed several books from the chair and sat down. He wasn't surprised the priest should so readily turn aside from it. 'He that is without sin among you, let him first cast a stone', had undoubtedly been prompted by self interest. But perhaps the text had served more as a reminder that if there was to be any stone throwing Father Roberto Kelly was more likely to be on the receiving end of the missiles. Not a comfortable message for the boozy old roué.

'I called to find out what you could tell me about the sisters at the convent,' Rafferty began as he glanced round the over-stuffed study and thought that even Llewellyn would have his work cut out getting it into some sort of order. Books and papers were piled everywhere: on the floor, on the cheek-by-jowl chairs, even on the mantelpiece where they balanced precariously above the roaring fire. Clearly the young housekeeper's talents didn't extend much to housework

Rafferty was surprised the infernal heat from the fire didn't, for Father Kelly, conjure up unpleasant visions of the Hellfire that must surely be awaiting him in eternity as punishment for his un-priest-like behaviour over the years. But if it did, his countenance retained a remarkable equanimity at the prospect.

'I'm sure you'll have heard on the grapevine by now that one of the sisters stumbled across a man's body there today, buried in a shallow grave,' Rafferty began.

Father Kelly stared unblinkingly at him, his rheumy eyes blotchy red circles of surprise. For a few seconds, he was uncharacteristically speechless. It seemed that, for once, the priest had signally failed in his usually masterful connection to the grapevine by which he kept tabs on his parishioners. But although losing the advantage, he quickly recovered the use of his tongue.

As if to show his lack of concern that his ignorance should be so apparent, he sat back and rubbed his hand over the grey stubble on his heavy jowls before he exclaimed, 'Well, I'll be buggered. A body, you say?' He sat even further back in the stout Windsor chair that was comfortably plumped with several fat cushions, and asked above the loud creaking protest of the chair as it accommodated the priest's adjusted bulk, 'Who was buried in the grave? Do you know?'

Rafferty shook his head. 'Not yet. But to return to the sisters. I understand you've known most of them and ministered to all of them, bar the two young ones, for years. I'm ready to bet you must know more about them than anyone else alive, including their families.'

'Is it gambling *and* breaking the secrets of the confessional, you'd be having me do, young Joseph Aloysius?' Father Kelly folded his black-clad arms and scolded. 'Shame on you for a well brought up Catholic boy. You must know I couldn't be doing either.'

Rafferty pretended to go along with this urban myth. 'No, Father. Of course not.' The fibbing old fart. Pity the sod of Ould Ireland hadn't been so concerned with confessional ethics when *I* was in and out of his box, he thought. Because, in his youth, his ma had somehow got to hear all about the things he shouldn't have been doing; things she could not possibly have learned from any other source.

Father Kelly was, unfortunately, a grass – one as green as Ould Ireland herself. The question was – would he be as enthusiastic a grass when it was nuns rather than unruly schoolboys he was ratting on? So far, the possibility didn't look promising.

Rafferty tried another tack. 'But surely you must also have learned things *outside* the confessional?'

Father Kelly didn't answer him. Instead, he posed a question of his own.

'It's not into suspecting the poor, holy sisters you're at now, is it? Shame on you, boy.' He rummaged in his desk and found what Rafferty presumed must be the keys to the church and threw them at him. 'You'd better away to the church and say ten Hail Marys as penance.'

Rafferty caught the keys with a Flintoff

flourish and tossed them on the nearest cluttered table. From the moment he had learned that Father Kelly was the priest who ministered to the sisters' spiritual welfare, he'd known he'd have trouble. How could he expect the priest to think of him as a respectable, responsible, adult Detective Inspector, when all the time he must have a picture in his mind of Rafferty the boy and youth who had been even more scruffy than his present day embodiment and whose Friday afternoon confessions took twice as long as anyone else's?

Rafferty knew, unless the priest was to continue to run rings around him, that he needed to be firm. Sternly, he reminded him, 'This *is* a murder investigation, Father and—'

'Sure and you don't need to be telling me that. Won't the darling ladies be on their knees, morning, noon and night, praying for the poor man's immortal soul?'

'It's not his immortal soul that concerns me, Father,' Rafferty reminded him. 'It's his mortal body and who ended its life. And given the enclosed nature of the sisters' order, I have no choice but to ask questions of, and learn about, everyone who had access to the grounds, even the holy sisters themselves.' Including *you*, you old reprobate, he thought, though he didn't push his luck by voicing the thought.

The priest studied Rafferty from his

whiskey-rheumed blue eyes, and asked, 'So, what is it you're thinking I can tell you, anyway? Is it details of the nightly orgies you're after? Or the black masses when the devil and all his imps dance before the altar?'

Rafferty counted to ten. Twice. Then he decided the best approach was to speak to Father Kelly in terms he was most familiar with: those of sin and retribution.

'Are you going to answer my questions, Father? Or do you want me to charge you with obstruction? I will,' Rafferty warned. 'If I have to.'

'There's no need to be issuing the threats to *me*, young Mr Detective Inspector. What would your mammy say if I told her?'

Rafferty could guess. But this was a path he had no interest in exploring. And as he had had more than his fill of religion and its practitioners for one day, he decided it was time to get tough and make the priest understand that his threat wasn't an idle one. Quietly, he began to intone the words of the official caution. 'Father Roberto Kelly—' was as far as he got before the priest interrupted him.

'Don't be starting on that nonsense with *me*,' the priest scornfully reprimanded, with all the sermonizing vigour that Rafferty recalled so well from his youth. 'I'm not some gullible gawbeen of a country boy just off the ferry from Ireland. You don't scare *me*. I watch *The Bill* and all those American cop films, too, you know. I'm aware of the usual form in these matters.'

Father Kelly's next words confirmed he was as conversant with the usual police arrest procedures as the most practised villain. He even had the usual vernacular off pat.

'I also know that my brief would get me sprung before you could get me as far as the cells.'

This interview was fast becoming as farcical as one of Brian Rix's West End shows, Rafferty acknowledged. But thankfully, before Father Kelly made him feel even more inadequate for the task of getting to the bottom of this inquiry than he already felt, the old priest confounded him once again by bursting into raucous laughter.

'Sure and I had you going for a minute there, didn't I?' he asked through his continuing loud guffaws. 'Just having a bit of fun with you, young Rafferty.' The priest's open mouth, from which the guffaws emerged unabated, displayed, behind the still fleshy lips of the born sensualist, an unedifying tombstone collection of decaying, nicotine-stained teeth. 'Just a bit of craic, boyo. Sermon writing can be nearly as dull as you always found sermon *listening*, you know. Especially when you've been doing it for as long as I have. And this Sunday's sermonizing hasn't been going well. Not well at all. Call it a religious writer's block, if you like.

Even the more serious minded and religiously resolute amongst the priesthood needs a bit of light relief from all the solemnity sometimes.'

Rafferty wondered if Father Kelly included himself amongst this doughty, religiously resolute breed.

'So, go on, go on,' the priest now encouraged with a wave of his stubby hand. 'What is it you're waiting for? Tell me, what is it you want to know.'

Relieved that he wasn't, after all, to be forced to cart the old bugger off to the station, Rafferty said, 'Basically, whatever you're able to tell me, Father. For instance, have there been any male visitors to the convent during the last few months who caused any kind of trouble? Anyone who had any sort of issues with one of the sisters?'

'*Issues*, is it?' The alcohol-induced thin veining on Father Kelly's nose and cheeks turned from red to regal purple as he tried to conceal the evening's second tendency to uncontrollable mirth beneath a pretended admiration. 'And isn't it up to the minute you are with the words?'

Rafferty knew he was being teased again. But this time he chose to grin and bear it. 'Too much PC for the PCs, Father,' Rafferty explained. 'Politically correct cant catches up with the best of us in the end.'

Father Kelly guffawed again at this. Suddenly the whole atmosphere eased. The priest even opened a drawer in his desk, fondled a bottle of Irish and poured two glasses kept so readily to hand that Rafferty guessed these sessions were a regular occurrence amongst the priest's habitual parishioner visitors. For while Father Kelly had signed up for the embrace of poverty, he wasn't keen on embracing too much of it. And he wasn't keen on it at all if it meant he was denied his favourite tipple.

Rafferty found himself wondering whether his ma had ever sought recourse to the priest's advice and his whiskey. Between her errant, late husband and her six kids, she must often have had cause to seek such solace. Maybe, she'd even succumbed to Father Kelly's *embrace*, as countless other sympathy-seeking women were reputed to have done.

But this was a thought beyond which even he wasn't prepared to venture and he quickly thrust it back from whence it had come.

The priest poured with a generous hand, not troubling to enquire whether Rafferty actually wanted a glass. A refusal of such alcoholic succour from a fellow with good, Irish blood in his veins was clearly beyond expectation or understanding.

It being beyond Rafferty's understanding also, he never thought of offering anything but a grateful 'Sláinte.'

Father Kelly sat back and sipped his whiskey thoughtfully. 'Troublesome visitors, you say?'

Rafferty nodded. 'Or anything else that struck you as out of the ordinary. Anything at all. Odd or not.' He didn't add that he was clutching at straws. But this inquiry was already causing him sufficient qualms that he was happy to clutch at anything, even Father Kelly and his unreliable whiskey-sodden memory.

The priest's stiff and plentiful yard brush-like eyebrows bristled and he looked at Rafferty with a narrowed gaze, as if suspecting *he* might be about to be accused of some sinful deviancy. Then his brow cleared, the realization that he was without sin was writ large, as he announced firmly, 'It's not those with drink taken you're thinking of, clearly. The sisters wouldn't let any drink-sodden man past the entrance gate.'

Not unless he's called Father Kelly, anyway, was Rafferty's irreverent thought, before he added, 'No, Father. I wasn't thinking of drunks.'

The priest merely twinkled at him as if he'd taken to reading minds as well as sermons, and topped up both their glasses. 'Now, I'm thinking, there *was* one young feller.' He peered at Rafferty from under his mad messiah's eyebrows. 'You did say within the last few months?'

Rafferty nodded.

'The timescale would be about right, then, I'm thinking, though you could confirm it with the dear Mother. And though he didn't cause any trouble, he was pretty upset. Not surprising in the circumstances. I gathered he was enquiring about poor Sister Clare. According to Sister Rita this man claimed he was some sort of relative.'

'Why 'poor' Sister Clare?' And why had Mother Catherine failed to mention this visitor when he had questioned her? Rafferty thought.

'Sure, and hasn't the dear woman been dead these thirty years? Died out in Africa. Ministering to the poor and the sick she was, when a murderous mob attacked the mission compound, killing Sister Clare and the other ministering angels. Sister Catherine, as the Mother Superior then was, was seriously injured. She was the only survivor and lucky to be so, something the church hierarchy clearly realized as when she sought permission to move to an enclosed order they proved sufficiently sympathetic to agree.'

'That's where Mother Catherine got those terrible burns?'

The priest nodded. 'Damaged her eyesight, too. That's why, even though, like the rest of us, she embraced poverty with her vows, she's provided with the funds to pay for those expensive tinted spectacles.

'Anyway.' Father Kelly tipped the last of his second Irish down his throat, poured a third and would have done the same to Rafferty's glass if he hadn't shook his head and moved the glass out of reach. 'To get back to that young man I was telling you about. Mother Catherine was cloistered in her office with him for some time, breaking the news to him about Sister Clare's terrible death. That would be sometime towards the end of August, I'm thinking.'

The priest frowned ferociously as he performed this prodigious feat of memory. 'As I said, Mother Catherine broke the news to him and the young man left, escorted out at the same time as me by Sister Rita. I hadn't seen him before that day and I haven't seen him since. Don't expect to. He had received the answer to his question and there was nothing else Mother Catherine could tell him. I imagine she would have much preferred not to have to speak about such a tragedy at all as it must have brought back some terrible memories for the dear lady.'

Rafferty nodded. After hearing Father Kelly's story, he felt more forgiving that Mother Catherine had failed to mention her August visitor. Presumably, her amnesia was essential if she was to save herself from a too-frequent exploration of such memories.

'That's all I can think of in the odd or troublesome visitors line. But of course, I'm not there that much. And what I'm able to tell you doesn't amount to much, either, does it, young Rafferty?'

Rafferty had to agree.

The priest changed the subject then and began to interrogate him.

'So, how's that young lady of yours doing since she lost her babby?' he asked with every indication of concern. 'I remember how set about was the poor little colleen when I saw her in hospital.'

Rafferty wasn't fooled by Father Kelly's show of concern. As usual, the priest had an ulterior motive concealed beneath his black religious robes and Rafferty suspected he knew where this was heading. But he answered anyway. 'She's fine, Father. Abra's fine now.'

'That's grand. That's grand. Glad I am to hear it. Be even finer, would be my guess, if you made an honest woman of her.'

But Rafferty, having obtained what he'd come for, not that that amounted to much, wasn't about to let the priest re-assert any kind of authoritarian Catholic hold over him now. So he simply thanked Father Kelly for the drink and the information, such as it was, bid him goodbye and made a rather swifter exit than he had entrance, chased by the question: 'And when can I expect to see you at Mass?'

'Sometime never,' Rafferty muttered under his breath. 'If I know what's good for me.'

'I know it's still very early in the investigation,' Llewellyn commented after Rafferty had returned to the station and recounted his conversation with Father Kelly, 'but, so far, we don't seem to have many promising leads.

'Before you rushed off so precipitously, I was about to tell you that Dr Peterson was able to tell me nothing helpful, either,' he revealed as Rafferty eased his tired body into his chair in his office. He hoped Llewellyn wasn't about to return to his earlier cross-questioning about his litter-bugging. But he was saved from this at least.

'It's not as if it's likely that any of the nuns can have some dark secret, apart from one of the novices perhaps, as they would certainly have lived in the sinful world more recently than the rest.'

Rafferty, thinking of his own recent encounter with a holy sinner, not to mention his blackmail letter which related to events months past, wasn't so convinced of these conclusions as Llewellyn seemed to be. 'We don't know that this man's death came about because of any recent event,' he pointed out. 'Maybe something from a time in one of their lives prior to taking the veil came back to haunt one of the sisters.'

'The timescale alone surely makes that unlikely?' Llewellyn replied. 'Apart from the novices, all the sisters have lived within an enclosed order for twenty years or more. Why would anyone seeking retribution for old secrets wait so long?'

'Why indeed?' Rafferty asked, as he again

thought of his own secret and the black-mailer who had himself been somewhat tardy in his approach. 'But they do have occasional visitors. Mother Catherine herself told us that the sisters' family and friends are allowed to make occasional visits, for instance. So anyone from one of the sisters' past lives could have gained access and slipped one of them a note along the lines of: "Meet me in the shrubbery after Compline. Come alone." That kind of thing.'

Llewellyn's inscrutable gaze gave little away, but Rafferty detected a hint of scepticism, a scepticism reduced only slightly when Rafferty reminded him what Father Kelly had told him. True it was, that although Mother Catherine had informed them there had been no such visitors to the convent during the relevant time, she had certainly suffered one memory lapse over the question. And although, unlike him, Llewellyn tended not to play favourites, the Welshman admitted his preferred suspects were the two men who had regular access to the convent: Father Kelly and Dr Peterson, particularly given the fact that the set of spare keys to the convent was missing.

'It's just the logistical aspect I'm thinking of,' Llewellyn said. 'Because whereas most of the nuns are given to abstinence, are on the slender side and have their days circumscribed by the demands of their Office, Dr Peterson is not only a big-built man, his time, although presumably as demanding as that of any busy GP, is capable of some flexibility. Given his size, he would surely not have too much difficulty in carrying a corpse across the sisters' extensive grounds.'

He paused, then asked: 'What about Father Kelly? Would he be capable of shouldering such a burden?'

'Doubtful,' Rafferty replied. 'Admittedly, Father Kelly is pretty hefty, too, but his is more of a whiskey-bloated stoutness. And he must be knocking on for seventy if he's a day. Not exactly designed for carrying heavy weights.' Not unless it was a parishioner's Christmas gift of a box of a dozen Jameson bottles. Rafferty suspected he'd manage that with no trouble at all.

Of course, unlike Rafferty, the Methodist-raised Welshman had no lingering Catholic issues from his youth, which probably explained his more logical thinking. Llewellyn harboured no resentments about the stern, repressive nature of his upbringing, even though, from what Rafferty had learned of his sergeant's own youth, the Methodists weren't above a bit of repression themselves.

Rafferty, struggling inwardly with his growing angst, was already finding the case a strain. How much more of a strain would it become, he wondered after he'd been encountering for several weeks on a daily basis, all the residual, ever present Catholic issues of guilt, sin and denial that he had hoped were, if not long behind him, at least far from sight, sound and conscience?

But the Catholic obsession with guilt and sin threw a long shadow. Rafferty suspected that, in time, he might even take to lighting candles in the hope that someone up there would help him bring this case to a swift conclusion. Because he was beginning to fear that Catholicism might yet manage to wrap its clinging, insidious tentacles around him for the second time in his life.

Perhaps, subconsciously, he hoped that if he was able to prove that, like Father Kelly, one of the holy sisters wasn't so holy after all, it might strengthen his defences against such ensnaring tentacles. It wasn't beyond the bounds of credibility, because, like fornicating priests, nuns, too, were capable of breaking the tenets of their faith – as many unfortunate orphans and young unmarried mothers in their 'care' in the past, in Ireland and elsewhere, could vouch for.

'Anyway,' he said as he rubbed eyes gritty from tiredness. 'The issues of weight and strength aside, in the morning, I want you to make a start on checking out the past lives of the ladies. You might as well begin with the novice, Cecile and Teresa, the postulant.' He threw Llewellyn a bone. 'As you said, given their ages, they're the ones most likely to have had recent entanglements of the masculine variety.

'While you're starting that particular ball

116

rolling, I shall, tomorrow morning, go and see Mother Catherine again and find out what she can tell me about this young man Father Kelly said visited in August enquiring about the late Sister Clare. I'd go tonight, but it's too late now. According to the list of their Offices that Mother Catherine gave me, they'll have finished their Great Silence and Compline by now and will be tucked up like good nuns in their hard and lonely little beds. I'd rather not end the first day by breaking my promise that I'd do my best to gear our questioning round their daily ritual.

'But if I can't speak to Mother Catherine tonight, I can at least speak to the troops. I want you to round up as many of the team that you can find and tell them to meet me in the Incident Room in ten minutes. I just want a brief chat to see if any of them can throw any ideas into the hopper before we call it a night.'

It was after ten o'clock already, Rafferty noted, as the bleary-eyed team trooped into the Incident Room. 'I know it's late,' he told them as he stood in front of them. 'I won't keep you long.'

But five minutes later, no one had volunteered any thoughts on the case that might move them forward. To this end, he said, 'I think what we have to ask ourselves, particularly, is why the body was buried in the grounds of the convent' – he'd already given up on calling it a monastery as it didn't feel right.

To his surprise, it was Timothy Smales who spoke up in response to his question, revealing that his improving ability wasn't restricted to learning how to preserve a crime scene. Clearly, he had grown sufficiently confident to voice an opinion in front of his more experienced colleagues.

'Easy, guv,' he said, glancing sideways at his colleagues, with a pleased little smile for his own knowingness. 'Because it was one of the nuns that killed the man. They don't hardly go out, so what chance would they have to bury the body anywhere else?'

Rafferty nodded. It was a valid point. Wasn't he thinking along the same lines himself? 'So you think it's an inside job, Smales?'

Smales nodded and looked to the rest of the team for support. When the young officer got no takers, he shuffled in his chair and swallowed past a suddenly too large Adam's apple. The expression behind the bum-fluff revealed his fear that he'd over-reached himself. But he plunged on.

'Got to be.' Smales reached for the support of formality. 'Sir. I did some Tudor history at school. Some of the goings on at those convents and monasteries would make your blood run cold. That's why Henry VIII shut most of them down.'

Rafferty rather thought Bluff King Hal's religious revolution had had more to do with

118

the fact that he wanted their land and their wealth. A burning desire to usurp the authority of the Pope who had failed to grant his divorce, by giving him a timely poke in the eye, doubtless also figured strongly.

But, aware that the rest of the team was watching him expectantly, waiting for him to reduce Smales to his usual inarticulate unconfident self and that he was waiting along with them, he surprised himself with the realization that he couldn't correct the poor booby in front of everyone. Perhaps the religious atmosphere of the day had made him more kind and saintly?

Or else, and, he admitted, far more likely, it was the picture he had in his mind of himself at a similar age, blurting out his opinion as a young, wet-behind-the-ears police constable at just such another gathering half a lifetime ago. It struck him that he must have looked and sounded an awful lot like Smales. He'd certainly never forget that feeling of being crushed under the weight of a superior's withering comments.

So, instead of making Smales feel small, he made him feel tall, by saying, 'That's a good point,' and was rewarded with a huge grin.

'Now.' He looked around the assembled faces. 'Has anyone else got a worthwhile observation to make?'

But nobody had. Maybe they feared that, having deprived himself of sarcastic indulgence at Smales' expense, he would be looking for another sacrificial victim. But like Smales in his seeking of support, Rafferty also got no takers.

He gave a wry smile. 'OK. If, unlike young Smales, you haven't anything useful to contribute, you might as well call it a night. I shall want you all here early tomorrow morning, so make sure you get sufficient beauty sleep.'

As the team shuffled out, muttering surreptitiously amongst themselves, Llewellyn murmured in his ear, 'You didn't tell them about the missing spare set of keys to the convent, sir.'

'So I didn't.' He called the team back, accompanied by smothered groans from several of them, and gave them this information before he dismissed them again.

It was an hour later before Rafferty felt able to dismiss himself and go home. Abra, his partner, had given up waiting for his return and had gone to bed with a book and a glass of wine.

As he shrugged off his clothes, dumped them in a heap on the floor and climbed in beside her, Rafferty glanced at the book and pulled a face as he saw that it was a hefty romance, and to judge from the cover, it had plenty of steam.

'Carrying on your love life without me now, Abs?' he asked plaintively.

Abra shrugged. 'What's a girl to do, when

she's abandoned for yet another corpse?' She put a marker on the page and closed the book. 'Or at least, I presume that's what's kept you so busy you forgot to ring?'

Ouch. 'Sorry. Spare me a "hello" kiss, at least, before you return to your fictional lover.'

Abra tossed her long, thick, chestnut plait provocatively and gave a secret smile. 'I think I might be able to manage that,' she told him and she pecked his cheek with a teasingly light touch. 'Maybe more than one.' She kissed him again, on the lips this time.

Although tired after the long, stressful day filled with assorted anxieties, Rafferty began to feel some of the strain dropping away. Abra always had the knack of doing that, even when she was cross with him – and God knew his job would give any woman plenty of reasons to be cross. But he knew that, with Abra, underneath, it was a reluctant crossness.

Encouraged by the second kiss, Rafferty leant close and put an arm around her shoulders, while his other hand deftly flipped the book to his side of the bed and opened it at random.

His gaze widened as he read a paragraph. 'Raunchy,' he commented. 'Get you a little hot under the collar?' he asked softly. Hopefully.

'Just a tad,' Abra admitted as she snuggled against his chest.

'Fancy getting hotter?'

'Yes, please, kind sir. I've only been sitting here, quietly steaming for the last hour, waiting for you to come home.'

'Then wait no longer, my Little Hotpot.'

They kissed. Soon, they were both pretty warm and the raunchy book fell unnoticed to the floor.

Later, as they lay still in each others' arms, Abra returned to an earlier conversation.

'So, tell me about the most recent competition for your attention.'

'Our latest cadaver, you mean?'

He felt her head nod against his chest. 'Mm. You know how I love your romantic pillow-talk.'

Rafferty gave a wry laugh. 'God, what a silver-tongued smoothie I am. But you did ask. And I bet you'll never guess where this one's turned up. I confess, it gave me a bit of a turn when I heard.'

Abra sighed, tossed her long, chestnut plait behind her shoulder, and said, 'Just tell me, Joe. It's too late for guessing games.'

'Our mystery male cadaver only turned up in the local RC convent of all places. In a shallow grave in their grounds. How do you like that for giving a man a Godly twist of the knife in the gut?'

Confidently, he awaited the comfort of some Abra magic. But magic of the sympathetic sort came there none. Not even when he called her 'Abracadabra'. Instead she got a fit of the giggles.

'It's not funny, Abs,' he rebuked as her giggles threatened to turn to hysteria.

'Oh, but it is,' she contradicted, once she'd got herself back under control. 'I hate to sound unfeeling and I admit it's clearly not funny from the dead man's point of view. But, that apart, I wish I'd seen your face when you got the news. Maybe I'll manage to witness it when you tell your ma all about it and how you're probably, even as I speak, plotting to fit up one of those poor nuns for the murder. Wouldn't want to miss such treats twice in one week.'

Aghast, Rafferty stared at her. He'd been so busy and preoccupied all day, between the blackmail letter and their religiously located corpse, that he hadn't given a thought to that aspect of the case.

But Abra was right, as he now realized with a sense of dismay. Sure as eggs were eggs, he could guarantee that his ma would have plenty to say when she heard the news. And when she discovered he regarded each and every one of the convent's community as a potential suspect none of her words was likely to be encouraging. And that wasn't even to bring her parish priest into the equation as another suspect.

The thought that an unkindly God had just given the knife another determined twist ensured that he was still awake long into the night.

# Seven

The next morning, Rafferty was out of the flat early, filled with a zeal so unusual that he hoped it wasn't an indication that the Catholic Church really was gaining an unwanted influence over him. Though he suspected that his zeal was at least partly to do with his desire to take himself out of his ma's reach before she read her morning newspaper.

OK, he knew he would be unable to long avoid hearing her inevitable championing of the sisters, but as he could guess the likely content of his ma's comments, any delay was to be welcomed. He was certain to receive sufficient ear-bashing from the media on this case, without his ma joining in. And a delay would give him a chance to prepare a few arguments of his own.

He just wished he could come up with a defence against the blackmailer. Or at least manage to figure out his or her identity and how he should proceed against the threat the blackmailer represented.

On his arrival at the police station, he spent an hour and a half working his way through the reports he should have read the previous evening. Then he glanced at his watch, thankful to find that if he went along to see Mother Catherine now he wouldn't be interrupting anything vital. The general domestic and other chores started at nine and Rafferty thought it unlikely that even the Prioress would object to his interrupting the dusting.

Behind the heavily tinted spectacles that protected her burn-damaged sight, Mother Catherine stared at Rafferty and repeated his question back at him. 'What happened to the man who visited us in August? I'm not sure I understand what you mean, Inspector. Of course, I apologize for forgetting to mention him and his visit when you spoke to me before. I admit it slipped my mind. I suppose because I didn't think his visit relevant. As you said Father Kelly confirmed, this visitor left the premises at the same time he did.

'But, certainly, I can tell you what the visitor wanted. As you said Father Kelly has already confirmed, he came to see me about poor Sister Clare. He told me she was a relative of his and that he had recently taken up an interest in researching his family tree.'

She almost faltered then and Rafferty felt a twinge of guilt that he was forcing her to again relive her undoubtedly tragic experiences. But, to his relief, she continued bravely on.

'I broke the sad news that she had died –

been murdered – many years ago in Africa. Then he left.'

She shrugged. 'I really don't know what else I can tell you. Sister Rita, who was escorting Father Kelly to the entrance as I opened my office door, showed my visitor out and, as far as I'm aware, he left with Father Kelly. As I didn't walk him to the front door myself, I can't swear that he actually left the premises, though I can't imagine that Sister Rita would have any reason to detain him. And she can't have done. As you've already said that Father Kelly confirmed she *did* escort this man to the gate and he left our premises, so I'm at a loss as to why you think I'm able to tell you any more about him.'

'Well no, I don't particularly,' Rafferty replied. 'But you must understand, Reverend Mother, that if I'm to discover the identity of the dead man and find his murderer, I need to check out visitors to the convent who are of the same age range and gender.'

'Yes, of course, I can see that. But surely his watch will be a help in identifying him? It looked expensive.'

'We're looking into that aspect.'

He had already arranged for a picture of the watch to be circulated to the media later today. He was hopeful some sharp-eyed member of the public might recognize it.

To Rafferty's surprise, given his suspicion that this case had been created by the

Almighty solely as a means to punish one of his back-sliding children, the dead man's watch *did* have an inscription on the back. Unfortunately, it was a simple one with no mention of surnames or dates. All it said was: 'To our dear son, Peter, on the occasion of his twenty-first birthday. From your loving parents'.

Rafferty suspected that God was merely teasing him. He might have given him a watch with an inscription, but He'd made sure that the wording was no help at all.

But he hadn't given up on it yet. The dead man's twenty-first birthday might well have occurred years earlier, but with such a pricey watch, there was still a chance they would get a lead on where it had been bought. They might even discover who had bought it. But he didn't allow himself to dwell too much on that possibility.

'What about other visitors?' he now asked the Prioress. Although he felt another guilty twinge that he should seem to imply that she could have had a memory failure about this as well, he couldn't let such scruples deter him. 'The sisters' families, for instance. Have any of them visited recently?'

She shook her head. 'You asked me that before and the answer's still "No". We have a sort of open day at Christmas and another at Easter. Those are the only occasions that families can visit. We don't encourage them to turn up out of the blue. It's too distracting. We all chose this life away from the world for its peace and contemplative aspects. If the world kept turning up on our doorstep whenever it chose, the whole point and meaning of our lives would be diminished.'

Rafferty nodded and drew her back to their previous conversation. 'This August visitor, I presume he had a name?'

For the first time, Mother Catherine looked flustered, embarrassed even. 'Yes, of course, but I didn't quite catch it. He had one of those quiet voices and my hearing isn't what it was. Maybe, as Sister Rita opened the front door to him and was told his business here, she will be able to tell you that?'

Rafferty nodded. 'Did he make an appointment to see you or did he just turn up on the off chance?'

The Mother Superior's brow puckered in thought. 'I'm fairly sure he just turned up. Wait a moment. Let me check the diary. If he made an appointment, it would be in there.'

She began rummaging in her desk, found the appointments diary and rifled through the pages till she reached the month of August. She shook her head. 'There's nothing here.'

Rafferty reached for the diary and checked through it himself. But she was correct. There was nothing.

'I'm sorry I'm unable to be more help,' she

told him. 'But I really don't think this chap can be one and the same as the dead man. How could he be, when our August visitor left? I'm sure that Sister Rita will be able to confirm it.'

'Did he say why he had come here, specifically?'

Mother Catherine nodded. 'He wanted to speak to me personally, he said. To question me about the late Sister Clare. And although he admitted his earlier enquiries had revealed that she had died, I got the impression he hadn't really believed it. It was at his insistence that the diocesan offices told him where to find me so I could confirm the facts of her death.'

'Did this visitor say what his relationship with Sister Clare was? Or why he was searching for her only now, thirty years after her death?'

Mother Catherine shook her head. 'He didn't tell me what the relationship was,' she explained. 'And I didn't like to pry. But, given his age, which must have been around the mid to late forties, as well as his general demeanour, I suspected he might have believed himself to be an illegitimate son of another family member. He seemed disinclined to believe that Sister Clare was dead. I suppose he assumed that, as one of the nuns who was in Africa at the time she was killed, I would be able to confirm the facts and maybe help him to accept them.'

Rafferty, prompted into bluntness by what he considered Mother Catherine's careful skirting around the details, asked, 'Is it possible that he could have been *Sister Clare's* illegitimate son?'

Mother Catherine seemed shocked at this blunt suggestion. It took her a few seconds before she replied. The reply was an emphatic, 'No. Certainly not. Whatever makes you think such a thing?'

Rafferty apologized. 'I'm sorry if I've offended you. It's just that Father Kelly told me this man seemed upset when he left. If, as you suggest, he was merely checking out his general family tree, and Sister Clare was his aunt, cousin, or whatever, I can't see why he should be so affected when her death was confirmed. But thank you, Mother, for your help.' He stood up. 'I'll have a word with Sister Rita as you suggested. I imagine I'll find her in the grounds?'

'Yes. She and Sister Benedicta are busy with the last of the fruit harvest in the orchard.'

He bid her good morning and went in search of Sister Rita. As Mother Catherine had told him, she was hard at work in the garden with Sister Benedicta, collecting apples and pears and boxing them carefully for storage.

Once she had hitched up her habit and climbed down the ladder, Sister Rita confirmed what the Mother Superior and

Father Kelly had already told him. Like Mother Catherine, Sister Rita was also unable to recall their visitor's name. Rafferty hadn't even bothered to ask Father Kelly the same question. The old priest had enough trouble remembering his own name most of the time.

'Here, Inspector. Catch.' Sister Rita took a shiny red apple from the box at her feet and threw it towards him. 'There's no need to wash it. All our produce is grown organically.' She laughed. 'Which sometimes means I'm out in the vegetable plot in the evening with a torch, picking off the slugs by hand. I'd set a competition to encourage the other sisters to lend a hand with the task, with a dish of garlic snails prepared by Sister Perpetua as the prize, only, apart from myself and Sister Benedicta, most of the other sisters, being born and bred city types, are too squeamish about touching such slimy things to be willing to enter.'

'They're in good company,' Rafferty told her. He bit into his apple. It tasted as sweet and juicy as he imagined the one with which Eve had tempted Adam must have been. 'Do you sell any of your produce?'

She nodded. 'Yes. Along with the sales of our brochures, crafts and other handiwork, it brings in a useful income. I'll add your name to the list if you like and send you details of our available seasonal produce.'

Rafferty did like. He thanked her and

added, 'You can send it to me care of the station.'

After Sister Rita had abandoned her labours for long enough to escort him from the convent, he stood on the street as the traffic rushed past him with its usual noise, exhaust fumes and bustle to get somewhere else. He was suddenly struck by the contrast between the two worlds. And for the first time, life inside the convent walls didn't come off second best in the comparison. In fact, he realized that he was beginning to find the cloistered life held a strange and growing appeal.

Yesterday, when the body had been found, the community had been shocked and subdued which had naturally depressed the atmosphere.

Yet today, the convent's normal aura had returned. With the sisters now over their initial shock, an atmosphere of joy and love permeated the place. It was there in the ready smiles of the sisters and in their care for one another. Completely immersed in the murder and its solution during the first day of the investigation, he had failed to notice these things. But he had noticed them now.

Even though he had only been enclosed by the convent's walls a couple of times, he realized how sharp was the contrast with 'real life'. It was, he realized with a shock, a contrast not to the world's advantage. The nuns' world was like a completely different planet. A soothing, loving place. In fact Rafferty, although feeling sheepish at the thought, would have been increasingly less willing to leave the place at all – even for Abra – if it wasn't for the embarrassment he felt that although the murder investigation impinged on their lives and disrupted their holy routines, the nuns mostly accepted it with a patient serenity that was an example to all. They simply offered their bizarre experience up to God and asked Him to help them deal with it, much as they asked His help in dealing with their threefold vows of poverty, chastity and obedience.

Rafferty had found his initial expectations of convent life had been wrong on every count. One of these expectations had been the presumption that the general atmosphere within the community would be one of bitterness at life from these 'failed' women. A bitterness overlaid with sexual repression. In short, he had expected a total lack of joy and laughter.

But joy – sheer, unbridled, radiant – shone from nearly every face. Most surprising of all was the discovery that convents didn't lack sensual pleasures of the simpler sort.

Sensuality was there in the sun-warmed scent of lavender and beeswax on the floor and the smooth wooden pews in the chapel. It was there in the pleasing slap of leather sandals on the stone floors in the rest of the convent. In the beauty of sunlight through the chapel's stained glass that cast its glorious glow on everything, lighting up the dancing dust motes that no amount of vigorous polishing could entirely remove. It picked out and enhanced the rich hues of the flowers and the deep and vivid green of the leaves in the vases which were filled to bursting with colours from a rainbow spectrum of flowers.

These flowers were everywhere. Their perfume, subtle and delightful, filled the place with sufficiently contrasting pleasing smells to make the senses reel. He was even getting used to the pervasive smell of incense.

The sisters knew how to laugh, too, as he had discovered. They hadn't abandoned their personalities or sense of humour when they rejected the world.

A grin curled its way round his lips as he recalled something that had happened a little earlier, as he was walking down the corridor to the back door to speak to Sister Rita. He'd noticed a half-sized door nearly concealed in a dark corner near the chapel and he had asked Sister Ursula, who had been hobbling towards him on her painful, arthritic legs, where it led.

The nun's face, as wrinkled as a walnut, had gazed back at him, deadpan, as she had replied: 'Oh that. It leads to the secret passage that allows us to smuggle lots of you lovely men into the convent.'

Rafferty recalled his own shock at the words of this nun, whose life was daily filled with the pain of arthritis and osteoporosis. But his shock had lasted for only a few seconds, before the wrinkled, humped and bent over old nun had roared with laughter and given him the greater shock of destroying all his previous certainties about religious life, when she told him: 'Your face is a picture, Inspector. And while I might have been glad of the odd, smuggled man in my novice days, I can't imagine what use I'd find for one now.'

Rafferty gave a rueful shake of his head at the recollection.

For the first time in his life, he felt he had lost out by so determinedly turning his back on religion. Another shock rocked him as a second realization hit him. The long-forgotten and unfamiliar urge to pray had subtly invaded his mind. Altogether, for a man who had spurned religion and all its works for years, this reaction was rather alarming.

In fact, these feelings so alarmed him that he subdued them and he hurried off to his car to return to the station, determined to continue with his normal routines. At least he knew where he was with them.

But this 'God' thing rather unnerved him. It challenged every tenet of his life. And he didn't like it.

'Not a lot to report yet on all but one of the

community,' was Llewellyn's response when Rafferty questioned him on his return.

'Most of the sisters, as we know, have been shut away from the world for a generation or more and their family members have died, moved away, married, divorced and lost touch generally. They're all going to require a lot more work to trace them than I've managed today. I suppose it's as Mother Catherine said, and keeping in touch all becomes, for the nuns' families, more of an effort with each passing year.'

Rafferty nodded. 'Continue with it, anyway, Dafyd. And even if the good sisters have failed to keep properly abreast of family house moves and so on, I'm sure government bureaucracy will have proved more tenacious.' He paused. 'You said "all but one". I suppose the exception is either the little novice, Cecile or Teresa Tattersall, the postulant?'

'Your first guess is correct. Sister Cecile's family still live at her old home. It's not that far from here, as the convent's records revealed. They still seemed a bit shell shocked at her decision to become a nun. Refused to believe that she really intended to take her life vows.'

'Understandable, I suppose. It must seem a strange vocation for a young woman nowadays, when so many prefer to go the illegitimate kids and welfare route.'

'Well no, it's not that. It's more a case that

they don't seem to believe in the sincerity of her vocation. They gave me the impression that they thought her taking up religion was simply a means for her to escape a persistent ex-boyfriend.'

'I can think of more attractive ways of escaping a troublesome boyfriend than joining a nunnery,' Rafferty retorted, determined to quell any return to his earlier worrying yen for religion. 'Though, I suppose what it lacks in attraction it makes up for in its efficient security.'

'Mm.'

'This boyfriend.' Rafferty had a sudden thought and he asked sharply: 'How old is he?'

'Old enough to be our cadaver, if that's what you're thinking. Even better from our point of view: he seems to have disappeared. Said disappearance was also in the right timeframe.'

The possibility that they might have discovered the identity of the dead man stirred jubilant juices in Rafferty's stomach. But he reined in his excitement as he reminded himself that too often, in the past, hopes of early achievement in a case had come to nothing. So he kept his voice level as he said, 'Tell me about him.'

Nathan McNally was forty-eight to Cecile's twenty-six. No wonder, as Llewellyn explained, that the young novice's family had been against the match from the start.

In addition to being in the same rough age range as their cadaver, which Dr Dally had already confirmed, this Nathan McNally was also, according to what Llewellyn had discovered, of a similar height to the dead man.

'Did you manage to get a photo of this McNally?' Rafferty asked.

'No. Unfortunately, Cecile's family were so delighted when their daughter finished with him that they threw away any photos of him.'

'Pity.'

'Though they were able to give me a fair description of him.' Llewellyn consulted his notebook. 'According to the family, McNally had short brown hair, hazel eyes and was around twelve and a half stone. He had a nasty temper, apparently.'

'Did he indeed? Sounds the sort to have a police record. You checked?'

'Yes, of course.' Llewellyn's lips thinned as if he considered the question not only unnecessary, but an insult to his intelligence. 'There was nothing on record.'

Rafferty swallowed his disappointment. 'Doesn't necessarily mean anything. There are any number of men out there prone to violence but who manage to keep their names off the police computer. This could still turn out to be a crime of passion, with the good sisters, in attempting to protect Cecile from her ex-boyfriend and his nasty temper, restraining him with a little too much vigour.

'I'm thinking Agatha Christie and the *Murder on the Orient Express*,' Rafferty revealed. 'You know, the one where the murder turned out to be a group effort.'

'Rather outlandish.'

'Outlandish it may be, but that doesn't mean it mightn't have happened that way. As I've always said to you, Dafyd, in this job, it's necessary to keep an open mind.'

Llewellyn's lips thinned again at this comment from his far from open-minded inspector, but he didn't rise to the bait. Instead, he said, 'Anyway, I've arranged for Cecile's parents to come into the station tomorrow and work on the computer with the police artist. If we have a face to go with the name we will hopefully either be able to trace and discount him as our victim or confirm that he is indeed our cadaver.'

The lack of a photo of Nathan McNally aside, Rafferty couldn't help but feel hopeful. But to prevent his hopes rising too enthusiastically, he issued himself another warning. It would be time enough to get excited when they had a confirmed ID for the dead man. But they were some way from that yet.

Still, he thought, if this Nathan McNally *did* turn out to be their victim – and if he failed to contact them once his details were circulated, this would be a strong pointer in this direction – it would mean all things were possible. The confirmed identity of the dead man would surely also provide a strong indication of the identity of his murderer ...

And as they had received confirmation from three sources that the man who had enquired about Sister Clare had indeed left the convent premises, it was good to have him replaced with another potential victim so quickly. Especially as this latest male had what was undoubtedly – in the shape of his ex-girlfriend, the novice, Cecile – what could be called a definite connection to the convent.

According to what Llewellyn had discovered, not only had Nathan McNally himself disappeared, but so had his family. They had long since moved away and none of the ex-neighbours whom Llewellyn had questioned knew where they had moved to.

It might take some time to trace them. But at least, once that was accomplished, their DNA would confirm whether or not Nathan was their cadaver. It could be a breakthrough. But to get even the possibility of one, so unexpectedly and so early in the case caused a little bubble of anxiety to replace the previous jubilant juices in Rafferty's stomach.

God, what's the matter with you? he asked himself. Here you are, possibly with a clear and early pointer to our cadaver's identity and still you're complaining. Don't tell me you're becoming like Llewellyn and logic's starting to edge out the optimism?

To make up for his earlier teasing, Rafferty slapped Llewellyn on the back with such enthusiasm that the Welshman winced. 'Good work, Dafyd. Of course, while we're trying to trace this McNally's family, we'll continue with the other strands of the investigation – checking the backgrounds of the other sisters and those of Father Kelly and Dr Peterson, as well as tracing the late Sister Clare's family. I still want to eliminate this man with no name who came to the convent to enquire about Sister Clare.'

He paused, then asked, 'Wasn't it another great detective who said that if you eliminate the impossible then what's left, however improbable, must be your answer?'

'Another great detective?' Llewellyn murmured. 'I wonder who it could be that you're thinking of for your first.'

Rafferty grinned. 'I'll let you guess. I'm sure you can figure it out.'

Rafferty admitted he was tempted to throw all his resources into the Cecile connection, but he put this temptation firmly behind him. Maybe his decision had something to do with the unwelcome part religion was currently playing in his life and it was helping lead him from such temptations? Or perhaps, as he preferred to think, he was just getting older and wiser.

# Eight

By noon the next day, Rafferty, finding his thoughts – about blackmailers, nuns and his mother – were chasing themselves round and round the grey caverns of his brain, decided he needed some fresh air.

But instead of wandering Elmhurst's ancient streets, he got in his car and headed for the open countryside surrounding the town. He didn't want people around him. He craved solitude and peace in the hope that he would manage to remove the sticky cobwebs currently binding his thought processes.

In spite of his desire for solitude and open country, he found himself stopping outside the convent instead of continuing to the countryside beyond. On an impulse, he parked up. He didn't even have to ring the bell to gain admittance. Sister Rita was in the entrance lobby and saw him through the grille.

She let him in and gave him a quiet greeting. 'Inspector. Back again, I see.'

He nodded. 'Afraid so.' He would be forced to keep turning up, like a bad penny, he acknowledged, until he had nailed the murderer.

Sister Rita studied him for a moment, then she smiled and said, 'You look in need of one of Sister Perpetua's famous tonics. Come into the kitchen. She's been experimenting with a new recipe. Something to do with apples, she said. She thinks it should be about ready for testing now.'

An hour later, the noise Rafferty, Sister Rita and Sister Perpetua were making after trying out Sister Perpetua's experimental and damn near lethal, 'apple drink', attracted the attention of Mother Catherine.

It didn't need communication with the Heavenly Father for the Prioress to realize that she was the only sternly sober one amongst them. After roundly chastising the two tipsy nuns and sending them to sleep off the effects of Sister Perpetua's experiment, she showed Rafferty to the door, like a stern headmistress who thought he was a bad influence.

But even after the door clanged shut behind him, Rafferty couldn't help but grin at the thought that Sister Perpetua, in her innocent experiment, like the ignorant savage who spontaneously invented the wheel, had, by accident, discovered how to concoct a heady brew of cider.

He was still chuckling (and staggering), after he had walked back to the edge of town and hailed a taxi – owing to the kitchen nun's concoction, being in no fit state to drive – to return to the station.

The evening darkness had long since descended when Rafferty, now suffering the after effects of Sister Perpetua's heady brew, put the phone down. He rubbed his aching head just as Llewellyn entered the office.

At least his sergeant had some welcome news. The artist's impression of Nathan Mc-Nally, the missing ex-boyfriend of the novice Cecile, that her parents had helped to compose, was now ready and could be circulated.

Rafferty acknowledged this with a nod. 'I'm glad *something's* moving on this investigation,' he said. 'I've just had Fraser on the phone. The dead man's fingerprints aren't on the national database. He's now checking the international one. But time's moving on and I don't want to delay any longer. So, in the meantime, while we're waiting to see if Fraser comes up with something, I think we're going to have to try to get a confirmed ID from dental records. And if that gets us nowhere, we'll have no choice but to go for facial reconstruction from the skull. Professor Amos at the university has got us some good results on that in the past. But getting a firm ID for this man is a priority. Without that, we haven't a hope of pinning down any of our suspects, never mind making an arrest.'

'Speaking of suspects,' Llewellyn said. 'I've just come from the Incident Room. Since the news broke on our cadaver there have been several anonymous telephone calls from members of the public about Dr Peterson, the convent's general practitioner. Their gist seems to be that back in the sixties, when he was a young doctor, he performed abortions at a time, before the 1967 Abortion Act, when, except in cases of the most extreme medical emergency, they were still illegal.'

Rafferty hunched forward over his desk and asked, 'And had he? Or is it just a case of unsubstantiated tittle-tattle? God knows all kinds of allegations come out of the woodwork during a murder inquiry. Most of them turn out to be nothing more than opportunistic spite, rather like the denunciations neighbour made against neighbour in the old communist states.'

'As yet, these allegations are unsubstantiated,' Llewellyn told him. 'But it's interesting that every one of the callers who rang on the matter said the same thing. Though, I must say that I can't see what possible connection these rumours can have to our current case. Even if one of the sisters at the convent had need of such a service back in her youth, why would they have gone to Dr Peterson?

'Apart from any other consideration, all the older nuns, bar the late Sister Clare, lived many miles away, so even if they had need of the skills of a doctor in Dr Peterson's line, they would scarcely approach him. It would be local knowledge and word of mouth an unwillingly pregnant woman would need in such circumstances. And she wouldn't get that by travelling halfway across the country to a completely strange place and then hoping for the best.'

Rafferty smiled. 'As ever, your logic is without flaw.' He grabbed his jacket. 'And much as I don't like having to drag a man back forty years in his life and ask him to explain his doings then, I suppose we have no choice. Most of us, over the years, move so far on from our youthful selves that we're unrecognizable as the same people.

'Still, we'll see what he's got to say for himself, even though, like you, I can't see that what he might or might not have done forty or more years ago can have to do with *our* murder.'

Rafferty sensed Llewellyn's intelligent brown gaze settle on him as they walked down the corridor to the stairs and the car park. He sensed a criticism coming. He wasn't wrong, he realized moments later, when Llewellyn voiced his thoughts.

'Strange,' the Welshman quietly commented, 'that you don't appear to harbour the same reservations about the ancient history of the sisters or Father Kelly.'

Pulled up by Llewellyn's comment, Rafferty glanced sideways at his colleague as they reached the first floor landing. 'No, I don't, do I?' he asked elliptically.

Of course Llewellyn knew nothing about the 'Road to Damascus' moment he'd experienced as he'd stood outside the convent's walls. And Rafferty, now that his earlier surprise at the experience had worn off, reverted to type and put the experience down to the fact that he hadn't had any breakfast. Fighting desperately to shrug off this new-found and unwanted 'God' thing, he added, 'Call it retribution of the less than Divine sort.'

'Payback time for youthful punishments received?'

'Perhaps.' Rafferty muttered, even though now he felt much less inclined to indulge the urge to get a bit of his own back on the Church. But preferring to keep his own counsel on the matter, he added, 'Or maybe it's just that I find more to empathize with in a young doctor trying to save frightened girls from the perils of the back street abortionist in the sixties than I do with a gaggle of nuns who spend their lives on their knees rather than doing something socially useful.'

He wished it were still true. He felt a hypocrite now, for saying it. For, in truth, he was finding much in the simple lives of the sisters to envy. Even if he was now inclined to shy away from again making such an admission to himself.

'Whatever happened to "Judgement is

mine, sayeth the Lord"?'

Rafferty, already anticipating his mother's judgement on the case and surprised that she hadn't yet confided it to him, was not in the mood to listen to his sergeant's also.

Anyway, he didn't know what Llewellyn was complaining about. Weren't they about to check out the doctor's past life and past doings, just as they had been doing and continued to do to those of the sisters? He would be less than human if, previously at any rate, some of the checks had appealed to him more than others. But that didn't mean he wouldn't be as thorough as possible in all of them.

In a voice that brooked no argument, Rafferty said: 'Judgement, like beauty, is in the eyes of the beholder. And as I'm the one doing the beholding—'

They reached the car park. Hungover and doubtless with Sister Perpetua's heady cider concoction still circulating in his body, Rafferty subsided into the passenger seat. Not another word was spoken till they reached Dr Peterson's Orchard Avenue surgery. Which suited Rafferty just fine.

Dr Stephen Peterson had just come to the end of morning surgery when Rafferty and Llewellyn arrived. The waiting room was empty. The receptionist rang the doctor on the internal line to advise him of their arrival and gave them the nod to go through to the office.

Dr Peterson was every bit as tall and broad as Llewellyn had indicated. He looked, to Rafferty, to be about six foot three and around seventeen stone. Even though he must be somewhere the wrong side of sixty-five and past the usual retirement age, he looked more than able, as Llewellyn had said, to heave corpses around without too much difficulty.

Had he, though? Rafferty speculated. And if so, why?

The doctor didn't look pleased to see them. Rafferty guessed he would look even less welcoming when he learned what they wanted to question him about.

'I've already told your sergeant here all I know about the body you found in the convent's grounds, which is precisely nothing,' Dr Peterson began irritably. 'I don't know what else you think I can—'

Rafferty held up his hand. 'Please, doctor. Actually, it wasn't about the body found at the convent that we wished to talk to you about.'

'No? What then? Whatever it is, I hope it won't take too long.' He glanced at his watch. 'I'm doing some filling-in and am due at the hospital in twenty minutes.'

'This shouldn't take more than a few minutes of your time, doctor,' Rafferty reassured him, adding the proviso: 'provided, that is, you're cooperative and answer our questions.'

Dr Peterson's lips pursed at this, but he contained any further inclination to temper. Instead, he asked shortly: 'And your questions are?'

Rafferty hesitated, glanced at Llewellyn, then said, 'We've received some allegations about you.'

'Allegations?' Peterson's thick grey brows almost met in the middle. 'What sort of allegations? And what could these allegations possibly have to do with the dead man found in the convent's grounds?'

'As for your last question, I suppose I have to say that that remains to be seen. But as for these allegations, they concern a time in your life when you were a young doctor. Over forty years ago. To before the 1967 Abortion Act, to be precise.'

Dr Peterson paled. The thin, aesthetic face which was such a mismatch with his muscular body, took on an anguished cast and he slumped heavily into his chair. 'Very well. What do you want to know?'

'These allegations, all of which took the same line, say you carried out illegal abortions as a young medic. I just want you to confirm or deny the allegations and we'll be on our way.'

To his surprise, Peterson didn't even attempt to deny them. Instead, he became aggressive once more.

'And what if I did?' he demanded. 'You've no idea of the butchers that were out there back then. Nor of the young girls who died of sepsis or who were permanently maimed at their hands.'

His voice turned sombre and suddenly, all the aggression went out of him. 'My elder sister died under the "care" of one such. She wasn't quite eighteen. She died in agony. I know, because I listened to her cries of torment.'

'Why wasn't she in hospital receiving treatment and pain relief?'

Dr Peterson's face contorted into a humourless mask. 'Well might you ask, Inspector.'

A haunted smile played briefly about the doctor's face, then he said, 'You're too young to know the social atmosphere of the time. It was rigid, unforgiving. My parents were "respectable". They would have been mortified if the shame of my sister's illegitimate pregnancy had become common knowledge. If they had taken her to hospital everyone would have known what she'd done.'

He raised a face still traumatized by past ghosts for their inspection. 'And they could not have that, you see. Their "respectability" demanded that she suffer in secret, died even, to protect it.'

Appalled at the man's revelations, Rafferty strove to get a grip. He knew he needed to challenge Dr Peterson, find a way through the defences of his still-present pain, if he was to obtain answers.

151

'But your parents must have known the reason for your sister's death would become common knowledge,' Rafferty pointed out, wincing at his own brutality. 'The death certificate—'

'The death certificate said my sister died from the complications of influenza,' Stephen Peterson told him flatly, as his face contorted into lines of bitter and pain-filled memory. 'My father had gone to school with the family GP,' he wearily explained. His tired, matter-of-fact manner seemed to imply that they should have understood this, at least. 'And my parents knew he would help them cover up my sister's shame.'

'I see.' Rafferty did see. Only too clearly. Diffidently, he asked, 'Is that why you decided to become a doctor?'

Stephen Peterson nodded. He even managed a smile, but it was a smile totally devoid of humour and merely emphasized the scored lines that gave his face such a cadaverous appearance.

'I was on a mission, I suppose. I was an idealist. An idealist who wanted to save the world. I thought I could make a difference. And I did, for some at least.'

His voice dropped and they had to strain to hear the rest. 'But not for enough of them. Not for nearly enough of them.'

He sighed, bent his head with its still thick salt and pepper hair and propped it on his hands, kneading his eyes with his forefingers and thumbs, before he brought his hands away from his face and let them fall into his lap. He looked back up.

He met their gaze squarely, one after the other, then said with a return of his former vigour: 'But I don't understand your interest in my idealism so late in the day. It's not as if the dead man found at the convent could have had any connection with my life back then. I doubt he was even born. I thought the newspaper report said he was believed to be somewhere around his mid to late forties?'

Rafferty nodded. 'But it's only a rough estimate. You're a doctor, so I imagine you're aware, that over a certain age, such estimates can be out by around ten years.'

Peterson nodded a vague assent to this statement. Then he said, 'But even if the dead man was fifty-odd rather than forty something, he would still have only been a child when I was a young doctor.

'No one with a grievance from that time has contacted me. So, if, as I presume, the implication is that I killed this man after he turned up accusing me of causing the death of his mother, sister, or other family member, in order to save myself from exposure, then you're way off the mark. Even if such a person *had* turned up and accused me of such a thing, it's half a lifetime ago.

'Besides, apart from any other objection to this man's death being anything to do with me, his body was found in the grounds of the convent, rather than my back garden. I might be the sisters' GP, but they haven't cut me a key for ease of access.'

An ironic mockery entered his voice as he added, 'You can't seriously believe that I was so worried that the British Medical Council would be so interested in raking over old gossip that I felt it necessary to kill some hate-filled vengeance-seeker from four decades ago.'

Rafferty thought it probable that the doctor was right about the latter. Didn't the BMA usually prefer to bury their heads in the sand when it came to one of their own being accused of malpractice or even worse, as in the recent, infamous multiple murders of his patients by Dr Harold Shipman?

Rafferty frowned and looked down at the once again seemingly penitently bent head of Dr Peterson, as he acknowledged that, when it came to the dead man, they only had the doctor's word for it that their murder victim hadn't contacted him and threatened him and his good name.

But even if he had, and the doctor had been provoked into attacking and killing him, it still didn't explain why the dead man had ended up buried in the grounds of the convent.

There again, though, as Rafferty grappled with his silent arguments, they only had the doctor's word for it that he hadn't been the one who had helped himself to the convent's spare keys.

Strangely, now that he'd explained himself, to his own satisfaction, at least, Stephen Peterson didn't seem particularly perturbed by their visit or by the provoking implications of their questions.

Perhaps he'd shed some of his idealism along the way and acquired instead, a protective layer of realism? Certainly, his remark about the inertia of the BMA indicated the possibility, Rafferty thought as he gazed at the doctor's bowed head.

But, whatever he'd acquired, it apparently didn't include the proclivity to breaking down and confessing. So he and Llewellyn said their goodbyes and headed back to the car and the station.

'Well, he didn't exactly try very hard to conceal the illegal abortions, did he? He was amazingly open, even gung ho about them,' Rafferty remarked as they waited to join the traffic on the roundabout by the shopping centre to the north west of Elmhurst.

Quietly, Llewellyn said, 'I suppose, after what happened to his sister, that's easy enough to understand. And given his tragic experience, who's to say, in the same circumstances, that the rest of us wouldn't have copied his example and done our best to help young girls in similar straits? I've read enough about that period to know how unforgiving was society if a young woman

155

made a single lapse from the expected virtue. Many a young girl, even as late as the sixties, ended up in a psychiatric hospital, often for years, if she fell pregnant outside marriage.'

Rafferty had heard enough, too, as he had eavesdropped on some of the conversations his ma had had with her female cronies amongst the neighbours. The conversations on which he had eavesdropped had not been ones for the fainthearted.

And, as he considered the latter, with all the in-built revelations about pain, suffering and death that he had, as a youth, overheard, it was some minutes before he felt able to make another comment.

In fact, he found he had to draw several deep breaths, before he could say anything else at all: 'Still, just because he freely admitted his culpability over the illegal abortions when we challenged him about them, doesn't mean he mightn't have other guilty secrets he's less keen to share. Take the location of the body, for instance.

'As the convent's medic, the body could be said to be practically buried in his back yard. And given that he, like Father Kelly, had the run of the place, either one could have helped themselves to the spare key from the key cabinet.'

As the flow of traffic eased sufficiently to allow even the cautious Llewellyn to press his foot on the gas pedal and enter the roundabout, he remarked, 'Perhaps that would be all the more reason for him to bury it there. He's presumably an intelligent man. Nobody would think he would be so foolish as to bury a body in a place with such close connections to himself.'

'Mm. Whatever *he* thought – I know what *I* think. And that's that it doesn't bring us any further forward.'

Rafferty thumped the dashboard in frustration. 'If only we can discover the victim's ID. His identity has got to be the key to his death. But until we have that key...'

Rafferty, although mostly lacking in reasons to be cheerful, at least had one cause for celebration. Because even though another working day was drawing to a close, his ma, unaccountably, had failed to get in touch with him and issue instructions as to how delicately he was to treat the holy sisters. It could hardly be that she hadn't by now heard the news, as the media, both print and TV, had seized on the discovery of the body in the convent with something approaching relish. He supposed that, for them, the story had it all: violent death, religion and presumed sexual repression.

Rafferty could only hope that no one tipped the media off about Dr Peterson's unorthodox and, at the time, illegal, early practices.

Because if they *did* and then also discovered what an old sinner was the nuns' priest, they would quickly put two and two together till they had come up with a complete, unabridged, unholy brew, that would put Rafferty and his investigation plumb in the middle of an extravagant media frenzy.

Tired at the end of another long day, Rafferty felt almost relieved to learn on his eventual arrival home that one of his many anxieties about the case was about to receive its validation.

For his ma was at the flat waiting for him.

# Nine

It seemed that his ma had decided to wait to give Rafferty the benefit of her opinion as to how he should conduct his current investigation until she was able to catch him at home and speak to him in person, it being so much more likely that she would be able to sway him to her views in the flesh than over the phone.

Rafferty opened the door to his living room and saw her, sitting near Abra on one of the new armchairs in their recently updated living room, a mug of tea, unusually for Kitty Rafferty, ignored and skinned over on the small table in front of her.

His ma, as anticipated, when he was foolish enough to blurt out the possibility, was scandalized that he could even think of suspecting one of the holy sisters of murder. She even wagged her work-worn forefinger at him as she told him: 'For shame.'

'Why shouldn't I suspect one of the sisters?' he demanded as he shrugged out of his coat and jacket and threw them towards the back of the settee, from whence, unnoticed and still entwined, they fell to the

159

floor. He threw himself on the second armchair. 'Or all of them, for that matter?

'OK,' he conceded as he saw his ma's scandalized expression, 'I agree, they may have more cause than the rest of us to suffer from housemaid's knee, but aren't the sisters human beings just like you and me?'

'Well of course they're not,' his ma told him, indignantly. 'The very idea.' Even her recently permed, unnaturally dark curls seemed to crackle with outrage at his remark. 'They gave up the world and all its sins when they took the veil. They're the latest in a long line of holy women. A fact you might recognize if you ever read that book about the lives of the saints that I lent you.'

His ma had, to Rafferty, the unfortunate habit of trying to rekindle what she called his 'lost' faith and was forever finding him religious books at the library. He wouldn't mind, but she also expected him to pay the library's fines when he forgot to return them. If she ever got an inkling that his rebuttal of Catholicism had just received a severe check...

He curbed the thought instantly, in case a process of osmosis transferred the thought to his ma's head. Instead, he set about arguing his corner.

'But a change of clothes and accommodation doesn't take the woman out of the nun. Or the propensity to sin out of her, either,' he pointed out. He warmed to his theme. 'And presumably, they all lived in the wicked world before the veil beckoned, so, equally, all must also have been as familiar with the temptation to sin as the rest of us. They all have pasts – lives they led before they entered the cloister. And no one, not even a woman convinced she has a religious vocation, becomes a saint overnight, in the same way that no one becomes a wicked sinner over a similar timescale. Each level of sainthood or sinning has to be built up, bit by bit. Probably takes years of practice, which seems to me to indicate that for a fair chunk of their lives, the sisters are likely to have fallen well short of sainthood.' He repeated what he had already said to Llewellyn. 'Maybe the past caught up with one of them?' And received an even more unwelcoming response.

'As it has with you so often?' his ma taunted. 'I seem to recall that you did your best to wriggle out of self-induced trouble more than once. For instance, look at what happened only this April just gone—'

Rafferty frowned warningly at her. But she had another, more urgent, argument she was keen to pursue, so she abandoned this reminder and continued with her religious inquisition. Thankfully.

Because Abra knew nothing about what had gone on in his life back in April. Neither did she know about the blackmail letter he

161

had received. And he would very much prefer it if both stayed that way.

Rafferty risked a quick, assessing glance at Abra. Her expression was thoughtful. Her gaze settled questioningly on his face, as if she was trying to discover clues to what his ma meant.

He scowled inwardly, which was as much as he dared do. But all he needed was for his ma's comment to spark questions from Abra.

Really, he thought, like Father Kelly, his ma knew way too many of his guilty secrets. But he refused to let that deter him from putting his point of view, even though he had never yet won a single debate or argument with his mother. Besides, he hoped it might yet distract Abra from pursuing any desire to question him herself.

He waited for his ma to pause for breath. It took some time – once Kitty Rafferty got into her stride there was no chance of stopping her till she ran out of oxygen – but at last, he had his chance.

'And as for the nuns being saints. Sainthood is as sainthood does, wouldn't you agree, Ma? I mean, look at St Thomas More as an example. He wrote scurrilous letters to Martin Luther, calling him all sorts of ugly, unchristian names for daring to find fault with the Catholic Church – though the Lord knows, given its many and varied corrupt practices, there was plenty of fault to find.

Hardly a Christian turning of the other cheek. Yet that didn't prevent More being made a saint. See what I mean? Even saints aren't always one hundred per cent saintly.'

'St Thomas More was defending his faith,' his ma told him, indignantly. 'Which he had every right to do. Maybe you'd find God smiled on you more often if you defended the faith a bit more. Or even practised it,' she added tartly.

Rafferty, accepting, at last, that he would never manage to persuade his ma that one of the holy nuns might be guilty of a greater sin than failing to defend their faith, decided not to waste his time in attempting the impossible any longer. He was too tired to take his mother on in an argument over religion. But he was convinced that it was in those years when one of the sisters' saintliness was in its lowest form – in their past lives, before they decided to take the veil – that he believed he was likely to find the richest pickings.

'OK,' he said, as if in capitulation. 'If you don't fancy one of the sisters as a suspect, what about their GP, Dr Peterson? Or Father Kelly? You've always said the priest was the "Greatest sinner in the parish", Ma,' he unkindly reminded her. 'Maybe it's time you enlightened me on some of his other sins?' he suggested. 'Apart, that is, from the booze and the women.'

But, for once in her life, his normally loquacious mother was discretion itself. And although Rafferty had guesses in plenty, he didn't actually *know* anything for sure. All he had were innuendoes, neighbourhood gossip and his ma's idle chitchat.

Father Kelly's fellow Catholic priests had proved – during countless scandals and Rafferty's own questioning of the two who shared the Priests' House with Father Kelly in particular – that they were as good as his ma at keeping secrets and protecting their own.

His ma had chosen an inauspicious time to copy Father Kelly's aversion to sharing secrets, whether those from the confessional, or any other sort.

Rafferty could see that his ma was in a quandary. She clearly, desperately, wanted someone other than one of the sisters to be in the frame for the murder. The difficulty about that, of course, was that the only other viable suspects were her parish priest and a doctor.

Clearly, the thought that the first was in some way implicated in a violent murder with the resultant corpse then secretly buried in an unconsecrated grave, was impossible for his ma to accept. Which left Dr Stephen Peterson as the least undesirable person in the frame. But the trouble for ma was that this also failed to provide a neat solution to her dilemma. For ma revered the medical profession. She thought doctors were gods and always had.

Rafferty wondered if she would still think this particular medical man quite so godlike if he revealed that he'd gone in for performing illegal abortions in his younger days.

But as his ma had never taken a vow of silence to still her wagging tongue, and as he felt that Peterson was entitled to expect discretion for forty-year-old sins, his ma's quandary continued as he decided not to reveal this particular titbit.

'There must be *someone* else,' she insisted. 'Someone you've missed.'

Rafferty shook his head. He was amused to see his ma's forehead crease in evidence of furious thought. Clearly, she was determined to come up with another suspect for him to seize on. He knew, from the light of triumph that appeared in her eyes but moments later that she had managed to hit on such a suspect. He waited, curious to find out the identity of this person.

'Big old house like that convent must need a lot of maintaining,' his ma, the builder's widow, pointed out. 'I know the sisters are pretty self-sufficient, but I don't suppose they're so self-sufficient that they are able to do all their own building repairs. You want to check if they've had any building work done recently, Joseph.'

No I don't, he thought. He had plenty of suspects already without trawling for more.

But his ma was right, of course, as he admitted to himself. Even if it pained her to need to pin the blame on someone in the building trade. It was the family business, after all and both Rafferty's younger brothers and most of his cousins and the uncles who hadn't retired, were involved in various aspects of the trade. It was a possibility he really should have thought of for himself.

It wasn't until Rafferty promised to further investigate this particular line of inquiry that ma finally decided to postpone more debate on the subject and allowed him to drive her home.

After he had pulled up at the kerb outside her council house, as usual, she managed to have the last word.

'You'd do well to go to confession, my lad,' she told him. 'You with so many heavy sins blackening your soul.'

'And what sins would they be, Ma?' he asked. 'It wasn't *me* who murdered the wretched man. All I'm doing is trying to find the person who did. Surely even God does not condone murder, or disapprove of those who try to catch the perpetrator?'

His comment received nothing more than a contemptuous sniff in reply. She didn't dignify it with more than that. Instead, she changed tack and reverted to reminding him of his sins. She even began to list them.

'You're living "over the brush", for one thing,' she informed him. 'And if you don't know that already, you should. Haven't I done my best to bring you up Christian?

'For another, I don't suppose the baby that Abra lost earlier this year was intended to be the first of many. So fornication can be added to the list.'

'Jesus.' Rafferty scowled as his mother's words reminded him what it was that he'd for years so hated about the Catholic religion. His 'Road to Damascus' revelation now seemed a long way in the past.

'And you take the Lord's name in vain way too often,' she briskly informed him. 'They are all sins, my son,' she reminded him, more gently. 'Whether you like it or not. Come the Day of Judgement you'll be called to account for them. All I'm saying is that you'd do well to get some of your sins squared away before that day comes.'

Why aren't I surprised? Rafferty asked himself, as his ma's voice shook with the tiniest trace of a sob, and she added, 'I don't want to think of you burning in Hellfire.'

It wasn't an appealing prospect to Rafferty, either. But he said nothing. Sometimes, with his ma, when she had her religious hat on, it was the best way.

Softly, before she got out of the car, she added another piece of advice. 'And I'm thinking it might be a good idea for you to make another confession. One to Abra. About what happened back in April. I take it you've never told her?'

Rafferty shook his head.

'You should, is my advice,' she told him.

'Secrets between couples are never a good idea. Take my word for it.'

Rafferty, after he had escorted his ma to her door, checked the house for burglars and said goodnight, was driving home when it occurred to him to wonder what secrets his ma might have concealed in *her* past.

Once again the thought popped into his head to wonder whether his mother, in her lonely, youthful widowhood, might have been one of the silver-tongued Father Kelly's lady conquests. His ma, like Father Kelly, was more than capable of berating a person about sin while their own sat comfortably upon them.

He shook his head. It was something he found impossible to contemplate. Besides, while his ma's sins might sit as comfortably upon her as a cat upon a sofa, she had too much pride to be numbered among the multitude of women who were reputed to have warmed the priest's bed.

But he wasn't to be left to wonder about his ma's secrets for *too* long. As he discovered when he got back to the flat he shared with Abra.

He would have done well to take his ma's advice, Rafferty realized within half an hour of returning home. Especially as it clearly hadn't been her secrets to which his ma had so elliptically referred.

Give Abra her due, he admitted. She had waited till their delayed evening meal was over, given him ample time to 'confess', before she pulled from her jeans a letter he had cause enough to instantly recognize.

Even so, she brought on galloping indigestion when she told him: 'This fell out of your pocket when I picked your jacket up off the floor where you dropped it the other night.'

Rafferty swore silently. For the first time he wished he was as careful about his clothes as his Beau Brummelesque sergeant. Llewellyn would never hang his clothes on the floor and leave Maureen, his wife, to find an incriminating blackmail letter. But then, of course, Llewellyn, his clever, logical, university-educated sergeant, would never be so foolish in the first place as to do something which might lead to threats of blackmail.

'So?' Abra said. And, try as he may, he couldn't miss the hurt in her voice as she continued, 'You *were* going to tell me about this, weren't you, Joe? Is it, as your mother suggested, that you were just waiting for the right moment?'

# Ten

At Abra's words, Rafferty clutched his aching belly with its shock-induced indigestion, and slumped on the settee. 'Tell you about it?' he said. 'What's the point? From the sound of things my ma's brought you pretty well up to speed.'

Abra shook her head, gazed at him steadily and said, 'No. When I showed her the blackmail letter, she said I should speak to you about what happened in April.'

Her face seemed to take on a feminist, 'I will survive', harmony, which sent Rafferty's already down-plunging hopes reaching Titanic depths. Especially when she added in sad tones, 'Which is what I'm doing.'

As his dinner sunk more stone-like than ever, Rafferty began to splutter. 'I can explain.'

'Can you?' Abra's expression left reason to doubt this. She looked sad. And he acknowledged that he had hurt her. Again.

'Go on, then,' Abra invited, as she sat back and crossed her arms over her chest. 'You can begin by explaining why you told me nothing about whatever it was that you got

170

up to in April. But before you do that, tell me, did my cousin Dafyd know all about it?'

'No. Of course not.'

But clearly, his hasty answer had warned Abra that he might be being economical with the truth.

'So when *did* he find out about your mysterious secret?'

'It wasn't till later. Till near the end of the investigation.'

'OK. I'll buy that.' She said nothing further, but simply sat, arms folded and waited for him to begin.

Stumblingly, Rafferty related the sorry tale of his signing up for the Made in Heaven dating agency and why it was that he had decided that using his cousin Nigel Blythe's name as an alias had seemed like a good idea.

'Apart from any other consideration, you know what a fuss ma would have made if she'd found out. And then there were my colleagues at the station to think about. I'd have been the butt of their jokes for weeks if they'd discovered what I'd done.'

As he drew his confession and his excuses to an end, Abra at first said nothing. Then, in a hurt voice, she asked, 'Have you got any other secrets you've kept from me? The odd axe murder, for instance?'

'No, there's nothing more, I swear.' And there wasn't. Nothing that he could recall, anyway. Though, in his family, there were

171

generally so many secrets of the criminally edged variety, that he couldn't hope to remember them all.

'So why didn't you tell me all about it?' Still sounding hurt, in that voice that made Rafferty squirm, she added softly: 'I suppose I was the only one who knew nothing?'

'No. That's not true,' he protested. 'Apart from Dafyd, who figured things out for himself during the case, only Deputy Assistant Chief Constable Jack Mulcahy and ma knew about it. No one else. And the way things panned out, I didn't really have any choice about telling the last two. Believe me, I'd have sooner not.'

'Aren't you forgetting someone else?' Abra waved the letter under his nose. 'Apparently your blackmailer knows all about it as well.'

Rafferty gave a mournful nod. 'Him, too, of course.' And the Lonely Hearts' case victims' murderer, he silently reminded himself. But he said that to himself rather than Abra.

'So, what are you thinking of doing to counter this blackmailer's threat?'

Rafferty shrugged. I was thinking of lighting a few candles in Father Kelly's church, he felt like saying. The bit of the universal God that hung around in that particular holy enclosure must, he thought, be an understanding sort, given that, unlike himself, the old priest always seemed to get away with *his* sins.

But he said none of this. Instead, he admitted, 'I don't know. Yet. But I'm exploring a few possibilities.'

'That must mean you've got some inkling as to who might be responsible for this letter,' she was quick to point out.

There were even fewer flies on Abra than on her smart cousin, Dafyd Llewellyn, Rafferty thought, as he admitted, 'Let's just say there are one or two' – or ten – 'who come to mind as possibles.'

Abra frowned at him for a few more seconds. Then she sighed heavily, rose and crossed decisively to the cupboard in the corner and removed a bottle of Jameson's and two glasses.

'Maybe a dram or two of this will help your head free up the identities of a few more potential suspects.'

Rafferty doubted it. He'd already travelled that particular path to enlightenment several times without reaching a firm destination. But at least, if whiskey provided no answers, it brought a welcome anaesthesia.

He held out his hand for the glass. Besides, it was how he was to neutralize the blackmailer that was what he needed to know. He already had his ten most likely suspects lined up in a row.

As he sipped the warming whiskey, it struck him that Abra had taken his revelations with an astonishing calm. He was just congratulating himself on being saved the

173

expected rants, raves, slamming doors and sulks when he realized they might have been preferable.

Because an Abra who reacted so calmly was simply another anxiety to add to his growing collection. What was she planning? Please God, he pleaded. Don't let her put her head together with Ma's and come up with some nefarious plot to save me from myself. If she does, he thought, I'm likely to end up in even more lumber than I'm in now, he thought.

But it seemed more a case that Abra had been brooding about the blackmail letter and his confession, rather than going over any ma-inspired plot for flaws. For later, when they had retired to bed, she became very quiet, which was unlike her. Usually, after a few drinks, she became talkative.

She waited until they had extinguished the bedside lights before she suddenly blurted out: 'Why didn't you tell me about all this before, Joe? And why didn't you tell me about the two dead women you took such a shine to?'

In the darkness, Abra's voice sounded small and distressed as if tears weren't far away.

Rafferty sat up, turned the bedside light back on, and reached for her. Cuddling her close, he kissed her hair, breathing in its fragrance. 'I'm sorry, sweetheart. I didn't mean to upset you. That's the last thing I want to do, now or ever. And yes, OK, I *did* take a shine to those women, but it's you that I'm living with. You that I love.

'I suppose,' he admitted, 'that I hoped to deal with it on my own without troubling—'

'My pretty head?'

Rafferty's lips drew back in a smile against her hair. 'Something like that.' He breathed deeply, thought for a second, then plunged on. 'Only remember, my Abracadabra, that this all happened before I met you. Can you really blame me that when Dafyd introduced us and we were struck by love's dart, that I wanted you to think well of me? Hardly impressive, I thought, to show myself a fool quite so early in the relationship.'

'No,' she agreed. 'It's always best, I've found, to try to conceal one's more foolish traits and actions, if possible. Certainly from the world at large, anyway. Only Joe, remember this; most women suspect in their hearts that they're partnered by fools. We can only help in the concealment of this truth if we're kept in the loop.'

Although stung by Abra's words, Rafferty's lips couldn't help but curl in unwilling amusement. For in his heart of hearts, he suspected she was right. All men were fools. Perhaps, he comforted himself, perhaps only a man who's a little less foolish than the rest is capable of acknowledging this truth.

'So? No more secrets, Joe?'

Rafferty kissed Abra and reached for the

light. 'No more secrets,' he agreed as he pressed the switch and plunged the bedroom into darkness. Though he was careful to cross his fingers under the bedclothes, just in case. After all, there were some secrets it would be too foolish to share. And with *his* family, Rafferty could never be sure that one such wasn't waiting just around the corner.

While Rafferty grappled with a murder case that seemed to be going nowhere, with a 6–8 week old corpse with no clothes, no ID, distinguishing marks, face or convenient criminal record, and waited for some obliging dentist to claim the body as his own, he strived to cope with his taunting blackmailer. A blackmailer, moreover, who, inexplicably, had so far failed to make any demands at all.

What was he waiting for? Rafferty wondered. But answer came there none. Though at least he'd come to a decision. After all, he thought, when dealing with a low-life such as a blackmailer, it must surely help to have the advice of another low-life?

To that end, Rafferty had decided to go to see his cousin, Nigel Blythe and ask his advice about what he should do about the blackmailer. If anyone in his family knew more about ducking and diving and getting himself out of self-induced trouble, his foppish, estate agent cousin was the man to do it.

But when Rafferty that evening turned up uninvited at Nigel's expensive apartment, he didn't exactly receive a cordial welcome. Not that he'd thought such a welcome at all probable. Nigel didn't like unexpected visitors.

Understandable really. As Nigel spent a lot of time avoiding disgruntled clients whose properties he had sold at under priced values to the benefit of himself and his roguish acquaintances. Not to mention those equally disgruntled husbands whose wives had submitted to Nigel's determined charm.

Eventually, Rafferty managed to persuade his cousin to let him past the outer door to the block. But even when Nigel opened his apartment door, the welcome was decidedly cool.

'It's not convenient,' Nigel immediately told him. 'I'm expecting a visitor.'

The ambience of dimmed lights and seductive music evident through the open door of the living room were confirmation that Nigel wasn't telling a porkie just to get rid of him. 'Sorry to intrude,' Rafferty said. 'It won't take long, I just wanted to ask your advice.'

'*My* advice?' Nigel's elegantly superior, salon-plucked eyebrows rose enquiringly. 'Thinking of selling that grotty little flat are you?'

'No. It's nothing to do with the flat. It wasn't your professional advice I was after.

It's to do with this.' Rafferty pulled the blackmail letter from his jacket pocket and thrust it at Nigel.

His cousin simply stared at the letter, skimmed fleetingly over it, but made no attempt to take it for a longer study.

'What makes you think I can help you?' he asked coolly.

'As you can see, it's a blackmail letter. I wanted to ask you about it.'

Still cool, Nigel seemed wary. 'Ask me what, exactly?' he demanded.

'Ask your advice as to what I should do about it,' Rafferty told him.

Nigel smiled, a more relaxed smile than he had hitherto given and said: 'I see. Well, don't stand on the door step. Come in, my dear fellow. Though I don't know what I can advise, exactly.'

Nigel led Rafferty through into the huge, starkly modern and supposedly stylish open-plan reception room. He even offered Rafferty a drink, which he declined.

Once they had both sat down on Nigel's latest extravagance – two enormous black leather sofas, Nigel said, 'So, I gather from the letter that this is about what you got up to in April?'

Rafferty nodded. It was humiliating to lay himself open to his cousin's contempt for the second time in less than a year. But he was desperate.

At least, to his credit, Nigel didn't laugh.

He even showed himself willing to read the correspondence once more. Again, it didn't take long as the letter was brief and to the point.

Suddenly, it hit Rafferty that the letter's brevity might have been deliberate, as if the blackmailer had been concerned that a longer epistle might enable him to guess the identity of his unwelcome correspondent.

'Sticky situation,' Nigel remarked as he handed the letter back. 'It certainly seems someone has you by the short and curlies, JAR. So what are you going to do about it?'

Rafferty shrugged. 'I don't see what I *can* do. I have my suspicions as to who might have sent it, though.'

'Oh really?' Nigel looked expectantly at him and asked: 'Who, exactly?'

Rafferty told him.

Nigel leant back against the leather-buffered comfort of his expensive settee, smiled and nodded. 'Makes sense. You haven't spoken to any of them yet, I take it?'

'No. There's the tricky matter of how I approach them. I still haven't found a way round it.'

'You could always try coming clean to your boss, of course,' Nigel suggested. 'It's what I'd do.'

Astonished at the suggestion, Rafferty stared at his cousin. To his knowledge, Nigel had never owned up to anything in his life.

'It would take away the blackmailer's

power over you,' Nigel pointed out smoothly. 'Have you considered doing that?'

Rafferty shook his head. 'Not an option. Given that Superintendent Bradley would love an excuse to boot me out of the police service, I'd rather continue to put up with this blackmailer. At least he's only likely to bleed me dry financially. Bradley would hang me out to dry and invite all the usual banes of a copper's life, like the media, the PC brigade and the politicians, to take chunks out of me too. Not to mention slapping a charge on me that was likely to land me in prison alongside some of the violent old lags I've banged up in the past.'

'Nasty. It would appear, my dear cousin, that you're between a rock and a hard place. Damned if you tell the truth and damned if you don't.'

Rafferty scowled at his cousin's unctuous observation and began to wish he hadn't come. 'Oh, well,' he said, 'I suppose I'd better be off home. Unless you've some other suggestion?'

Nigel shook his head. 'Sorry, dear boy. Wish I could help. But nothing springs to mind.'

In spite of Nigel's show of sympathy, as his cousin showed him out and waved him off, Rafferty thought he detected a hint of amusement briefly cross Nigel's handsome features. Damn the man, he thought as he went down the elegant stairs to the entrance lobby, I swear he's *enjoying* this. But then, had he really expected anything else? He supposed he should be grateful that Nigel hadn't laughed out loud at his predicament.

After promising his ma that he would check whether the convent had had any recent building work done, the next morning, Rafferty waited till Mass and Terce were over before he took himself over to the convent to question Mother Catherine.

She seemed surprised at the question, but answered it readily enough.

'Yes,' she said. 'We did have a builder in, actually. It was some weeks ago. We had a persistent leak and although Sister Rita is pretty handy about such practical tasks, she was unable to resolve the problem.'

'Which firm did you use?'

'It was a local firm. Bell and Son.'

Rafferty smiled. Given that the sisters lived their lives by the summons of a bell, the name of the building firm struck him as singularly appropriate.

'We've used them before and found them reliable, which I imagine is why my predecessor chose them.'

'Your predecessor? You've not been the Mother Superior for a long time, then?'

'No. Six months only. I'm "keeping the seat warm" for Mother Joseph. Should the good Lord see fit to return her to us. She has an advanced form of breast cancer. At the moment, she is being nursed in the infirmary of one of our sister houses that has more extensive medical facilities than we can provide.'

'So, if Sister Joseph doesn't return, you will be confirmed as Prioress?'

Mother Catherine raised her shoulders in the tiniest of shrugs. 'Perhaps. It is in the Lord's hands. Anyway, as I said, Mother Joseph found Bell and Sons reliable, but this time they were less so. The first man who turned up failed to find the cause of the problem and didn't bother to come back. I have their card in the address book.'

She reached into her desk drawer, extracted a business card and handed it to Rafferty. He jotted down the details and returned the card.

'Do you recall when they were here?'

'I can't remember precisely, but between the visit of the first man and the second one who managed to repair the leak, it spread over the latter part of August and into early September.'

Rafferty thanked her and a few minutes later he left and headed across town to the premises of the building firm, resolving that he should listen to his ma more often.

The builder's yard was cluttered with ladders, concrete mixers and a van, into the back of which two men were loading toolboxes.

Rafferty introduced himself and asked,

'Are either of you men Mr Bell Senior?'

The older man, tall, grey-haired and with the weather-beaten face of an outdoor worker, nodded. 'That's me. What can I do for you, Inspector?'

'I'm in charge of the murder investigation at the local convent,' Rafferty explained.

Immediately, the man's pleasantly open features became wary. 'Oh, yes?'

Rafferty nodded. 'I understand your firm did some work there back in the summer, repairing a leak.'

'That's right.' Mr Bell turned to the younger man and said, 'It was Nat that we sent first to do the job, wasn't it, Harry?'

The younger man, so much like Mr Bell that he must have been the 'and Son' part of the firm's name, confirmed it. 'Nat's not with us any more. Turned out to be too unreliable. Bit of a free spirit was Nat.'

A bell – not of the 'and Son' variety – rang in Rafferty's head. 'This Nat – his full name wouldn't be Nathan McNally, would it?'

'That's him,' the senior of the two Bells confirmed. 'Harry called him a free spirit a moment ago, but he was mostly into freeing up our cash takings and the more portable of our expensive equipment.' Mr Bell pulled a face. 'The insurance has refused to pay out, so we've had to bear the cost. That'll teach me to take anyone on trust. Normally, I would insist on proper references, but we were so snowed under with work at the time that I broke my own rule and lived to regret it.'

Rafferty checked the date that Nathan McNally had worked at the convent. It tallied with what Mother Catherine had told him. 'Do you have an address for him?'

Mr Bell Senior nodded. 'Not that you'll find him there now. I went round to have it out with him when I discovered the money and tools were missing, but he'd done a flit. He was staying at a lodging house in East Street, the other side of the bridge over the River Tiffey. No 55.'

Rafferty was thoughtful as he made for Nathan McNally's ex-lodging house. It was interesting that McNally should have had access to the convent during the period that Dr Sam Dally and the forensic entomologist estimated that their man had died.

Mrs Norris, the owner of the lodging house from where Nathan McNally had flitted with the Bells' cash and equipment, was able to tell Rafferty little about her ex-lodger, apart from the fact that he was a surly sort who thought the world owed him a living.

'He didn't like it when I insisted he paid up front. But I've had experience of these itinerant building workers in the past,' she explained. 'Way too fond of doing moonlight flits for my liking. Now, I make it a rule that if they don't pay, they don't stay.'

'Very wise. Have you any idea where he

went when he left here?'

Mrs Norris shook her head. 'None. As I said, he was a surly sort. Barely spoke unless he wanted something. I was glad to see the back of him. I pity the poor woman who takes up with him.'

'Oh? Still, it doesn't sound like he'd get too many women if he was as surly as you say.'

Mrs Norris smiled. 'You'd be surprised. He wasn't a bad looking man. Muscular. Struck you as the strong, silent type, till you got to know him. The sort that appeals to some women. One thing I do remember about him – he had a lovely smile. It quite altered his face. Not that he used it too often on me. But I suppose it could be enough to turn some girls' heads if he chose to point it in their direction. As I said, I certainly didn't see much of it. I don't suppose he thought me and my demands for rent up front worth many smiles.'

With Nathan McNally long gone from his lodgings and with no hint as to his current whereabouts, Rafferty headed back to the station. When he reached his office, he discussed this latest discovery with Llewellyn.

'I think we're going to have to try a bit harder to find this Nathan McNally, Dafyd, don't you?'

Llewellyn nodded. 'Though whether we'll find him alive or whether we've *already* found him – in the grave – is open to debate.'

As this wasn't a debate in which Rafferty

felt keen to indulge, he just said, 'See to it, will you?' and made a pretence of reading the latest reports until Llewellyn took himself off. Then he raised his head and stared into space, reports and the need to get on top of them forgotten as his mind was again invaded by worries about his blackmailer's intentions.

It really was becoming intolerable. He wasn't sure how much longer he could carry on with the constant strain his curiously undemanding blackmailer was causing him without cracking up. The pity of it was that he had reason to doubt that Superintendent Bradley would make as understanding a confessor as Father Kelly should he be so foolish as to take Nigel's advice and seek absolution.

# Eleven

The investigation into the rest of the religious community was still on-going. During the course of it, they had made the discovery that Father Kelly wasn't the only holy sinner in the case.

As Rafferty had suspected and pointed out to his mother, not all of the sisters at the convent had previously led lives that had been totally pure. Old Sister Ursula, she of the arthritic limbs and playful manner, admitted to having been even more playful in her youth. For she had borne an illegitimate baby by an American serviceman that she had given up for adoption.

Even Mother Catherine wasn't without the stain of sin. She had admitted to the sin of pride in achieving her current rank. It was, she told him, the mark of a lifetime's devotion to God and the community. She confessed to Rafferty that she prayed daily for the death of her pride.

Rafferty told the Prioress that he thought she was being unnecessarily harsh on herself. 'Surely,' he said, 'if God wanted to encourage His children to use the talents He gave them, as indicated by the parable, then He would understand that when our efforts are successful they bring a measure of satisfaction, even pride?'

'Maybe so,' Mother Catherine had replied. 'But what is it they say? *A haughty spirit goeth before a fall.*'

'A little pride in genuine achievement is unlikely to cause a fall, in my experience,' Rafferty had replied before he recalled several occasions when pride had caused that very thing. He wished the words, which were supposed to comfort, were true. But at least, he thought, from Mother Catherine's response, he had carried this white lie off with aplomb and nary a blush.

But later he discovered that his words hadn't after all proved of much comfort to Mother Catherine. As Sister Rita, one of the Prioress's closest intimates, confided, 'The death of this man has affected our Mother Catherine very badly. She hasn't been Prioress for very long. Until now, she had been quietly learning about the demands of her new role, determined to do it to the best of her ability. But because this man's death and burial occurred on *her* watch, all her previous pleasure in her new role seems to have gone. She appears to consider her elevation and her quiet satisfaction at it on a par with pride in one of the more worldly prizes. She seems to feel her pleasure at her attainment of rank in the community indicative of an emptiness within, a lack of holy virtue.

'Certainly, I have never seen her so affected by a death as she has been over this man's. And we have both of us seen a few. Before she joined this community, Mother Catherine was a sister in an unenclosed order and worked at a Catholic mission in Africa. She saw more than her share of difficult deaths there. In fact, she was the only survivor of an attack by a frenzied mob on the mission school and clinic she helped run.'

'Father Kelly told me about that. I gather that's where she incurred her terrible burns?'

Sister Rita nodded. 'Strange in a way, but her dreadful experiences and suffering in Africa strengthened her faith. Soon after, she sought permission to move to an enclosed order. Normally,' she explained, 'once you have taken your final vows as a nun, you remain in the order in which you spent your novitiate. But she was given special dispensation and joined the Order of Carmel here in Elmhurst in 1975, as soon as she came out of hospital.'

From up a ladder which was propped against one of the apple trees in the orchard, Sister Benedicta's voice chimed in. 'Talking of Mother Catherine wrestling with her pride, Inspector, you might like to know that we all wrestle with one or more aspects of the life. For me, it was the vow of poverty that caused most anguish, particularly in my younger days as a nun.' She smiled down at him through the leaves. 'You might not think so to look at me now, but I had a good figure once. I used to be something of a clothes horse and loved clothes and treated myself to regular bouts of retail therapy, as they now call it. I earned good money before I entered the convent. I could be extravagant. It's especially hard not to have your own money so as to be able to buy family birthday and Christmas presents, for instance. I still feel it most at such times. Anyway, that's my major bête noire. Whereas with my friend, Sister Rita, here, it's the celibacy she's always had most trouble with.'

'Really, Sister Benedicta, I'm sure the inspector doesn't want to hear all this. You're making a fool of yourself.'

'So be it,' Sister Benedicta cheerfully replied from her ladder. 'It's understandable, I suppose, as she was married once, did she tell you?' she asked Rafferty. 'She only joined the order after she was widowed. She always likes to tease the sisters who retained their virginity that they don't know what they're missing. The implication being that, for them, the giving up of what you've never known isn't much of a giving up at all.'

'I suppose, in a way, she's got a point,' Rafferty's smile attempted to ease Sister Rita's discomfiture at her fellow nun's disclosures.

'Perhaps. Mother Catherine advises us that

we must offer ourselves, our strengths and our weaknesses, up to God, much as she confesses that she offers up her pride. Though I think she's too hard on herself.' Her comment was an echo of Rafferty's own. 'I don't think pride in one's achievements can be so wrong, do you, Inspector? If God has enabled you to do things in this life, it always strikes me as churlish not to take pleasure in His gift.'

'Talking of achievements...' Rafferty, who had parked his behind on one of the boxes used for storing the fruit, stood up. 'If you'll excuse me, Sisters, I still have a case to solve, so I'd better get on with it or it'll be failure I'll have to offer up to God *and* my superintendent.' He smiled and added, 'though sometimes, I'm not too sure if they're not one and the same.'

The results from both the national and international fingerprint checks on their victim had come back negative, as had the request put out to the nation's dentists.

Nathan McNally, Sister Cecile's ex-boyfriend, had still not been traced in spite of the artist's impression that her parents had contributed and which had been circulated to the media. Nor had he or any of his family contacted the police; though whether this was because he was indeed the cadaver currently lying in the mortuary or because he and they had their own reasons for wanting to remain out of the police's radar,

Rafferty couldn't guess.

With so little to help their investigation, Rafferty decided now was a good time to speak to the novice Cecile, and find out if she was able to give them any idea about the possible whereabouts of McNally or his family. He would also like to learn more from her own lips about her own prior life. Because Llewellyn's further digging had revealed that the novice, although appearing 'breathless with adoration' in the expected mode, and hoping to be allowed to take her final vows within the next few years, hadn't always been breathless from the adoration of God.

Before finding her vocation – if vocation it was, as even her family doubted – and entering the convent, she had been a rather promiscuous young woman with – in McNally – a violent and jealous boyfriend, the last in a long line of such boyfriends.

Rafferty couldn't help but wonder if Cecile's past life could be entirely unknown to the other residents of the convent or the diocesan hierarchy. Certainly Mother Catherine had let slip that she had been aware of something of the novice's troubled past. Indeed, she had struck Rafferty as acting more like a mother hen than a Mother Superior in her desire to protect Cecile. Was it merely because she *did* feel motherly towards the young novice? Or was there some other reason?

Rafferty shrugged. Maybe he'd stand a better chance of getting answers from the more vulnerable younger woman than he had from the stronger older one? It was certainly worth a try. To this end, he went in search of Cecile.

He found her in the convent's chapel, on her knees on the hard wooden floor before the altar. A natural enough place to find a young girl who professed to have a vocation for the life of a contemplative.

But it wasn't the young novice's prayers that made him hesitate, it was the sound of her weeping. A weeping that seemed to be wrenched from her soul and that betokened great misery muffled only by the thick material of her veil.

She must have heard his quiet approach in spite of her tears, because she turned and stumbled to her feet. More like a guilty thing surprised than a woman who professed a desire for the religious life.

'I'm sorry,' Rafferty apologized. 'I didn't mean to startle you.'

Slowly, after genuflecting to the altar, she approached him, wiping her wet face as she came towards him.

'Tears?' he questioned. 'What's upset you, Sister?'

'Nothing. Nothing. Really,' she was quick to reassure. She gave him a watery smile that made her previous words even less convincing, before she said, 'Well, not *nothing* really,

193

I suppose. Not to me. Only the usual. It's just that I spent another sleepless night questioning my vocation. I – I'm not sure I'll ever be ready to take my final vows.'

What had brought about this doubt? Rafferty wondered. The uncertainty of a pretty girl who was unsure that she really wanted to give up all the pleasure that her looks might provide for her in a more worldly life? Or was it an attack of conscience from a soul troubled by violent death?

'Perhaps we could walk in the grounds and you can compose yourself,' he quietly suggested. 'There are a few questions I need to ask you.'

'Questions?' She shot an anxious glance at him from behind her veil. 'About what, exactly?'

*About the fact that we've got this dead body with marks of violence on him, whose identity is still unknown*, he might have answered. But he didn't say this to her. He didn't say anything immediately.

Instead he explained, as if she were an innocent child rather than a young woman mature enough to have considered making a life-long religious commitment, 'As I'm sure you're aware, when there's a suspicious death we need to check out all the possibilities.'

She nodded, but said nothing.

'And one of these possibilities, as we have learned, is that the dead man might be someone you know.'

She stared at him. 'Some one *I* know? Who?'

'Nathan McNally.'

'Nathan?' She tried to laugh off his suggestion, but her laugh sounded strained. Indeed, her breath was starting to become a little ragged. 'But why would you think that? Nathan didn't even know where I'd gone. I certainly didn't tell him. Why should you think Nathan would turn up here? That he – ' she gulped – 'might even be that dead man that Sister Rita stumbled over?'

'No reason that would currently stand up in a court of law. No reason at all, beyond the fact that I understand he was unwilling to let you go, unwilling to let God have you. And now he seems to have gone missing. And because it seems he did some building work here towards the end of the summer—'

'Building work? Nathan? Well, I never saw him.'

Cecile had been quick to deny that she had seen her ex-boyfriend working at the convent. But how likely was it that she wouldn't have seen him around the place?

'You said he'd gone missing? What do you mean, exactly?'

'He hasn't responded to our requests that he contact us. Neither has his family.'

'That sounds like Nathan. He and his family always travelled a lot.'

'Hmm. Well, unless he's travelled to the ends of the earth this time, he must surely have seen our requests that he contact us. They've been in all the national newspapers and on the TV and radio. Yet, as I said, we haven't heard a murmur from any of the family.'

'Nathan was never much of a reader, Inspector.'

Again, Rafferty couldn't help but notice her use of the past tense. 'Travelled a lot', 'was never'.

She seemed aware of it, too, because in her next sentence she immediately corrected the tense. 'He's not much of a one for the television either. When I was with him, he always complained that there was nothing on but soaps and idiotic reality shows. Mostly, when he watched the box at all, he hired videos or DVDs.'

It was a convenient explanation. It might even be true.

Rafferty cleared his throat, fingered the epistle from his undemanding blackmailer that was back in its pocket home, and sighed. 'What I wanted to ask you was if you have any idea where Nathan might have gone?'

Cecile shook her head and continued, Rafferty noted, in her determined mention of Nathan in the *present* tense.

'Nathan is a free spirit. That was what attracted me to him at first. Unfortunately, as I discovered, he isn't so keen on others also having a free spirit.'

'Yet, from inquiries instigated during this investigation, I've learned that you made rather a habit of dating young men of – shall we say? – *repressive* instincts when it came to their girlfriends.'

Cecile smiled. It was the first genuine smile he had seen since he had found her in tears in the chapel.

'Let's just say that I have always been a slow learner, Inspector. But I finally learned that I didn't want such men in my life any more. I grew up and stopped thinking that bad lads or men were attractive. I learned I didn't want a man at all.' She frowned and bit her lip. 'At least, I thought I didn't. It's only since I've had the peace of the convent around me that I've begun to wonder if I wasn't doing what everyone outside always thinks nuns are doing – running away from life, rather than walking willingly to God.'

They strolled for another ten minutes during which Cecile confided that, apart from being a loner, a drifter, who came from a travelling family, with no discernable past beyond the few pieces of maybe-truthful information that he had told the young and naïve Chrissie before she had found herself as Cecile, and which seemed to her in retrospect more likely to be the comments of a fantasist, Nathan McNally was also a 'nowhere man', at least as far as the government was concerned.

Nathan McNally avoided government bureaucracy and earned his living by his wits. Unlike normal citizens, he had left no paper trail, or none that Rafferty, Llewellyn and the team had been able to find. Certainly the paper trail he had left in his younger years had come to an abrupt halt shortly after he had left school at sixteen. Mr Bell Senior had reluctantly confirmed when Rafferty had telephoned him that he had taken McNally on as a casual labourer and paid him cash in hand.

It explained why Mr Bell's insurers had declined to make good the builder's losses at McNally's hands. It also explained why Mr Bell had failed to report the thefts to the police. Presumably he had been anxious to avoid answering awkward questions from Revenue and Customs. It was a sentiment most of Rafferty's family shared.

McNally's known past was limited and brief, his present indeterminable, and his future – if he *was* the corpse – non-existent.

Cecile had confided to Rafferty during their ramble that Nathan had seemed to feel that her love of God and her wish to dedicate her life to Him, was a rejection of *him*.

She had explained that she had told Nathan that it was nothing of the kind. It was more a case that, along with him, she would, by her prayers, show her love for *all* mankind. But, Rafferty read between the lines the words the young novice failed to confide, rather than placating him, her claim to have an overpowering love of God had made Nathan McNally more angry.

According to Cecile, her ex had been a man with a grudge against her sex. She had never met his mother, never heard him so much as mention her. If they had a permanent home, which in retrospect seemed unlikely, she had never been invited to it.

Nathan McNally's reaction, when the young Chrissie had tentatively confided to him the growth of her vocation and her desire to become a nun, had been violent. His reaction had made her wonder if his family might have some religious connection which he had repudiated.

Cecile's suggestion had Rafferty wondering at the possibility that Nathan McNally might have been one of the by-blows Father Kelly's busy loins were suspected of fathering. It would certainly explain any religion aversion on McNally's part.

But just then the bell tolled, signalling that it was time for Sext, and Rafferty let Sister Cecile go. The young nun seemed eager to answer the summons to prayer. He found such eagerness strange in a young woman whose increasing doubt that she had a religious vocation at all had caused such anguished tears but a short time earlier.

He continued his stroll in the grounds after Cecile had gladly hurried off. He gazed across to the back of the convent's main structure, where Sisters Rita and Benedicta were washing their soiled hands under the outside tap preparatory to answering the summons to prayer.

As he watched, the two muscular nuns completed their ablutions and strode athletically down the path leading to the rear entrance. And into his head, for the second time, popped a thought both monstrous and intriguing.

What if the sisters, the entire community, truly *had* been forced to collude in the death and cover-up of same of the novice's threatening ex-boyfriend, as he had previously thought a possibility? A bunch of holy nuns involuntarily re-enacting Agatha Christie's famous novel *Murder on the Orient Express*, where all the train's passengers had come together to kill the victim?

Even Rafferty had to admit that he found such a possibility a bizarre one. But it would be less bizarre if Cecile's ex-boyfriend had come across her while he was at the convent doing building work. What if he had turned violent when Cecile continued to reject him in favour of God? It was possible that, in an attempt to restrain him and help Cecile fight off his assault, one or more of the nuns had been forced to hit him on the head rather *too* strongly. Certainly, looked at from that viewpoint, it wasn't a wholly unbelievable scenario.

For while the convent was a holy religious order, given over entirely to prayer and silent contemplation, it was an integral part of the Catholic Church. Whether accidental or deliberate, the man's death, his burial here, was a physical reminder of the less forgiving, far more violent aspects of the Church's history. Violence had for centuries formed a large part of the Church's way of going about its business. Who was to say the holy sisters of the Carmelite Monastery of the Immaculate Conception, its latest adherents, hadn't been willing to carry that behaviour over into the present, in order to protect a threatened member of the faith from an irreligious, heretical, violent and threatening outsider?

Such behaviour was far from unprecedented. Nor was it entirely unbelievable, given that, apart from Cecile herself and the postulant Teresa Tattersall, the other nuns were all around sixty or more. They had been taught their faith in a more fire-and-brimstone age, an age when, much like Rafferty's ma, preachers had spoken of hell-fire and damnation.

Again like his mother, as young women the sisters had not signed up to a milk and water faith like the modern 'anything goes' Church of England with its happy-clappy preachers, tambourines and guitars.

The religious teaching of *their* youth, even more than the one Rafferty remembered with such vividly unpleasant recall, would have been a harsh, demanding doctrine. One all about defending the Faith and being Soldiers of Christ. Presumably, also, one that defended its adherents from ungodly types like Nathan McNally. But, of course, as Rafferty admitted, that was all supposition. And although he might suspect the convent's religious community of inadvertently killing the young novice's ex-boyfriend to protect her, he – they – had still been unable to positively ID the corpse. And even though the dead man's expensive watch *had* turned out to have an inscription, it was too simple a one to help them identify him.

They had found the shop from which the watch had been purchased, but it had turned into a dead end. The current owner had only held the lease for a year and had no paperwork going back as far as the year of the watch's manufacture. The previous long-term owner had died and his papers had long since been thrown away.

They were still awaiting a response from a member of the public with a claim that they recognized the dead man's costly timepiece. He had arranged for a second appeal on this in case a relevant member of the public had missed the request. But while this appeal might yet come good, the days were passing.

Perhaps it was now time to admit defeat on the normal fingerprint and dental identification route and try something else? After all, time and the superintendent were pressing.

Conscious that all their man hours had so far achieved little, that the country's dentists were still failing to come forward with a match for their cadaver, Rafferty was unwilling to delay any longer. He decided it was time to try another method to identify him.

# Twelve

Before Rafferty took himself off to organize this alternative means of identifying their cadaver, he spied Sister Rita returning from Sext, and thought it might repay him if he put some of his thoughts to the community's most earthy sister. Apart from anything of interest he might learn from her, she had seen him in earnest conversation with Cecile so, if he had stumbled on the truth and the murder of their man had been a joint effort by the sisters, he might be able to make her believe that Sister Cecile had inadvertently blurted something out.

He was hesitant to openly suggest that his current thinking was that this might have been a crime of passion or at least a crime provoked by passion spurned.

But, to his embarrassment, his lack of forthrightness seemed to encourage Sister Rita the earth-mother nun, doubtless supported by Sister Benedicta's earlier disclosures, to think his questions were born of more prurient motives, that what he wanted was enlightening about nuns and sex in general, and that he had chosen her for his enlightenment.

She seemed amused by his approach and wasn't slow to provide him with answers, even though they weren't the answers he actually wanted.

'God love you, Inspector,' she said matter-of-factly. 'The normal human urges don't just vanish when you adopt the life of a celibate. A nun is still a human being, so sexual desire is naturally still part of you. Most of the time it is somehow changed, metamorphosed if you like, into the love of God. So while we deny ourselves physical love, we're open to the energy of it.

'Though – and this might surprise you, Inspector, whatever Sister Benedicta told you – celibacy isn't the most difficult demand placed on a nun. For the majority of the sisters *obedience* is regarded as the most challenging of the three vows. OK, it's no longer the blind obedience that was once demanded of those leading a cloistered life – we have regular house meetings to discuss and usually mutually agree on things that affect the community – but it's still a submission of self, a dropping of the ego. Not a very popular concept in our hedonistic, ego-driven modern society.

'But to get back to the sex thing. If you find it difficult to think of nuns and sex in the same sentence, let me give you an analogy you might, as a man and a policeman, find easier to understand. Think of it as you

205

would of a hardened drinker swearing off alcohol. Do you think *his* urge ever goes away?'

Amused and bemused in about equal measure by Sister Rita's stout forthrightness, Rafferty shook his head.

'The sexual energy is still there, still demanding fulfilment, much like the hardened drinker's urge to have *just the one*.' Sister Rita laughed. 'Just the one can be all it takes, can't it? Whether that one be having a drink or losing your virginity. The first can lead you straight back to alcohol and the second can leave you pregnant.'

With a muscular heave, she lifted another box full of apples into the wheelbarrow and trundled it towards the shed while Rafferty walked companionably beside her.

'As Sister Benedicta told you, I was married once. And I always enjoyed the physical aspect of marriage. But when my husband died, I started to become interested in the more spiritual side of life. I suppose you could say I got the call, if that doesn't sound presumptuous, ridiculous even, in this day and age. But abstinence from sex is still, even now, a big thing for me. Though I received my last sexual proposition from a man a long time ago. So I guess I'm pretty safe in my celibacy now.'

They had by now reached the shed. 'Allow me,' Rafferty said as he heaved the box off the wheelbarrow and on to the shelf. The shed was large and almost full of such boxes.

'That's the last of the apples harvested,' Sister Rita told him with satisfaction. 'Now, I must get on with spreading the compost.'

He accompanied her back down the path to the vegetable plot and watched as she picked up the spade left ready earlier for the purpose and began shovelling rich dark compost out of the large green bins and on to the soil that had produced their summer crops. She worked quickly, methodically, and Rafferty watched her industry with the fascination of the idle bystander.

'You never had children?' he asked her bent back after some five minutes. 'I ask only because, from my understanding, the contemplatives' opportunities to see their families are very limited.'

Sister Rita raised her eyes from her energetic compost-spreading to look quizzically at him. She took the opportunity to stand upright and ease her back for a few seconds.

'No,' she confided sadly. 'I was never afforded the joy of motherhood. It was, for many years, a great sadness to me. If I had been granted such a blessing, I would never have entered an enclosed order; probably, for that matter, never become a nun at all.'

Until then, she had worked in that diligent wholehearted manner which, she had previously explained to him, God expected from all His Brides, whatever their current endeavour.

*Even murder?* he mused. Did God expect that, also, to be offered up? It didn't seem likely. But hey, he thought, immediately back in his normal cynical, lapsed, mode, this *is* the Catholic Church, we're talking about here. Killings were their forte, whether burnings, hangings or disembowelments. In his heart he doubted that the soul of the Catholic Church had really changed much over the centuries. It was simply that the law no longer permitted their previous indulgence in blood-letting.

Sister Rita dug her fork into the soil, but this time she didn't turn it over. Instead, she leaned on its cross-member, staring down at the turned soil, and – proving that she had understood his drift all along and had been merely teasing him – she neatly wrong-footed his intention to imply that Sister Cecile had confided rather more than was wise.

'I get the impression, Inspector, that you feel this man's death might be a crime of passion. Am I right?'

'It's one possibility we're considering,' Rafferty admitted.

Smiling, she nodded. 'Let me guess. I noticed you having an earnest conversation with young Cecile before the tolling of the bell for Sext. You're thinking of our little novice, am I right? Our little novice and her undesirable ex-boyfriend?'

Rafferty neither confirmed nor denied it.

But he rather thought he'd given himself away.

Undeterred by his silence, Sister Rita continued. 'Cecile, a pretty young novice with a violent and obsessive ex-boyfriend, would, I suppose, in a policeman's eyes, be a natural for a crime of passion, especially with most of the rest of us being so old and raddled. But you're mistaken, Inspector. Do you think we wouldn't notice if her old boyfriend turned up on our doorstep, demanding to see Cecile? He hasn't.'

Was Sister Rita lying? he wondered. Or was she simply unaware that Nathan McNally had been the first of the building firm's employees to turn up to repair their leak?

Quietly, he observed. 'You seem very protective of her, Sister.'

'Of course I'm protective of her. Apart from the fact that I'm Mistress of Novices, we're family here. We care for one another. It's what families do, most of them anyway. And it's good to have some young blood around the place. She and Teresa liven us old women up no end.'

Rafferty was thoughtful as he took his leave of Sister Rita. She had admitted that she felt protective of the young novice. It seemed likely that a similar desire to protect her was felt by the other older nuns. He had certainly noticed something similar in Mother Catherine.

What would they do? he wondered again, if

Cecile's ex *had* spotted her while he was here trying and failing to repair the leak, and had turned violent? Surely, as he had earlier believed, they would attempt to restrain him? Even nuns wouldn't put up with a violent male destroying the peace of their home without doing something to stop it. Especially *Catholic* nuns, with the entirety of their faith urging them on to protect one of their own against the violent unbeliever.

And when you thought that the one they would at the same time be protecting was one of their two newest chicks...

It was certainly a possibility that Nathan McNally had bumped into Cecile while he had been working at the convent. And given that he didn't sound the type to turn the other cheek when he had an unexpected opportunity to revenge himself for her rejection of him, it was plausible that he could have ended up being somehow mortally injured during any struggle to restrain him. Was it also possible that the sisters had decided, most *un*-Christianly, to deny him medical aid?

Or had he died too quickly for such aid to be summoned? If the latter was the case, had they then held an impromptu house meeting, taken a majority vote and decided that least said was soonest mended, for Cecile's sake?

Rafferty didn't know and wouldn't even have the scenario as a definite possibility until they had identified the corpse.

He had already decided to waste no more time in trying to get that identity established. And now he took out his mobile phone. But it rang before he could make the call.

His caller was Llewellyn, who was still tracking down the elusive past lives of the sisters. He had turned up some information from the past life of Teresa Tattersall, the young postulant, which seemed to offer as many possibilities for murderous protectionism from the other sisters as did that of Cecile.

Like so many youngsters of today, Teresa had been tempted by the shallow pleasures afforded by drugs, lured on by a 'loving' boyfriend who had had ulterior motives for turning her into a drug addict.

'Apparently, she got hooked very quickly,' Llewellyn's quiet voice murmured into Rafferty's ear. 'Her dealer, like most of that breed, first got her to fall in love with him and then used the innocent naiveté of his young victim to get her hooked on drugs. Once she was hooked, and unable to afford the increasing quantities she craved, he pushed her into prostitution.'

'More a case of Mary Magdalen than Holy Mary, then?' Rafferty replied. 'Though, seeing as she's nearly at the end of her six months as a postulant and is about to be "dressed" as a novice, it seems our particular Magdalen must have managed to renounce prostitution and drugs.'

'True. But not before she suffered several relapses. She found religion after the last one of these.'

'I suppose even young women who find religion are likely to suffer the usual temptations of this modern generation, including drugs. Why wouldn't they, when it's well known that so-called respectable doctors, bankers, financial types and even politicians aren't averse to using drugs to unwind?'

'Also true. But unfortunately Teresa Tattersall went in for something rather more serious than weekend unwinding. Her dealer boyfriend got her on crack cocaine, which as we know is one of the most difficult forms of addiction from which to wean one's body.'

'Nice chap. And how did he respond when it dawned on him that her getting religion had lost him the income he gained from selling her body?'

'He responded much as you might expect. Violently. She had to flee in the night to escape him, with just the clothes she stood up in. She was fortunate in that she was picked up wandering the streets in a distressed state by Dr Peterson while he was out on his rounds. He got her into a clinic and once they had managed to help her on the road to recovery, rather than have her living in some cheap bed-sit and at risk of falling back into the old routine, he persuaded Mother Catherine to let her come on retreat to the convent.'

'Where she found her vocation.'

'As you say.'

After instructing Llewellyn that he would meet him back at the station, Rafferty ended the call and went in search of Teresa.

'I'm not proud of what I did,' Teresa told Rafferty earnestly when he questioned her. 'But who hasn't done things in their lives of which they're ashamed?'

*Not me, that's for sure,* thought Rafferty. And as he recalled Father Kelly and his 'casting stones' sermon, not to mention the white lies that had attracted the attentions of a blackmailer, he was forced to acknowledge the truth of this thought. It was certain that, like Father Kelly himself, *he* was unlikely to be in a position any time soon to start picking up stones.

But it was a continuing revelation that a person could still join a religious order even if their entire life didn't match some perfect ideal. Just as well, probably, he thought. As he'd pointed out to his mother, even nuns, like priests and policemen, were only human.

What was it Sister Rita had said about modern society? That it was hedonistic. Hedonistic and, presumably, rather too fond of its shallow pleasures than was good for it.

As he left the convent and walked towards his car, Rafferty found himself wondering if the Teresa who had found ordinary life

213

required the prop of drugs, wouldn't find the more demanding life of a nun required the same prop.

Could she have relapsed and contacted her old boyfriend dealer? Asked him to come to the convent? Trading what? Surely not her body? But she had nothing else to trade, as the nuns were permitted only sufficient income to buy soap and other personal necessities.

Was it possible the foolish girl had allowed the peace of the convent and the quiet goodness of the other nuns to blind her to past reality? Had she hoped to persuade her ex-dealing boyfriend to part with the drugs for free, for the good of his soul?'

Surely even a young nun couldn't be that naïve? Particularly one who had already been lured into prostitution once?

Still, as Rafferty drove to the station, he turned the possibility over in his mind and found it an interesting one. For all he knew, it might even be what had happened and with the same result as he had envisaged with regard to Cecile and *her* undesirable ex-boyfriend.

After all, Teresa had already proved sufficiently naïve to let herself be duped into addiction and prostitution. And, as his experience as a policeman had sadly taught him, there were no depths of gullibility into which young girls who thought themselves in love weren't capable of falling.

Clearly, they would have to speak to Teresa again and try to discover if she had indeed fallen by the wayside in her vocation and her life. But that would have to wait. For Rafferty currently had the bit between his teeth and had already set his next course. He wasn't about to be distracted from it now.

The expert they used for facial reconstruction was based at the university. Professor Amos was, first and foremost, a forensic anthropologist, but he was also a talented artist, one with flair, imagination and a remarkable propensity for accurate facial reconstruction. It was a rare combination of talents.

The professor had done some astonishing reconstructions for them in the past. And Rafferty, as he shook the professor's hand and he and Llewellyn followed him into his office, was hopeful he would be able to perform his magic again.

After he had once more explained precisely who they were and what they wanted – Alexander Amos carried the stereotype of the absentminded professor to its ultimate, and Rafferty was never sure whether he was truly that absentminded or whether it amused him to pretend to be so – the professor, who was still only thirty-eight, nodded his head with its shock of prematurely grey hair.

'Of course, Inspector Rafferty. I remember now. You said on the phone that you wanted a reconstruction done on the skull of a man found in the convent at Elmhurst.'

Rafferty nodded. 'That's right, Professor. We've had no luck in identifying him using other means, so I'm in your hands and hoping you can work your usual magic.'

Professor Amos smiled. 'I suppose, to the lay person, it *is* magic.' He stood up and, with all the eagerness of the born enthusiast, asked, 'Would you like to see a reconstruction I was working on earlier?'

Rafferty, amused by the deliberate use of the expression familiar from the *Blue Peter* of their childhoods, said, 'I'd love to. Should I bring the sticky-back plastic?'

Professor Amos grinned and shook his head. 'No sticky-back plastic required. Come with me.' He led the way into his workroom and pointed to what looked like an almost-finished reconstruction. The face appeared incredibly lifelike.

'This one's a rush job for one of your colleagues in Braintree. The skull wasn't complete, but as your colleagues didn't manage to find the torso, it was all we had, incomplete or not. It was a difficult reconstruction because of that. The skull underpins the basic form and structure of the face and this one came to us in over eighteen separate pieces. It was like piecing together a jigsaw, a three-dimensional jigsaw. We were fortunate in that we had sufficient pieces that we were able to build them into a skull, cast it and then use it as the foundation for the facial reconstruction.'

'How do you decide on the form of the face?' To Rafferty all skulls looked remarkably similar; he found it difficult to understand how anyone could build up a recognizable face from so little.

'As I said, it's the skull that provides the form and structure for the overlying flesh. The layman, of course, finds it all but impossible to see beyond the dreadful rictus grin and gaping eye sockets so popular in horror films. And when the skin and muscles decay, the character goes with them. It's our job to put it back. We work from a knowledge of around twenty to thirty-five anatomical landmarks. Key tissue depths that are scattered all around the face: their greatest concentration is around the mouth and between the eyes.

'The reconstruction starts with small pegs used as depth indicators for each landmark, which are fixed to the skull or a cast of it to indicate the flesh depth, and then we apply the clay between the pegs. With these basic flesh depth markers in place, it's possible then to fill the gaps and start on the features. The width of a nose, for example, is roughly the same as the distance between the inner corners of the eyes. The corners of the mouth lie directly below the inner borders of the iris, and lie over the back edges of the canine teeth. Ears are roughly the same length as the nose, apart from in the elderly where the ears are proportionately longer.

'It's not an exact science, of course. Fortunately, an exact likeness is not always necessary. As I'm sure you and Sergeant Llewellyn know from your own experiences, often it's enough simply to provide a sufficient likeness to jog someone's memory.'

'Makes you wonder how we managed without it,' Rafferty commented. 'We'd certainly be stumped in our current case if facial reconstruction wasn't available. Who was the bright spark who came up with the idea, professor?'

'Systematic facial reconstruction really began with the work of a Russian anthropologist back in the 1920s and 30s. He used to measure the tissue depth on the faces of cadavers awaiting dissection at Moscow's medical college.'

Llewellyn nodded. 'I remember reading about that. Wasn't his most famous reconstruction the face of Tamerlane, the Mongol king?'

The professor beamed at this show of interest. 'Quite right, sergeant. You're well-informed.'

Rafferty, always hyper-sensitive to his own feelings of inferiority that he wasn't likewise well-informed, forced back the ready frown and made himself concentrate on what the professor was saying.

Professor Amos looked down at the skull his hands were caressing. 'Anyway, to continue the lecture, the human skull, gentle-men, is a veritable mine of information to the anthropologist. This chap, for instance, is a *caucasoid*. You can tell that by the skull's high and wide appearance and by the fact that neither the cheekbones nor the jaw project. The jaw falls behind a vertical line from the forehead.

'The africoid skull, by contrast, can be easily recognized by several features: the wide nose opening, the tendency to larger teeth than other races and that the skull tends to be long and narrow with moderately projecting cheek bones.'

'OK,' said Rafferty. 'I understand that – I think. But how do you know he's male if you haven't even got the pelvis to work on?'

Llewellyn answered before the professor could reply. 'Because the skull itself, just like the pelvis, is also a prime indicator of gender. Isn't that so, professor?'

Much to Rafferty's irritation, Llewellyn received another approving beam. 'Right again, sergeant. For the gender, we look at three particular points on the skull: the ridges above the eyes; this bone here, below the ear; and this one – the occiput – at the lower back of the skull. The last two are what are known as muscle attachment sites and are more prominent in males than in females.'

'With you so far,' Rafferty said in an attempt to regain some of the intellectual ground that he had managed to lose to Llewellyn. 'So how old would he have been, this chap, if he'd lived to see his next birthday?'

The professor laughed. 'You've got me there, Inspector. It's impossible to be precise on age. But this chap is likely to be somewhere around the late teens or early twenties as two of his four wisdom teeth have appeared.'

'Very impressive. What's his name? Arnold?'

'I don't know this one's name. Not yet. But that one,' he nodded towards another reconstruction. 'He's called Anthony. We had a confirmed ID just before your arrival.'

The face certainly looked incredibly lifelike. Rafferty wasn't surprised that it had gained a confirmed ID. He just hoped they were as lucky with their cadaver.

'So when will you be able to fit in our chap?' Rafferty asked.

'I've almost finished this one. It's the only customer I have at the moment. So if you send your man's skull over this afternoon, I'll make a start.'

'Not having his identification has delayed things terribly,' Rafferty began.

'Don't tell me, Inspector; you want a rush job. Right?'

'You're a mind reader, too?'

'No. Let's just say that police officers are no more patient than the rest of the human race when it comes to wanting things done. I'll be as quick as I can.'

Rafferty thanked Professor Amos for his time, his explanations and his agreement to get the reconstruction done as speedily as possible, then he left, his mobile clutched to his ear as he went, in order to arrange the transport of their John Doe's skull from the mortuary to the professor's work room. Now that he had set the reconstruction in motion, Rafferty was keen to waste no more time.

Llewellyn, undoubtedly aware that, in showing off his knowledge about the professor's work, he had trodden on one of Rafferty's most sensitive corns, trailed some way behind. But he trailed with the sprightly step that told Rafferty his sergeant had gained some little amusement, in his dry way, for his nicely judged irritation of his superior officer.

# Thirteen

While they waited for Professor Amos to perform his 'magic', Rafferty, with Llewellyn in tow, returned to the convent to again question the postulant, Teresa Tattersall, about her past.

Unsurprisingly, as on the earlier occasion that Rafferty had questioned her about it, she showed a marked reluctance to talk about her previous life at all. It was only when Rafferty appealed to Mother Catherine to speak to the young woman in her care that Teresa agreed to open up further.

Rafferty, believing she would speak more easily out in the open and away from the rest of the community, found them a bench well away from the vegetable garden where Sisters Rita and Benedicta were working. Rafferty sat beside her, with Llewellyn propped a few feet away against a tree, so the young woman didn't feel they were crowding her.

'You know Mother thinks it would help you to talk about your past experiences more fully?' Rafferty began.

Teresa smoothed her calf-length brown

skirt and raised a distressed gaze to Rafferty. 'I'm not sure Mother is right in this instance. It's a life I want to put behind me.'

'Understandably.' Rafferty was surprised that he hadn't previously noted the remains of the ravages left by drug use. He could only suppose he had unconsciously put the hollow-cheeked pallor and the dark-smudged eyes down to a life too devoted to proving her vocation. 'And you're succeeding in doing that?'

Teresa bit her lip and began to blink rapidly. It was an indication to Rafferty that the young postulant wasn't at all sure that she was succeeding. Certainly, she didn't attempt a reply.

'It must be hard for you.'

She nodded. 'Yes. But the sisters are very supportive. And Mother is patient with me. She tells me to take one day at a time and to pray to God for strength. She has been very kind and has even tried to convince me that my sin wasn't so great that it is beyond God's forgiveness.' A ragged smile appeared and was as quickly gone. 'Though I'm not sure I agree with her.'

'You haven't had any contact with your ex-boyfriend since the sisters agreed to take you in?'

'Contact? With him? No. I haven't had any dealings with him.'

*Unfortunate choice of word*, was Rafferty's thought. He couldn't help but wonder what

sort of 'dealing' she might actually be refer-
ring to. However, he didn't push it. If they
could find her ex-dealer, it would remove
him from the list of possible cadaver candi-
dates. Besides, if they managed to trace the
scumbag, Rafferty was sure he would find it
far more satisfying to direct any questions to
him.

'I'd like you to let us have the name of your
ex-dealer, Miss Tattersall,' he said.

She looked alarmed at this. 'Why? I'm not
looking to have him punished for what he
did to me. I was weak and foolish, I admit
that, but that is no one's fault but my own.'

'Maybe so. But you were encouraged in
your weak foolishness by this man.' Only half
ironically, he added, 'Maybe I can succeed in
bringing him to the path of enlightenment?
Not to mention prevent him leading other
young women astray.'

Even the naïve Teresa seemed to find this
possibility unlikely for she looked askance at
him before she shrugged. 'Anything is
possible, under God's guidance, Inspector. I
wish you joy in your quest.' She paused, then
reluctantly added, 'His name was Ray Payne.
He always used to spend a lot of time at the
Green Man in the High Street. He used it
virtually as his office. I think he gave the
landlord a percentage to encourage him to
turn a blind eye to his drug dealing.'

Rafferty nodded and noted the information for further investigation. He was curious

to note that, like Cecile, Teresa had used the past tense in describing her ex-boyfriend. But maybe that was simply because he was part of the past tense of *her* life rather than his own. The same reasoning could, of course, apply to Cecile also.

Previously, Rafferty had wondered if someone had been making threats against the convent – a property developer, perhaps, as the convent was on a prime site, just crying out to be purchased and redeveloped. But he had put aside this possibility when it occurred to him that it would, presumably, be the bishop of the diocese who would make any decision to sell the property rather than the sisters.

But later that day they learned that someone had indeed been making threats. Though not against the nuns, which was one of the possible reasons Rafferty had thought the body could have ended up in the convent's grounds.

No, the threats had been made against Dr Peterson. Their reluctant but voluntary informant had been Dr Peterson's wife

She had rung the station and asked to speak to Rafferty. Intrigued, he had made an appointment for himself and Llewellyn to go and see her.

Dr and Mrs Peterson lived in a large, detached house in the exclusive residential district on the eastern extremities of Elmhurst. Among the wide and leafy avenues lived some of the more successful of the town's residents. The Oakhill Estate housed doctors like Dr Peterson, barristers like Toby Rufford-Lyle – he of the Made in Heaven investigation – and other comfortably off professionals.

Mrs Peterson herself opened the door. She was tall and slim. A nervy slenderness, Rafferty thought as he observed the tightly-clenched hands and the anxious way she kept smiling at them once they were all seated in the too-fussy drawing room.

Her smiles were those of a person over-anxious to please. From the thin lips that looked more naturally inclined to purse than smile, to the way she kept fiddling with her clothes and hair, to the way she kept fidgeting in her seat, she exuded tension.

'I hope you didn't mind me contacting you?' she asked Rafferty.

Even her voice betrayed her anxiety. It was high and breathy, quick, too, as if she was scared that if she didn't get the words out in a rush she wouldn't get them out at all.

'Indeed not. We're always grateful for assistance from the public.' Hoping to encourage her, Rafferty said, 'You mentioned that someone has been making threats against your husband.'

'Yes. Yes.' A muscle fluttered high in her cheek. 'Oh, I do hope Stephen isn't going to be annoyed that I called you. He told me to ignore the threats made against him. He said the man would soon tire of making them and stop.'

'And he hasn't?' Llewellyn put in.

Mrs Peterson gazed anxiously between the two policeman as if worried they would think her a fool, then she admitted, in another breathy rush, 'Well, yes. He has stopped, actually. Certainly Stephen, my husband, has said nothing for some time about receiving more threats. But he could be keeping them from me. He knows how anxious they made me.'

'What exactly was this man making threats about?' Rafferty now asked. He had asked the same question when he had spoken to her on the phone, but she had been almost incoherent. He hoped, by now, she had managed to gain some clarity. 'Was this man a patient of your husband's, perhaps? One unhappy with the treatment your husband had given him?'

She shook her head. 'No. He wasn't a patient. It was nothing like that.' She began to play with the fussy bow at the neck of her blouse, winding the dangling string round and round her finger. 'Oh,' she exclaimed. 'This is very difficult. I'm beginning to think I shouldn't have rung you. Stephen told me not to. He said it might get him into trouble. But really, it was all so long ago and—'

'This man,' Rafferty interrupted, afraid that unless they nudged her forward Mrs

Peterson would continue in this far-from-enlightening manner for the rest of the day. 'Who was he, if he wasn't a patient? Do you know?'

'I don't know his name. All I know is that he had some grievance with Stephen about his mother's death. Apparently, she died of some pregnancy complication. I don't know the details. But he seemed to blame Stephen.'

'Do you know when this man's mother died?' Rafferty asked. 'Was it recently? And what else can you tell us about him? For instance, did he ever turn up at your home to issue his threats? Or were they all made by telephone and letter? Did you see him? Could you describe him?'

'My goodness. What a lot of questions.'

Rafferty realized he had flustered her and he cursed himself for his clumsiness. Now, slowly, he repeated his questions one at a time, not moving on to the next till he had received an answer to the previous one.

Bit by bit, slowly, tortuously, they got the story from her. The mother of the man who had made the threats against Dr Peterson had died back in the early sixties. Mrs Peterson wasn't very clear what exactly had caused the woman's death apart from the already-given explanation of 'pregnancy complications'. She confirmed that this man had turned up at their home several times, the last appearance being more than two

228

months earlier.

Rafferty and Llewellyn exchanged discreet glances as the significance of the timescale hit them. The cadaver in its shallow grave had been dead for around that length of time. He wondered why Mrs Peterson had waited till now to confide in them and when he asked her, she simply said that the man's silence had worried her more than his threats. She had become scared he might have been plotting something.

Mrs Peterson told them that the man issuing the threats had looked to be somewhere in his forties. 'He was well-built and strong-looking. He seemed wild if not a little mad,' she confided. 'He frightened me. I was scared he might turn up here when I was on my own and break in.'

'Understandably.' Her description told them this man shared several traits with their still unidentified cadaver. 'But your husband refused to allow you to contact us?'

'Yes. Stephen just said he was a sad creature who, to judge from his eyes and general demeanour, was on drugs and was to be pitied rather than reported to the police. He said the man needed help, not harassment.'

By now, overcome with her daring in defying her husband, Mrs Peterson looked ready to burst into tears.

'You did right to tell us all this, Mrs Peterson,' Rafferty said quickly, in an attempt to avert the possibility. 'I'm sure your husband

229

will understand why you felt you had to contact us. Any such threat should be taken seriously.'

She gave them another of her tremulous smiles. 'Thank you, Inspector. That's exactly what I thought. Exactly what I told Stephen.' She sighed, pulled a tissue from her pocket and dabbed at her eyes. 'I just wish he would listen to me sometimes, that's all.'

'Poor lady,' was Llewellyn's comment fifteen minutes later, after they had finally managed to extricate themselves from Mrs Peterson's clingy desire for further reassurance. 'She really doesn't seem to have grasped that we're investigating the murder of a middle-aged man. Or that the death could involve her husband. No wonder he tried to forbid her to speak to us about it. We'll have to question him again, of course.'

'Nothing more certain,' Rafferty agreed. 'Let's just hope, for her sake and her husband's, that this man is still alive and well and just got bored with making his threats.'

They found Dr Peterson in his Orchard Road surgery where they had previously spoken to him.

As on the last occasion, he didn't look pleased to see them. Though when Rafferty explained the reason for their visit, he seemed more exasperated than worried.

'My wife is of a nervous disposition, Inspector,' he unnecessarily explained. 'I'm sorry she's troubled you over such a trivial matter. The man issuing the threats against me finally listened to reason and understood when I explained the circumstances of his mother's death to him: that I had tried to *save* her life, even if it was to no avail. The blood poisoning had too strong a grip by the time she was brought to the hospital. I couldn't save her.'

'What was she?' Rafferty asked. 'Another victim of a backstreet abortionist?'

Dr Peterson just nodded.

'I'd like this man's name, please doctor. His address, too, if you have it. I'd also like to know why, when we spoke to you before, you told us that no one with any connection to the sixties, when you performed your illegal abortions, had contacted you.'

'His name's Barry Anders. I don't know where he lives. He never told me. Though I suspect he may be living rough or in a squat somewhere in the town. As to why I chose to conceal the fact of this man's existence and the threats he made against me...' The doctor shrugged. 'I suppose I just thought telling you about him wouldn't help and might even delay your investigation. *I* knew the dead man wasn't Anders, so it seemed a needless complication, easier just to keep quiet.'

'Not so easy now that we've found out about him and that you lied to us, doctor. You must appreciate how bad it looks.' Dr

231

Peterson shrugged again, but made no further attempt to defend his deceit. 'Your wife said he looked to be in his forties,' Rafferty continued. 'Would you agree with that?'

'Something like that, I imagine. Though if, as I said, he *was* living rough, the life might well have made him look older than he was. I have reason to believe he was a drug-taker, too.'

'So, what did he look like, this man? Can you describe him?' It would be interesting, Rafferty thought, if the doctor attempted to give them a different description from the one already supplied by his wife. However, he wasn't so foolish as to compound his errors.

'He was tallish. He looked surprisingly well-built for a drug-taker, most of whom seem to eat little, but I wonder now whether that was more down to all the layers of clothes he wore rather than to his having well-fleshed bones. He had a scrabby beard and unkempt hair, much as you'd expect.'

'Your wife also said he turned up at your home several times, making his threats. That must have been unpleasant. Your wife certainly found it so.'

'I told you, my wife is highly strung. Naturally, she became upset out of all proportion. I didn't feel the man was any real threat. I told her I'd sort it out and deal with him.'

'And *did* he, I wonder?' Rafferty commented as, five minutes later, he and Llewellyn returned to the car and drove back through the pleasant, leafy avenues to the far from leafy environs of Elmhurst's police station. 'Better get a few bodies out to check the doss houses, street sleepers and known squats, Daff, and see if we can find this Barry Anders. If he still exists at all, that is, and wasn't *dealt with* by the good doctor and buried before his threatening behaviour could escalate and cause Dr Peterson problems he would rather have avoided.'

But, fortunately for the doctor, Barry Anders, the man who had issued threats against Dr Peterson, was quickly traced through the Department of Work and Pensions. Social Services had, in the interim, found him a bed-sit and promised to get him on a drug rehabilitation programme as soon as a place became available.

As soon as he set eyes on him, Rafferty could see why Dr Peterson had dismissed his threats as nothing to worry about. Because Anders was a sorry soul, one of those pathetic individuals who become full of bravura with drugs or alcohol, but when without either courage-inducing substance relapses into weak self-pity.

But, Rafferty presumed, as he gazed at the watery-eyed and sorry-for-himself individual Barry Anders, that the early loss of his mother had dealt him a cruel blow, one from which he had never recovered.

Nowadays, with so many broken families,

there were thousands like Anders in the country: people who needed propping up by Social Services and charitable organizations. All needed help and support just to live, to do the basic things that most people took for granted. For a moment, Rafferty had the urge to take Anders home to his ma for some much-needed mothering, but he restrained the impulse. If she discovered a taste for taking in stray dogs, who knew where it would end?

So after asking for a look at the few documents Anders hadn't managed to lose so they could confirm his ID, they left. Rafferty, for one, couldn't help but feeling he was, somehow, walking by on the other side in leaving Anders alone in his drab comfortless bed-sit and at the tender mercies of the 'Social'. But he didn't see what else he could do.

# Fourteen

While Ray Payne, Teresa Tattersall's drug-dealing ex-boyfriend, was proving as low-profile and hard to find as most who earn their living on the wrong side of the law, to Rafferty's relief the Almighty had condescended to give them a helping hand in one area at least.

But, even more than the Almighty, he had to thank Professor Amos who had completed the job of reconstruction with a remarkable and commendable speed.

Armed with pictures of Professor Amos's facial reconstruction of the dead man, Rafferty went yet again to the convent. He hoped to get confirmation that the reconstruction was a good likeness of one of their possible victims: the man who had visited the convent to learn about the late Sister Clare; Nathan McNally, Cecile's missing boyfriend; or Ray Payne, Teresa's ex-drug dealer boyfriend *cum* pimp.

Both Teresa and Cecile were adamant the photograph of the reconstruction bore no resemblance to either of their ex-boyfriends – claims easily checked out, in Cecile's case at least, since her parents and the Bells, the father and son building team, also confirmed that the reconstruction bore no resemblance to Nathan McNally. Certainly Professor Amos's reconstruction was widely at odds with the facial features Cecile's parents had worked on with the police artist. As for Ray Payne, he was a well-known local scumbag. They should have been able to discount him as being the victim as they had McNally. Unfortunately, Payne's features weren't dissimilar to those of the dead man as reconstructed by the professor.

And while Sister Rita and Father Kelly – who was paying one of his regular visits – were not sure either way, Mother Catherine seemed far more positive and insisted it was a good likeness of the convent's anonymous visitor in the latter part of August.

After such a time lapse, Rafferty couldn't allow himself to get too excited about Mother Catherine's certainty, particularly as it was a certainty which neither Sister Rita nor Father Kelly shared. He knew that the memory plays tricks and that in spite of the Prioress's good intentions in trying to help, she might very well be mistaken. Her weak and damaged eyesight didn't help in encouraging any such certainty.

Rafferty turned back to Father Kelly. 'You said you left with this visitor back in August, Father. Did he take the opportunity to speak to you at all or mention where he might be going once he left the convent?'

Father Kelly gave him a sheepish smile. 'Is that what I said? Ah, to be sure and I think I might have unintentionally misled you, Inspector. Now that you mention it, this young man didn't actually leave at the precise same time as me.'

It was Rafferty's turn to frown. 'But you said—'

'Sure and I know what I said. Haven't I just admitted as much? I made a simple misake.'

'How can you have made such a mistake? You gave me the distinct impression that he *had* left with you.'

'Well, and so he didn't. It's a small enough matter, I'm thinking. And amn't I telling you now? No, this young man hung back to speak to Sister Rita. And as a man of the cloth, eager to get on with the saving of souls, I was in a rush to perform my other priestly duties, so I left them to it.'

Rafferty swallowed hard on the cynical eruption that Father Kelly's pious statement encouraged and turned to Sister Rita. 'Strange, but I also gained the impression from you, Sister, that this visitor left with Father Kelly.'

Before the nun could respond, Mother Catherine broke in. 'I'm sure Sister Rita didn't intend to mislead you, Inspector, any more than did Father Kelly. It *is* some time ago, as Father Kelly said. Such a small matter could become confused in anyone's mind.'

Never mind those of an ageing nun and an even more ageing toper? He wasn't sure whether it had been Mother Catherine's intention to plant such an inference in his mind. But intentionally or no, she had succeeded, and Rafferty inclined his head in acknowledgement.

Still, he reflected, as he and Llewellyn bid them all good day, it was curious that both the holy father and the holy sister had had the same memory failure.

In spite of the contradictory information he had received from the nuns and Father Kelly, whose acquaintance with the August visitor was now revealed to have been even briefer than he had been led to believe, Rafferty was hopeful that someone who knew the dead man rather better than any of the religious parties concerned would see the reconstruction, recognize the dead man's face and his watch, and come forward.

In this he wasn't disappointed. In fact, when it came to responses, he soon had an embarrassment of riches. Because after the pictures of the facial reconstruction had been issued to the media, many members of the public rang in to say they recognized the dead man.

Each of these claims had to be checked. That would take a few days. In the mean-time, Rafferty decided he would direct a

238

little more effort into finding Ray Payne, Teresa's drug-dealing ex-boyfriend who had got her hooked so he could pimp her body. So far, they had had no luck in finding him. In fact, information from assorted snouts soon made it clear that he hadn't been seen for some weeks.

After a long discussion amongst the team in the Incident Room, it was concluded that he had last been seen within the time frame during which their cadaver had been killed.

Rafferty thought for a few moments, then he said, 'OK, we'd better try a bit harder to see if we can find out what's happened to him. It could be he's decided to keep a low profile for a while. Maybe a more subtle approach will winkle him out.'

To this end, Rafferty asked for the temporary secondment to CID of PC Allen. He set her the task of finding Teresa's drug-dealing ex-boyfriend. He had chosen her for the job because she was young and hadn't been on the strength for long, so there was less chance that any of Ray Payne's law-breaking druggie friends would be familiar with her face – a possibility made even less likely when, several hours later, after she had been sent home to change her clothes, Rafferty saw the transformation to PC Allen's appearance made by her thigh-high jean skirt, the long flowing natural blonde hair freed from its top-knot, and an application of cosmetics that was so subtle it made her look about sixteen. An innocent sixteen with a hint of promise. Just the sort of fodder that any self-respecting drug dealer and pimp would be glad to hook into for future earnings.

Predictably, Llewellyn had protested about his plans.

'You can't send this young woman out to lure a violent drug dealer from his lair. She's too naïve, too inexperienced.'

'That's the whole point, Dafyd,' Rafferty told him, unsurprised at the discovery that the shy-with-women Llewellyn should have hidden depths of gallantry.

'You should at least arrange some back up.'

Rafferty took the wind out of the Welshman's sails. 'I have,' he told him.

Llewellyn's dark eyes regarded him suspiciously. 'Who?'

'Timothy Smales.'

'*Smales?*'

Rafferty nodded. 'He's not as dozy as he looks. Trust me.'

'You realize you're sending out two innocents?'

Rafferty nodded. 'That's what will keep them safe.' One of the things, anyway. But as one of the other safeguards was unofficial, Rafferty thought it best to keep this information to himself.

Llewellyn didn't look convinced, but given Superintendent Bradley's complaint that he'd already gone over his overtime budget for the month, Rafferty didn't relish giving the Super yet another reason to carp. Which was why he had taken the option of co-opting one of his cousins, just in case.

And this cousin was a rough and ready builder who wouldn't look out of place in the scruffy pub which was Ray Payne's usual hangout. His cousin had a mobile. All he would have to do was ring them if things looked like turning ugly. He and Llewellyn could be there in a jiffy. Not that he thought they'd be needed.

Rafferty's cousin was a big bloke, six foot six. And he loathed drugs. And dealers. No harm would come to the two innocents.

Rafferty turned away from Llewellyn to give some final instructions to Claire Allen.

'Be casual. Just ask if chummy's around and hint you're looking to score. Act as if you know him and are a regular customer.' Rafferty paused and looked at the bright-eyed, healthily glowing young woman standing eagerly in front of him and frowned.

'Can you fake some pallor? And make your eyes a bit less bright and shiny. You're meant to be a druggie. No one will believe that if you look like a Pollyanna.'

The young PC Allen looked puzzled at the reference, but she was quick to reassure. 'Don't worry, sir,' she told him. 'I've got some pale foundation at home. I used to wear it when I was younger and wanted to make my mum think I was too sick to go to school.'

'Did it work?'

She grinned. 'Every time.'

'Yes, well. Just remember these boys aren't likely to be as gullible as your mum. All I want is for you to find out where this Ray Payne is to be found. Stay away from dark alleys and crack dens, OK?'

As it turned out, neither Rafferty nor Llewellyn had any cause for concern. PC Claire Allen sailed back into the station two hours later looking like death warmed up and as desperate a druggie as any Colombian drug baron with future profits to think of could wish for. To no avail, unfortunately.

'The rumours are right,' she reported. 'Ray Payne's gone to ground. The word is he's been treading on some heavy rival's toes, not to mention his patch, and the rival's put the word out that he's dead meat.'

*Dead meat, gone to ground.* In the circumstances, the phrases were unfortunate. And after he had dismissed Claire Allen, Rafferty couldn't help but wonder if the heavy rival to Teresa Tattersall's ex had succeeded in his threat and had thought it amusing to plant the *dead meat* of the unwanted competition in the grounds of the convent of his one-time girlfriend.

And although it seemed probable that Cecile's ex, at least, was now out of the running as their victim, it was unfortunate that the ex-boyfriends of both Cecile and Teresa lived such unsettled and unpredictable lives. Checking them out had taken much valuable time.

*You'd think you could rely on would-be nuns to have dated nice settled mummy's boys*, Rafferty thought crossly. What was the world coming to?

Hearing the returned Smales' youthful footsteps passing outside his office, Rafferty shouted his name and when the young PC stuck his head round the door, ordered him to the canteen for tea, hot, strong and – for him at least – well-sugared.

Once the tea was delivered, Rafferty sat back and gazed at Llewellyn. 'OK,' he said. 'Let's do a bit of wheat and chaff sorting. So far, apart from old Sister Ursula and the baby she bore courtesy of her American GI during the war, the only detrimental discoveries we've made concern the two young ones, Cecile and Teresa, with the former, at least, apparently now out of the running.

'And as far as the two male suspects in the case are concerned, all we have that is recent is the fact that they both had the opportunity to help themselves to the convent's spare key.'

'Don't forget that Dr Peterson has shown himself not only capable of lying, but also of taking the law into his own hands if he felt it warranted.'

'Mm.' Father Kelly, too, wasn't above

breaking a few laws, though in his case they were the laws of God rather than man. This was information that so far Rafferty had managed to keep close to his chest. He had allocated no one but himself to checking the priest out, thinking it likely that if Father Kelly suspected his doings were about to become common gossip around the station, he might just return the favour and encourage the gossip to switch to Rafferty's recent doings. Though if he was prepared to break what he surely considered *higher* laws, breaking those of man would presumably be unlikely to trouble the priest over much.

'Anyway, lies or not, Dr Peterson seems to be out of it. Unless he made a habit of attracting threatening men in their middle years to his door.'

Half an hour later, their wheat and chaff sorting hadn't noticeably advanced the investigation and Rafferty brought the discussion to a close.

'Looks like we'll have to wait for the prof's recon to bear some riper fruit than it's so far managed,' Rafferty commented after he had drained the cold dregs of his tea. 'Pray that it does. Because if not, I don't know where else we can turn to get a lead on this case.'

The team allocated to checking the responses to the calls that had come in from the public after the release of Professor Amos's facial reconstruction finally got round to a Mr Mike Mitchelson. Mr Mitchelson had been insistent that the body in question was that of one of his tenants, a Mr Peter Bodham. He even claimed to recognize the dead man's watch.

Initial questioning of Mitchelson revealed that Peter Bodham was, if nothing else, certainly the right age and height to be their cadaver. The name on the watch's inscription matched too.

But it was only after Mr Mitchelson had used his key to let the officers doing the initial checking into his tenant's flat, and they had taken surface fingerprints and hair from the brush in the bathroom for DNA checks, and the fingerprint results had come back positive, that Rafferty knew he was finally moving forward.

They at last had a confirmed identity for their cadaver.

# Fifteen

Rafferty and Llewellyn drove to London to speak to Mr Mitchelson, the dead man's landlord. He lived in the same small private block of flats as his tenant, Peter Bodham, south of the river at Wandsworth.

Now they had a confirmed identity for the dead man, Rafferty was anxious to search Bodham's flat. He was hopeful they might turn up some clues as to what had been going on in his life that might have caused him to wind up dead and buried in Elmhurst's RC convent.

After first paying a courtesy call to the local police station, they drove to the flats and found a visibly upset Mr Mitchelson waiting on his late tenant's doorstep. The landlord, tall, wiry and inclined to pugnacity, launched into a verbal attack the moment he saw them.

'Maybe if you people had listened to me and done something when I reported Peter missing, he might still be alive.'

Rafferty, although he thought it unusual that the dead man's landlord, of all people, should become so upset at the violent death of a tenant, did his best to calm the man.

'I'm sorry, sir. But adults go missing all the time. And if there are no grounds to suspect foul play, there's unlikely to be an investigation. There's no law to prevent a grown man or woman going walkabout if they choose.' Privately, Rafferty admitted it had been carelessness that had allowed Peter Bodham to be missed on their trawl of missing persons. Particularly as, physically, he was a match for the dead man. The latter was unsurprising. Because the checks on his fingerprints and DNA proved conclusively that Bodham *was* their previously unidentified cadaver.

Fortunately, Mr Mitchelson seemed unaware that nowadays missing persons were computerized, so supposedly easily matched to bodies. At any rate, to Rafferty's relief, he did no more than mutter fretfully, 'Yes, well, maybe there ought to be such a law.'

Although Mr Mitchelson's belligerence appeared to fade, a raw anger could still be detected just below the surface. Rafferty could feel it in the tension emanating from the man, he could see it in the thinning of the lips as they struggled to keep back any further outbursts. Again he wondered why the landlord should be so upset about the death of Peter Bodham. He asked if Bodham had been a relative. And when Mr Mitchelson shook his head, Rafferty wondered whether the landlord's emotional outburst

247

was derived less from personal grief and more from mercenary concerns. Maybe his late tenant owed him rent?

Rafferty, concerned to ward off another outburst, concentrated some more on calming Mitchelson. 'You told my colleagues who contacted you after your response to our call for information that your tenant had said he might be going away,' he reminded the man. He paused then, in the hope that any further information Mr Mitchelson was able to give them would help in their understanding. 'You said that you last saw Peter Bodham at the beginning of September.'

At least Mr Mitchelson's nod of agreement confirmed that Bodham *had* left the convent after his August visit. And given that his visit had provided closure on the fact of Sister Clare's thirty-year-old death, it seemed unlikely that Peter Bodham would feel a follow-up visit necessary. Though, of course, that conclusion didn't explain how he'd wound up buried in the convent's grounds, a burial that made clear there *had* been a second visit to the convent. The question was whether that visit had been voluntary or *in*voluntary...

'Did Mr Bodham mention where he might have been planning to go on his travels?'

Mike Mitchelson nodded. 'He seemed upset. Peter wasn't the hysterical sort, but he'd seemed depressed for several days, and though he refused to tell me why, he did talk about going abroad. He seemed set on going to Africa, of all places.'

'What part of Africa?' Rafferty asked. 'Did he say?'

'Well, yes, he did. It was one of those places that's changed its name. Someplace that now begins with a Z. I don't rightly remember. It might have been Zaire. Or maybe Zimbabwe. Unless there's another country on the continent beginning with a Z.'

Rafferty glanced at Llewellyn. Father Kelly had mentioned that it had been Zaire where Sister Clare had been murdered all those years ago. He could only suppose that Peter Bodham had wanted to travel there to learn the facts at first hand from some villager of the time. If that was still possible given the lapse of years and the usual African death rate.

'As I said,' Mitchelson continued. 'One day he'd been totally set on going to Africa. He'd even got some foreign currency. Then a few days later, he simply dropped the idea. I was surprised, because Peter was one of those determined people who – when they decide on something – invariably carry it through. It can't have been a shortage of money that made him change his mind, either. Because he'd been made redundant from his job only a couple of months before, so had his redundancy cash as well as savings. Not that he was what could be called extravagant with his money when he was employed. He'd never gone on holiday in the three years I knew him, yet he was filled with the idea of taking this expensive trip to Africa. That's why it's so odd that he should change his mind about the trip shortly before he was due to travel.'

Rafferty questioned him about Peter Bodham's previous employers and Llewellyn noted the details.

'How did he seem when he told you about the trip? Was he excited?'

'No. That's the curious thing. Although, as I said, he was determined on going, the thought of the trip didn't seem to excite him at all. Rather the reverse. And then, as I said, a day or so before he was due to set off, he told me he wasn't going after all. Even more oddly, cancelling his trip *did* seem to excite him. I wondered if his decision to cancel the trip might have had something to do with the letter he received that morning.'

Rafferty questioned Mr Mitchelson as to when the letter had been received and what else he could remember about it.

The man shrugged. 'It came early in September. It was just an ordinary letter, you know, in one of those small white envelopes. I was down in the lobby when the postman arrived, and I noticed him placing it in Peter's mailbox. The address was handwritten rather than typed. It was unusual for Peter to get personal correspondence, which is why I remembered it. But he never told me what was in it to get him so hyper.'

'What else can you tell us about Mr Bodham? Was he married, or did he have a regular girlfriend?'

Mr Mitchelson shook his head. 'Peter had lived here three years. He'd never had a girlfriend in all that time. I suppose you could say he was a loner, like me. Kept himself to himself. Even more so when he lost his job. He was never any trouble, not like some tenants I've had in the past. I felt we'd become friends of a sort.' For some reason he looked awkward at the admission.

'What about other friends? Work colleagues from his last job?'

Mitchelson shrugged. 'I never saw any. I told you, he was a loner. He didn't seem to be close to anybody, so it's hard to imagine who could want him dead.'

That was the last thing Rafferty wanted to hear. But he was still hopeful that Bodham's flat would yield some clues. He thanked the landlord, borrowed his key and let himself and Llewellyn into the dead man's home.

'What do you think about this Michael Mitchelson, Bodham's landlord?' Rafferty asked once they were in Bodham's flat with the door closed. 'I wondered if he's so upset about Bodham because his late tenant was behind with his rent. But then another possibility occurred to me. Mitchelson said they'd been friends. Do you think they might have been rather *more* than friends?'

Llewellyn shrugged. 'It's possible, I suppose. Mr Mitchelson did say that Peter Bodham hadn't had a girlfriend in all the time he'd known him. Shall I assign one of the team to look into their relationship?'

Rafferty nodded. 'Put Mary Carmody on to it. She's good at drawing people out and she's got a strong bladder, which is just as well. It's the sort of assignment which demands the ability to drink tea by the gallon. And our Mair can drink any sort of tea going – weak, strong, sugared and unsugared – *and* look as if she's enjoying it. A rare skill.' Rafferty pulled on some gloves, and said, 'Right, give Carmody a bell, get those checks organized, and then we can get on with this search.'

Bodham's home wasn't large. There was just a living room, a single bedroom and a kitchenette with bathroom off. Peter Bodham hadn't troubled to stamp his identity on the place; it looked more like a largish though comfortless hermit's cell than a home. There were no pictures or ornaments of any kind and not much in the way of furniture beyond a bureau, a couple of armchairs, a nest of three cheap occasional tables and a dining table with two chairs which stood against the window wall and which housed a computer. The computer was the only expensive item.

Rafferty nodded at the computer. 'We'll take that back to Elmhurst with us, Dafyd.

You can study its innards at your leisure. Meanwhile, let's get on and check the rest of this place.'

They divided the room search. Rafferty made a start in the living room while Llewellyn took the bedroom. Rafferty opened the cheap bureau and found just the usual files for household bills, utilities and so on. He'd only been checking through these for a minute or two, wanting to be certain he'd missed nothing, when Llewellyn called through from the bedroom.

'Inspector.'

Rafferty walked the couple of paces through to the bedroom and asked, 'What have you got, Daff?'

Dafyd tapped his fingers on a lever arch file and indicated several more stored in a large plastic box. 'According to these notes, the late Mr Bodham was researching his family tree.'

Rafferty nodded. 'That agrees with what Mother Catherine and Father Kelly told us.'

They sat down and studied the paperwork the late Peter Bodham had amassed. There was a surprising amount of it. It was clear that most of it had been printed out from various genealogical websites. They found papers confirming that Bonham had been adopted at birth. There were also two death certificates, one for each of his adoptive parents. They had died within a few months of each other earlier in the summer; perhaps that had been what had prompted Peter Bodham to search for his birth family.

Rafferty was momentarily distracted by a photograph on the window sill. He hadn't noticed it before and it was only when the breeze through the draughty window blew the curtains back that the photo had caught his eye. It was a head shot of a young man with unusually vivid green eyes. A middle-aged man and woman stood on either side of him; presumably his adoptive parents.

'Reckon this is our victim?' he asked Llewellyn. It certainly looked a good match for Professor Amos's recon.

Llewellyn took the photograph and studied it for a moment, then, with his usual logic, he said, 'The quickest way to find out is to ask the landlord,' and made for the door.

As the landlord lived across the hall from Bodham's flat, Llewellyn was back in five minutes. 'The landlord confirms that Peter Bodham and the man in the photograph are one and the same,' he said.

While Llewellyn was speaking to the landlord, Rafferty had been studying Peter Bodham's paperwork. As he did so he found himself wondering what the late Sister Clare's birth name had been. Even though he had, on the spur of the moment, suggested to Mother Catherine that Bodham might have been the late nun's illegitimate son, he hadn't really considered it a likely possibility and had failed to follow up on it.

Maybe he should do so now?

He took out his mobile and rang the convent. But their phone was engaged, so instead, he rang the diocesan offices. It didn't take long to get the information he sought.

*Well, well,* he thought as he cut the connection and returned the mobile to his pocket. Bingo. Or is it? he wondered as he glanced again at the assorted papers, one of which categorically denied any connection between Bodham and Sister Clare.

On Llewellyn's return, he handed several pieces of this paperwork over.

'Looks like he was stymied on the family tree front. He's managed to find his original birth certificate – or so he must have thought. And though the woman named as the mother bears the same name as the late Sister Clare – Annemarie Jones – it's a surname that goes way beyond common. But at least it explains his visit to the convent. If he thought Sister Clare was really his mother, he must have been shattered when both the diocesan office and Mother Catherine confirmed she had long since died.

'There's no father mentioned on the birth certificate. And I found a letter from a woman he thought was a maternal aunt, who insists he's got the wrong family and that her sister Annemarie Jones was *not* his natural mother.'

'Still, it's a curious coincidence,' Llewellyn

pointed out.

'Mm.'

It was the only personal letter amongst Peter Bodham's meagre and otherwise soon-searched possessions. Unlike the letter that Mike Mitchelson had mentioned Bodham receiving, its envelope had an August, not a September, postmark. There was no trace of the later one.

Next, Rafferty handed over a newspaper cutting. It was a death notice and apparently reported the death of Peter Bodham's correspondent; a Mrs Sophia Ansell, the woman he had believed to be his maternal aunt.

'Shame this woman's dead. She might have been telling the truth, of course, that her sister wasn't Peter's natural mother at all.'

'Equally, she might have lied to him to keep a family secret. Either way, we're unlikely to find out now. Unless we can get permission for an exhumation for DNA purposes on such flimsy proofs, it looks like we may have got round one dead end only to find another.'

He stood up. 'See if you can find some carrier bags, Dafyd. Along with the computer and the photograph, I want to take all this paperwork back to the station so we can study it at our leisure. But before we do that, and once we've dropped this stuff back at the station, we'll pay a visit to the address of Bodham's late correspondent and speak to the neighbours. Maybe if this Mrs Ansell was lying when she told Bodham her sister Annemarie wasn't his natural mother, any old neighbours might be able to shed some light one way or the other.'

Rafferty's excitement about their latest discoveries was tempered when they returned to the station and he saw what he had no trouble in recognizing as another of the blackmailer's missives. It was sitting, impertinently, right at the top of his in-tray.

Warily, keeping one ear cocked for Llewellyn, who had stopped off in the Incident Room to check if there had been any further developments, Rafferty ripped the envelope open and quickly scanned its contents.

Inexplicably, the blackmailer had again failed to make any demands, financial or otherwise. This strange new strain of 'no demand' blackmail was disconcerting. It alarmed rather than reassured, especially as its taunting nature had increased since the first letter. He didn't know what to make of it. What did this creature *want*?

But he didn't have time to dwell on this latest worrying missive. When he heard Llewellyn's light tread in the corridor, he quickly stuffed both letter and envelope in the pocket in which he kept the previous one. He said nothing, but his mind was racing as they headed back to the car. He still had no real idea of the blackmailer's identity: he had so far failed to come up with a plausible approach to questioning his previous fellow members of the Made in Heaven dating agency. Even his cousin Nigel had been unable to help him decide how best to act.

But even if he somehow managed to come up with a believable excuse to approach his fellow dating agency members, meeting them again would require him to once more don the disguise he had found it necessary to adopt in order to investigate the two murders that had occurred during that previous case. And as that would require that he again grow a beard and wear the prescription glasses of his late father that had almost blinded him before, he wasn't keen. Broodingly, as he handed over the keys to the car to Llewellyn and climbed in the passenger side, he thought his only option would be to wait until the blackmailer *did* play his demand card. There was bound to be one eventually, as he suspected his tormentor was providing himself with further sport by making him wait to learn what his demand would turn out to be. He would just have to possess his soul in patience till his tormentor got bored and made his demand. He would see then if he could meet it. He now rather regretted having given Abra *carte blanche* to redecorate the flat. The makeover had put a serious dent in his limited savings. He could only hope that the blackmailer's demands, when they did finally arrive, weren't beyond his means to meet. Because if they were, he suspected that Abra's previous calm acceptance of his foolish behaviour in April might just change to something less calm and restrained.

# Sixteen

To Rafferty's relief, when he and Llewellyn spoke to the long-standing neighbours of the Jones family, it was to discover that the Annemarie Jones who had lived at the old family address in Mercers' Lane, behind East Hill, had indeed gone on to become a nun. It had been the talk of the neighbourhood at the time, as Mrs Smithson, the elderly woman who still lived in the next-door terrace house, confirmed once the three of them were seated round her kitchen table, the tea had been poured, and Rafferty had led up to this question.

'I must say, I didn't expect her to go through with it,' Mrs Smithson told them as she sipped her tea. 'I was surprised when I heard that she was serious about it. Annemarie had always been an impetuous sort of girl, given to sudden enthusiasms. I assumed this interest in religion would be another such.'

Mrs Smithson, when questioned, admitted she knew nothing of any early pregnancy. But even given the disparity between Sister Clare's family address and the address given on Peter Bodham's birth certificate, it struck Rafferty as unlikely in the extreme that the two women weren't one and the same. And now that Mrs Smithson had confirmed that her Annemarie Jones had become a nun …

Rafferty thought it probable that Annemarie had turned to religion after giving up her baby; such a devastating loss would tend to make any young woman more seriously inclined, particularly back in 1957, the year Peter Bodham was born. At that time, the moral climate and the attitude to unmarried mothers and their illegitimate offspring was far less tolerant than it was today. Annemarie had been not quite eighteen at the time. She must have felt very alone.

Mrs Smithson told them that Sophia Ansell, the eldest of the Jones daughters and the one who had written to Bodham denying the family connection, had remained in the family home and had lived in it till her death.

'It's a shame this Mrs Ansell died so recently,' Rafferty quietly remarked to Llewellyn as he accepted a second cup of tea from Mrs Smithson. 'If we could have spoken to her we might have been able to get her to tell us more about the family.'

Although Mrs Smithson was certainly in her eighties, there was clearly nothing wrong with her hearing. For she gave him a curious look and carefully replaced the brown earthenware teapot on the table before she said, 'But surely you know there was a third sister?'

'A third sister? No,' Rafferty admitted, 'we didn't know.'

'Well, there was. Still is, come to that. If you want to know more about the family, you can always speak to Rosalind. Rosalind Wilson, Rosalind Jones as was. She's still alive. I even have her address.'

Slowly, Rafferty lowered his tea cup to its saucer.

Like her late sister, Rosalind Wilson was as adamant in the spoken word as Sophia Ansell had been in the written, that Anne-marie had not given birth to an illegitimate child and was certainly *not* Peter Bodham's natural mother. Only she was more verbose in her denials.

Less laid-back in her entertaining than Mrs Smithson, Mrs Wilson had chosen to entertain them in her lounge rather than her kitchen. Her house was semi-detached, but of the older sort, more roomy than the cubby-holes that modern builders erected. Unlike the friendly and gossipy older woman, she didn't offer to make them tea.

Perhaps, Rafferty thought, after he had explained the reason for their visit, her natural affront that he should imply that the stigma of illegitimacy applied to a member of her family was sufficient to remove the basic social graces. Or perhaps she just didn't like entertaining policemen in her home. The way Rosalind Wilson sat, stiff-backed in her armchair, wearing an outraged expression, seemed to confirm this possibility.

'I assure you, Inspector, my sister Annemarie did *not* give birth to an illegitimate baby as a young woman. The very idea!'

Clearly, Mrs Wilson was of the mind-set that such things might happen to other women's sisters, but they certainly did not happen to hers.

Perhaps she thought she had been a bit too vehement in her rejection of the idea, because now she softened and provided a more reasoned argument. 'Don't you think I would have known if she had? How could I not? We lived in the same house. Shared the same bedroom even. I admit we weren't close – she was always closer to our elder sister, Sophia – but we *were* sisters. Why anyone would want to tell you such wicked lies when Annemarie's been dead for thirty years, I can't imagine. But when I find out who they are, they'll get the sharp edge of my tongue.'

Rafferty studied Rosalind Wilson, from her neatly French-plaited, subtly red-tinted hair to the stylish tailored trousers and well-cut linen top. He got the impression that, after his phone call arranging their visit, she had dressed smartly to make them understand that she was a respectable woman from a respectable family. He also got another impression: that the sharp edge of her tongue would be very sharp indeed. He admitted to himself that she seemed unshakeable in her conviction, even genuinely sincere in what she was saying. But during their conversation she had not only revealed herself to be an extremely garrulous woman, who would use ten words where three would suffice, she had also admitted that, at fifty-nine, she was the youngest of the three Jones sisters, seven years younger than Annemarie the middle sibling. She had admitted she and Annemarie hadn't been close, so it was quite possible that she would have been kept in ignorance of Annemarie's teenage shame.

Many young girls at the time, pregnant with illegitimate babies, had been packed off to distant aunts, cousins or whatever to await the birth, long before any pregnancy would be visible. Some, as Llewellyn had said, had even ended up in the old county asylums, it being a prevalent belief back then that young women who became pregnant out of wedlock were mentally below par, not to say degenerate, and needed locking up.

So it was possible that, to this day, the youngest sister, with her unfortunate tendency to let her tongue run away with her, had been kept completely in the dark. The neighbours, too, would likely have been told some falsehood to account for the months of Annemarie's absence. But what of the older sister, the late Mrs Ansell? Again, Ruffilly found himself regretting this sister's recent death. Rosalind Wilson had told them that both her late sisters had been close. Had Sophia Ansell known about, or at least suspected, Annemarie's plight? Surely Annemarie would have confided in someone? Who better than the older, wiser sister to whom she was so close?

It seemed possible, maybe even probable, was Rafferty's conclusion, even though Sophia Ansell's letter to Peter Bodham had denied that Annemarie might be his natural mother. In Rafferty's experience, moral attitudes learned early tended to remain with a person throughout their life. That was why all religions liked to imbue children with their ideology and the younger the better. Hadn't *he* spent most of his life weighed down with Catholic guilt and with a hard taskmaster for a conscience?

'Your sister decided she had a religious vocation while still in her teens, I understand?' Rafferty remarked to Mrs Wilson.

Mrs Wilson gave a quick nod and looked set to comment at length, but Rafferty held up his hand to stay her tongue.

'So she would, I presume, have gone on Catholic retreats of some months' duration during this time?'

'As you rightly point out, Inspector, my late sister had a religious vocation, though she didn't actually enter the religious life as a postulant until she was almost twenty-one.'

She paused and gazed indignantly at him as if what he had implied had just sunk in. 'Just a minute, Inspector! You can't seriously be implying that Annemarie would have used her faith as a cloak to bring a pregnancy to term and to give birth secretly at the address you say is on this Peter Bodham's birth certificate?'

Put baldly like that it did seem unlikely, Rafferty admitted to himself. And given that, if Sister Clare *had* given birth prior to entering a convent as a postulant proper, the birth and her own death were all so long ago, and any birth so wrapped in secrecy and denial, that getting to the truth so far down the line seemed unlikely. Particularly as the sole remaining member of her immediate family clearly knew nothing at all of any value to them and would probably have continued in her denials even if she had known.

For a moment, he considered asking her to agree to provide a DNA sample so they could compare it with that of the dead man. But she looked so closed up and determined to rebut any suggestion of immorality in her family that he knew she would be certain to refuse. Maybe later, if curiosity overcame her outrage, she would agree.

Their visit had been a disappointing one and Rafferty felt a bit deflated. But then it occurred to him that there might be a way to get at the truth.

When they got back to the station, Rafferty asked Llewellyn to find out if the late Mrs Ansell had left a will.

'A will?' Llewellyn questioned.

'Yes, Little Sir Echo, a will. If I'm right and the missing letter that Peter Bodham received was from Mrs Ansell – a Mrs Ansell, moreover, who knew she was dying – she might have had a crisis of conscience in that in denying that Annemarie was his natural mother she was also denying him knowledge of his own parentage.

'We already know that Sophia Ansell died at home, with her family gathered round her for comfort. I wonder whether it didn't strike her as cruel that she had denied the solitary Bodham any hope of the same source of comfort from which she drew strength. Maybe she finally accepted that everyone was entitled to know where they came from.'

'You think she might have also left him something in her will?'

'That's the general idea. If she did, it would prove beyond any reasonable doubt that our Annemarie was also the late Peter Bodham's Annemarie. Why would Mrs Ansell leave him anything if he was the total stranger she had previously told him he was?'

Llewellyn nodded. Rafferty could see that his sergeant's logical mind approved of his theory. 'I'll get on to it right away.'

Rafferty continued with checking the rest

of his post after Llewellyn had left. He didn't get very far with it, as the next item in his in-tray was a note from the Incident Room staff concerning Father Kelly. An anonymous tip-off, the note said. Rafferty began to snigger. He'd barely got his sniggers under control when Mary Carmody knocked and entered.

'So did you manage to find anything on Bodham's landlord or the precise nature of their relationship?' Rafferty asked, forcing his gaze away from the note in case the sniggers should break out again.

'Nothing doing on the lover angle,' his DS reported. 'I asked discreetly all round the neighbourhood. Not a whisper of any relationship beyond friendship. From what I discovered, I think it was just that Mr Mitchelson lost his own wife and adult son eighteen months ago. He's a long way from being over their loss and I gather that Peter Bodham resembled his dead son a fair bit.'

Rafferty rubbed tired eyes. 'OK, Mary. Thanks. It was never a likely angle, especially given where Bodham's body ended up, but it had to be checked out. At least your efforts mean another possibility has been squared away. Take a canteen break, have something to eat. Then come back here. I want to have another little chat with Father Kelly.'

Mary looked quizzically at him and asked, 'You wouldn't prefer to wait till Sergeant Llewellyn's available?'

Rafferty smiled. 'Mary, believe me when I

say that this interview isn't one suited to DS Llewellyn. He had a sheltered upbringing and I think he might be shocked by some of the questions I'm going to have to ask our man of the cloth.'

'Ah. Like that, is it?'

'Exactly like that,' Rafferty confirmed. Apart from any other considerations, he would prefer that Llewellyn didn't hear whatever accusations his questions might prompt from Father Kelly. He tapped the Incident Room note. 'This call came while I was out. Anonymous, of course. It implies that Father Kelly's a closet homosexual and might well have had a relationship with Bodham.' The implication struck Rafferty as absurd in the face of the priest's previous form with the ladies of the parish. 'I suspect it's just a woman scorned who has started to spread this rumour about our good Father, because I hadn't heard a whisper to suggest the possibility before today. But given that his landlord said that he'd never known Bodham to have a girlfriend, the fact that the two men had met and that the good Father had access to the convent's spare keys, means I'd better look into the possibility. Anyway, off you go and I'll see you in an hour.'

'A sodomite? Me? How dare you, young Rafferty!' Father Kelly glanced at Mary Carmody as if inviting her to share his outrage.

'And to make such a suggestion in front of a young woman too! I have never lusted after young men in my life.'

'That's what I thought, Father. But when the possibility was mentioned—'

'*Who* mentioned such a possibility?'

Father Kelly was righteously indignant. Of course, he had a well-deserved reputation as a Lothario to be upheld. At least in his own eyes.

'You know I can't tell you that, Father. Not that I know who the person was anyway, as it was an anonymous caller. But it had to be checked, especially in view of the fact that Peter Bodham, the man in the grave, was never seen with a girlfriend.'

Father Kelly was so outraged that, perhaps for the first time in his life, his normally ready tongue was stilled.

Rafferty took advantage of this golden-silence gift from the gods to bid Father Kelly goodbye. He and Mary Carmody made good their escape before the priest's outrage could find further voice.

Back at the police station, Rafferty gazed unenthusiastically at the day's remaining post still piled in his in-tray. Desultorily, he reached for it.

He hoped that if Llewellyn managed to confirm that Sophia Ansell had remembered Peter Bodham in her will, it would be a firm indication that Sister Clare must indeed be Bodham's natural mother. He had hoped that such a confirmation would move them forward. But now he wondered whether this was likely. He had had time to think it through, and he was inclined to feel that his latest suspicion would make no difference at all. How could it? What difference would it make to their inquiry when such a central figure had been in her grave for three decades?

'Jesus,' Rafferty muttered as he fought his way through the Sellotape confining the topmost item of post and stared at the thickness of the file. 'Three quarters of an inch of waffle on why criminals commit crime,' he muttered disbelievingly. 'I could tell 'em in six words, with one of them saved to describe the idiot who wrote this report. Criminals commit crime because they're too stupid, work-shy, immoral, lazy and unpunctual to get a legal income. And the idiot who wrote this trash is too blinkered to look beyond poverty as a reason for crime. Bumf.'

Impatiently, he threw the fat file in his pending tray.

'More bumf.' A second weighty missive joined the first in a 'pend' likely to last for all eternity if Rafferty had anything to do with it. Unless, that was, Llewellyn chose to ruin his eyesight on it and give him the gist.

After so precipitously disposing of the first two items in his in-tray, Rafferty stared at the third letter. It had been concealed by the fat bumfery. He immediately recognized the envelope – addressed to 'Inspector 'N' Rafferty' – as *another* letter from the blackmailer, his second that day. He'd hoped that morning – since there hadn't been one for some time – that the blackmailer had tired of his taunts. But now, here he was receiving double bubble.

Slowly, with a growing feeling of foreboding, he slit open the envelope and quickly perused the contents. The letter was short, as the others had been. And still there was no demand for money. This was getting beyond a joke. Why didn't the bastard stop torturing him and just say what it was he wanted?

He supposed he should at least be thankful he could now talk to Abra about it. He could even discuss this latest letter with Llewellyn if he wanted to, as Abra had persuaded him that it might be a good idea to make use of the logical brain of her cousin in order to figure out a likely identity for the blackmailer. Not, though, that Llewellyn had been either help or comfort. If ever a person had been designed for the description *Job's comforter*, that person was Dafyd Llewellyn.

'Be sure our sins will find us out,' Llewellyn had mournfully intoned immediately after Rafferty had told him about the blackmailer.

Abra wasn't much better. And although she had taken his confession in good part, she was less understanding about the extent of the angst he was suffering from his current investigation. Because, although she felt sorry for the dead Peter Bodham, she was unable to hide her quiet amusement that his current murder investigation meant that a Catholic backslider like him should find himself tangled up with a bunch of nuns.

The only member of Rafferty's family who didn't find his current case a cause for mournful wise-after-the-fact proclamations, or quiet amusement, was Rafferty's ma.

But Rafferty felt he would rather bear either of the first two options than be forced to listen to any more of his ma's continuing admonishments or her attempts to persuade him to take himself off to St Boniface Church and Father Kelly and confess the evil suspicions that were blackening his soul. After his latest questioning of the priest, he guessed he would receive such a sizable penance that he wouldn't get out of the church for a decade or more. If he got out at all.

*God*, he thought, *if only I can prove one of those ruddy nuns is guilty.* It was the only way he would be able to get his mother to shut up about the subject. Or maybe not. Maybe it would be a guarantee that she would continue to harp on and on about his wicked pursuit of holy women. If, on the other hand, he managed to prove them all as innocent as his mother thought they were, in his mother's estimation he would practically be elevated to sainthood himself. Sinner or saint. Saint or sinner. He didn't much fancy either title, much preferring to rub along in the middle ground, like most people. Perhaps, if he wasn't being persecuted by the attentions of this blackmailer, he might have half a chance of solving this case. He stared down at the letter clutched tightly in his hands, his eyes narrowed to slits of frustrated impotence. And as he stared at the missive, barely seeing it, one sentence seemed to hit him squarely between the eyes.

'What?' he gasped. 'But – but– How the hell does this bastard know *that*?'

No one other than his family – not even Llewellyn – knew that he had nearly killed his sister when they were both still kids. Yet there it was, in black and white.

Everyone believed, once the suspect was arrested, that your Nigel Blythe alter ego was innocent of the murders of those two girls in the Lonely Hearts case. And maybe you were. But then, Inspector, they didn't know about your earlier predilection for violence against females, did they? Perhaps if they had known about your attempt to kill your sister Maggie, they mightn't have been so ready to accept your protestations of innocence.

Slowly, unbelievingly, a possibility dawned on him. Could these blackmail letters be one of his family's idea of a *joke*?

Stunned, Rafferty folded the letter – carefully, as if it might yet blow up in his hands – and put it in his pocket with the others, as he wondered who, amongst his family, possessed a sense of humour so warped that they could do this to him?

But Rafferty really didn't need to think about it for long. For while his family might have more than its share of those who bent the law for their own advantage, none of them was inclined to this level of spite. No, he decided, this wasn't one of his family's idea of a joke. This was revenge, not so pure but very simple.

And what member of his family believed they had reason to extract that revenge? None other than his cousin, Nigel Blythe. The Nigel who had pretended to commiserate with him in his dilemma. His cousin must have nearly bust a gut to prevent himself laughing out loud when Rafferty had sought his advice on the letters.

Rafferty couldn't understand why it hadn't occurred to him before that his cousin, Jerry Kelly – or Nigel Blythe as he currently preferred to call himself – would want to get back at him and cause him as much pain and anxiety as he was capable of drumming up. It was, of course, in retaliation for him being the cause of Nigel's name being bandied about back in April as a possible double murderer.

Now he wondered how he'd let the wool be pulled over his eyes to the extent that he'd never considered his cousin might be the person writing these letters. But then he excused his blindness. Why would he have reason to suspect him? While Nigel might be many things that most decent people despised – the fact that he was an estate agent featuring at the top of most lists – he was *family*. Rafferty had believed that his cousin – even if Nigel's list of things he most despised would certainly feature that institution somewhere near the top – wouldn't stoop as low as blackmail.

Besides, the events that had given rise to the blackmail letters had occurred months ago. Why would his permanently cash-strapped cousin wait so long to extract the readies? Especially when Rafferty himself had provided him with the means, motive and opportunity to put himself in line for a nice little earner in the blackmail line.

Even more curious – why would he, after making the initial approach – fail to even mention money at all? No wonder the possibility of Nigel as the blackmailer hadn't occurred to him. It wasn't that Nigel was such a saintly sort; Rafferty was aware that Nigel could raise spite to heights never previously achieved if he had a mind to. It was the blackmailer's failure to demand money that meant he had overlooked Nigel for the role. Why would the permanently cash-strapped Nigel, with his ruinously expensive tastes, neglect to claim the prize? Especially when, for all his high hopes and ambitions, Nigel had yet to make his income match his expenditure?

The more Rafferty considered the matter, the more his mind went round in circles. He would have to wait and hope his cousin enlightened him. Still, the more he thought about it, the more he realized that the role of blackmailer suited Nigel's personality to a T. But, in spite of the oddness of the money angle – or rather, the no-money angle – he was certainly considering him now. More than considering. He was certain that Nigel Blythe was guilty.

And to think he had believed that Nigel – apart from the continual sly digs – had long since put any propensity for revenge behind him! But now the scales had dropped from his eyes. The letters made clear that his dear cousin had been plotting his revenge for months. Clearly cousin Nigel, the devious bastard, was a believer that revenge was a dish best eaten cold.

It was certainly colder than Rafferty's anger which, fuelled by the worry he had suffered since the first letter's arrival, was quickly raised to the white-hot heat of rage.

And while he admitted to himself that Nigel – Jerry Kelly as was, before his upper income bracket property buying and selling clientele had prompted the move to the more upmarket Nigel Blythe moniker – might feel he had good reason for grudge-bearing, his way of acting out that grudge was way out of order.

Yet, Rafferty was fair-minded enough to acknowledge that *he* had been the one who had caused Nigel's name to be bandied about as a suspected double murderer in the Lonely Hearts case. Nigel had been sly enough to make him believe he'd put any rankles about it behind him. After all, it *had* been over six months ago. But clearly Nigel, in the world of grudge bearers, was an Olympic contender.

And while Rafferty's rage still burned, it wasn't so out of control that he didn't realize he couldn't just blunder his way into his cousin's flash apartment and throw accusations about. Like Father Roberto Kelly, Nigel knew way too many of his guilty secrets for that. Stoking the fires of Nigel's resentment wouldn't be a sensible move. But while he would be denied the opportunity to let fly at Nigel, Rafferty nonetheless intended to tackle him about the letters. At the very least, he hoped to be able to persuade his cousin to confirm that he, rather than one of Rafferty's fellow Made In Heaven lonely hearts, was the letter writer. Such a confirmation would at least save him any potential embarrassment – or worse – at the hands of the Made in Heaven lot should he ever manage to come up with a few questions of the non-self-incriminatory sort to put to them.

Perhaps, Rafferty thought, he should go round to Nigel's apartment after work this evening, and get his wretched cousin to admit that he had written the blackmailing letters.

But as there were some few hours before he could put his accusations to his cousin face-to-face, Rafferty tried to put Nigel to the back of his mind and think about the current investigation.

He was helped in this by Llewellyn's return with the confirmation that the late Mrs Ansell had indeed remembered Peter Bodham in her will.

'She altered her will shortly before she died, to leave him a substantial legacy, though one he never took up, which is yet another confirmation, should we need one, that Peter Bodham and Annemarie Jones' illegitimate son are one and the same.'

Rafferty nodded. But then they had pretty much suspected he would be. Getting confirmation though, as he had earlier noted, didn't bring them any further forward. Identifying their cadaver still left them with the difficulty of finding someone with a motive to kill him. And they were still no closer to discovering who that person might be and what their motive was.

But then, as his gaze fell on the topmost pile of bureaucratic bumf in his pending tray, with its predictable title *Why Criminals*

*Commit Crime,* and recalled what actions of his own had provided the blackmailer with his weapon, he began to get a glimmer of an idea as to why this *particular* crime had been committed.

He said nothing to Llewellyn, though. He'd had glimmers of ideas before that had died in the face of the facts. He wasn't about to offer this one up prematurely for his sergeant's brand of clinical dissection.

# Seventeen

When Rafferty called round to his cousin's apartment on his way home that evening in order to confront him, Nigel didn't even trouble to deny that he had been the writer of the blackmail letters. In fact, although clearly a touch peeved that he'd been found out, Nigel seemed rather pleased with himself and inclined to gloat.

'Bet those letters got you nicely rattled, didn't they?' he taunted while vainly checking via the mantel mirror perched above the Italian marble fireplace that the hair he had raked back from his forehead had flopped forward again in a satisfactory manner.

*I'd like to smash his vain face in*, thought Rafferty, as he stared at the preening cousin who had caused him such anguish. But, of course, this was merely another temptation he daren't give into.

'Serves you right,' Nigel turned back from admiring himself. 'Count yourself lucky that letter writing is all I did. Because after all the trouble you caused me back in April, I was tempted to contact your boss and bring him up to speed on a few things.'

Rafferty did his best to conceal the shudder that this revelation brought. But he refused to give Nigel the satisfaction of admitting that he had been seriously rattled for days. Instead, he remarked in a throwaway manner: 'You've had your fun now, so can I take it that you're going to call it a day on the letter writing front?'

Nigel shrugged his designer-suited shoulders. 'No point in continuing with them now that you know it was me.' He smirked. 'Though it might be amusing to think up another means of getting under your skin.'

'And why would you want to do that?' Rafferty demanded. 'As I said, you've had your fun and—'

'Had my *fun*?' Nigel's previously nonchalant leaning figure sprang indignantly away from his mantelpiece. 'Do you have any idea how little *fun* I've had since you started the rumour that I was a double murderer? This might come as news to you, *JAR*,' – contemptuously he used the family nickname spelt from Rafferty's initials – 'but strangely enough, most girls don't fancy the prospect of dating a man who's had his name splashed round for all the wrong reasons. Being branded a dangerous headcase tends to worry the ladies that the foreplay might involve an axe – or three.'

Nigel paused as if remembering something more pleasant. Then his gaze became unfocused, and a smile played cat and mouse with his lips as he added, 'Apart, that is, from the weird ones who find dicing with such danger a great turn on.'

'There you are then,' Rafferty exclaimed, glad to discover that his cousin's fifteen minutes of fame hadn't been *all* bad. 'Sounds to me like you've had some fun you wouldn't have had but for me.'

Nigel's gaze narrowed unappreciatively. 'There's fun and *fun*. Like there's weird and *weirder*, dear boy. One or two of those ladies were so into S and M that they scared the life out of me. And they know where I live.'

Rafferty restrained the urge to grin and give Nigel an inkling of just how much S rather than M pleasure this information afforded him. There was no point in antagonizing his cousin and giving him reason to make good his threat to try some other means of meting out a retaliatory punishment.

There was one aspect of Nigel's blackmail letters that still puzzled Rafferty, and he decided he might as well get as many answers as he could while his cousin was in this expansive gloating mood.

'So why didn't you demand money from me?' he asked. He still found it inexplicable that his extravagant, permanently in-hock cousin had failed to follow through on his taunts with a demand for money.

'Demand *money*?' Nigel drew his slick and stylish self to his full height, the better to

283

display to advantage both his affront at this unwarranted slur on his character and the cut of his designer suit.

This impressive show of indignation almost managed to persuade Rafferty that he'd been wrong, all these years, to put his cousin down as a greedy chancer. Almost, but not quite.

'I might be many things,' Nigel replied, his affronted dignity surely now of Oscar-winning proportions. 'But, unlike so many members of *your* family, I'm not a *criminal*.'

That Rafferty's family were undoubtedly also Nigel's family, Rafferty didn't bother to point out.

'A joke's one thing, and the police can't touch you for it,' Nigel went on, his ruffled dignity rising to the occasion with even more aplomb, 'but if I'd started demanding money, it would put me into a different league. I was merely offering advice. As far as I'm aware, no one can touch you for that.'

'Advice?' Rafferty queried. 'Your missives all read like blackmail letters to me.'

'Blackmail? Surely not, dear boy. As I said, that would be against the law. Read the letters again. I think you'll find I simply offered to help you *resolve* your difficulties. Nothing illegal in that.'

'So, if you were so keen to help why didn't you make your identity plain?'

'Why? Because I didn't want my good name sullied by association with yours a second time should your secret ever become common knowledge.'

Nigel got down off his high horse for long enough to make an unusually honest admission: 'Though I can't deny I was tempted to follow through.' He waved an elegant arm around his huge warehouse apartment. 'Do you think this place comes so cheap that a little extra in the spondulicks department wouldn't be welcome? But even if I'd been tempted, I couldn't. Warned off, wasn't I? Just after I posted that last letter. As if you didn't know.'

Alarmed by Nigel's admission, he was deaf to the final sentence. 'Warned off? Who by?' he demanded. *God*, thought Rafferty, *don't tell me there's yet another person in the know on this business. How many more are there?*

'Don't come the innocent with me, Joe,' Nigel scoffed. 'We both know who did the warning-off.'

'Humour me.'

'Your dear mama, of course. I might have known you'd go running to her with your little sob story. There's a woman who has no crisis of conscience when it comes to getting in the first low blow, I can tell you. She came here with some long-haired lovely in tow. The pair of them actually *threatened* me.'

Rafferty bit down hard as another grin made a bid for freedom. He had little difficulty in concluding the identity of the 'long-haired lovely'. Abra, of course. Nigel had

285

never met her – which, given Nigel's indiscriminate amorality where the female of the species was concerned – was something Rafferty had taken pains to ensure.

What more natural than that Abra should have confided in Ma after she'd found the blackmail letter that had dropped from his pocket? She'd obviously had more confidence in Ma's ability to get to the bottom of the problem and find the solution than she had in his. She'd been right too, because clearly Ma's superior detection skills had hit on Nigel as a potential blackmailer before he had managed to come to the same conclusion. And *he'd* had the last letter as an added pointer.

Not only that, by Nigel's own admission Ma had sufficient on his cousin to actually threaten him should he take the action his letters implied to the ultimate conclusion.

'So which of *your* sordid little secrets did Ma find useful as a blackmail stopper?' Rafferty asked.

'Never you mind. It's enough that your mother knows. With a bit of luck she'll take the knowledge – and the evidence – to the grave with her.'

Rafferty couldn't resist saying, 'I wouldn't bet on it.'

From his suddenly down-turned lips, it seemed this was also Nigel's belated conclusion. For he nodded and said, 'No. Not a woman to lose track of the important things in life, Kitty Rafferty.' He couldn't help but add the taunt: 'And who knows what sort of pickle her little soldier's going to get himself in next that needs some back-up evidence of the incriminating sort to get him out of hock?'

A little while later, after he and his cousin had exchanged a few more pleasantries, Rafferty left, confident that his ma's blackmail stopper, whatever it was, had halted his cousin's fun in its tracks.

It was fortunate for him that his ma had something on his cousin. Because if it wasn't for that, he wouldn't have held out much hope. The man was an estate agent, for God's sake. And, much as he might refute the possibility, Nigel was unlikely to have continued to deny himself the lure of easy money for much longer without Ma's timely intervention.

And while, after what he'd put him through, Rafferty might like the idea of one of Nigel's weirder new lady friends inflicting some serious damage on his cousin, he didn't allow himself to dwell on the possibility for too long. After all, he knew from bitter experience that it wasn't wise to wish for things. You might just get them.

And the last thing he wanted was Nigel demanding the police provide him with protection from one of his more sadistic S and M ladies. If he did, in spite of Ma and Abra's valiant efforts on his behalf, the whole April business might yet come out.

*No*, Rafferty counselled himself. *Keep your mouth shut, your wishes firmly in check and everything crossed. You know it makes sense.* Besides, with a bit of luck, Nigel would soon tire naturally of any inclination to indulge in such vindictive games.

This, thankfully, wasn't an impossible hope. Nigel's enthusiasms – apart from the continuing ones for more swank and lots more money – were rarely long-lived. He was inclined to lethargy to the extent that, if a woman or a property deal demanded too much effort, Nigel wasn't inclined to put in the hours to win either. It was one of the reasons his income always failed to match or exceed his expenditure.

Nigel would always prefer an easy ride and easier money. *Let the wage slaves break their backs while he reaped the rewards* had always been Nigel's philosophy, inasmuch as he had a philosophy at all.

Abra put the light on as Rafferty, trying and failing to creep into bed in the dark and not disturb her, stumbled over a bedroom chair that had moved its position since that morning. He fell to the floor with a crash and a string of curses.

Dragged from a deep sleep, Abra stared groggily at him, before she fell back against her pillows with a sigh. 'How did I know it was you?'

'Rather than one of your other lovers, you mean? Sorry. I did try to be quiet. But how was I to know you'd decide to move the bedroom furniture around while I was at work?'

'I had a sudden urge.'

'Another one? What a woman you are for urges. I was round at Nigel's earlier,' he explained.

'Ah.'

'Ah indeed.'

'Your mother and I just put our *pretty little heads* together like the sensible women we are. You shouldn't complain when your womenfolk get your little problems sorted, Joe. At least it means you can get on with solving your murder. How's it going anyway?'

'One step forward and two steps back would about cover it.'

'That good, huh?'

Rafferty stripped off his clothes and fell into bed, too exhausted to even hang his suit up, something he had resolved to do after Abra found the first blackmail letter that fell from his carelessly discarded jacket.

'If I'm ever to solve this blasted murder, I must get some sleep,' he muttered as he turned the light out again and aimed a kiss at Abra's cheek. 'Night, sweetheart. Pleasant dreams.'

It took him a while to enter the Land of Nod. His mind roved over his various experiences during the investigation, and he smiled into the darkness as he remembered Abra's reaction when he had confided that, much to his surprise, he had begun to enjoy the peace of the cloister.

'God, Joe,' she had said, 'Don't tell me you're getting the call!'

Rafferty had smiled and replied, 'No. I doubt there's a monastery in the country who'd have me. I'm too fond of my vices and have no desire to even try to wrestle with any of them.'

Abra had stared at him, unconvinced. 'Vices or not, I think that place has affected you more than you know. I think you've got God.'

'God forbid!' But although he chose to joke and rebut her claim, Rafferty was beginning to wonder if she mightn't be right.

After all, he'd even let Nigel off without a roasting. Though, of course, that might be less because he'd become a Holy Joe than because of self-preservation. Rafferty had been surprised that Nigel admitted the truth so easily. But then he hadn't reckoned on Ma and Abra issuing a counter-threat. And, as his ma would be sure to tell him when she finally got round to boasting of her intercession, the Nigels of this world were prone to leave themselves wide open to retaliatory blackmail. Certainly, judging from Nigel's reaction, he had had his strings pulled so comprehensively that Ma had tied him up in knots.

With this cheering thought to comfort him, Rafferty finally dropped off to sleep. But, in spite of the resolution of his blackmail dilemma, his sleep was restless. He tossed and turned, and found himself dreaming of corpses and killers and nuns coming at him with incense burners. A nun with no face was the other side of an open grave, swinging one such burner at him, violence writ large on her wiped-smooth countenance. But rather than incense, what came wafting over to him across the grave was something that smelt very noxious indeed.

He tried not to breathe, but as his legs seemed to have turned to an uncooperative jelly, he was unable to hold his breath for long enough to get away. Not that he could get away anyway, because the half-decayed body in the grave had a fleshless hand fast around his ankle. The broken watch on the wrist slid down the dead man's arm each time Rafferty tried to tug his leg free, and then flew up the arm again when the skeleton pulled him back.

Rafferty made one final heave in this macabre tug-of-war and managed to release himself from the cadaver's grasp. He fell backwards and landed heavily on the ground, such was the force needed to break the deadly grip. The broken watch flew off the skeletal wrist and hit Rafferty on the cheek with some force as a voice shouted in his left ear, 'Will you stop all that heaving about?'

His cheek was hit a second time. Startled, Rafferty opened his eyes and sat up.

'What's happening?' he demanded gruffly.

'You're keeping me awake, that's what's happening,' Abra complained crossly. 'Do you know what time it is?'

'Time?' Still groggy, Rafferty turned his head and gazed at the illuminated clock radio on the bedside table. 'It's two o'clock,' he replied, as if he thought Abra really did want to know what time it was.

'Exactly. What's the matter with you, anyway? Not been practising incense-swinging in your sleep to get ready for life as a Holy Joe, have you?'

'No. I was trying to get out of the clutches of a corpse.'

'Ugh.' Abra shuddered, then suggested, 'Put him back in his coffin, nail it down, and let's get some sleep.'

'Aye, aye, my little ghoul. Should I dance on his grave while I'm about it?'

'With *your* dancing? Certainly not. Hire a professional if you must. Now, will you please shut up or I'll tie you to the bed in the spare room.'

Faced with such a threat, Rafferty lay quiet. His mind wandered back to the idea about the murder that had come to him before his second visit to Nigel. After wrestling with the idea for ten minutes, his eyelids flew open and he sat up again. That was odd, he thought. How did—?

Beside him, he heard Abra give a long-suffering sigh.

'Now what?' she demanded as she thumped him. 'I was nearly nodding off. For the *fourth* time tonight.'

'Sorry. It's nothing, sweetheart. Go back to sleep. I promise I won't disturb you again.'

And he didn't. He lay very still, listening to Abra's breathing and watching the play of the lights of passing cars reflected on the ceiling. But if his body was as still as the grave, his mind was anything but and was filled with thoughts as numerous as the insect life that colonized freshly dead flesh.

By the time dawn's rosy fingers began to clutch at the room's shadows, Rafferty was congratulating himself on the selfless sacrifice of a night's sleep. He thought it had been worth it. Because his frightening dream had helped him make a connection he had failed to see before.

Of course, it might yet turn out to be nothing. He'd find out if his conclusion was right later today. But if it was, and if the other suspicions that had started to edge into his mind proved correct, he believed it meant he might have found the murderer. Rafferty believed his bad dream had provided him with answers. And, to a point, it had. The trouble was the answers raised even more questions, none of them with any answers. None that his sleep-deprived brain was able to find, anyway.

Morosely, he stumped off to work. It was an unseasonably hot day for October, too, which didn't improve his temper. The car felt like the gaping maw of Hell itself. The plastic seat stuck his shirt to his back, the steering wheel singed his fingers, and the glare through the windscreen seemed likely to seer his eyeballs. Imagine this for all eternity, he thought, appalled. Maybe, he thought, maybe now's the time to become un-lapsed.

Just then, the vagaries of the British weather, which had chosen to turn as sultry as the Masai Mara, made a second connection click in his brain. At first, he dismissed it. It seemed too bizarre. But once he had reached his sticky office and sweated some more, he began to think it through. And he realized he might, this time, actually have some answers. And to think at least one of them had been staring him plainly in the face from the first day...

However bizarre his theories, they all fitted together with a logical neatness that was entirely foreign to him. This fact gave him pause for thought as well as reason to doubt his conclusions. For Llewellyn was right when he claimed that his inspector's theories *never* panned out so neatly, with every 'i' dotted and every 't' crossed.

The never-before-experienced actuality of

several of his theories coming together into a perfect whole unsettled him. He wasn't sure he dare trust his own conclusions.

Later that same day, as he had intended to do anyway, he sought out Sister Rita and Sister Perpetua and questioned them. Their answers proved that at least one of his conclusions was correct.

Even Llewellyn was impressed that Rafferty had made a connection that he had himself missed. And given his sergeant's logical, intellectual mind-set, Rafferty decided not to reveal that he had found the answer not through logical thought and reasoning, but via a dream. He could only presume that, with the blackmailing distraction dealt with, his mind had relaxed sufficiently to recognize something he should have seen much earlier in the case. But at least he *had* finally seen it. And now he found that the idea that had occurred to him earlier, when put together with other aspects of the case, made shocking but believable sense.

The only drawback was that he wouldn't be his ma's blue-eyed boy any more. But every silver lining has a cloud. He just hoped this one didn't decide to rain on his parade after all.

# Eighteen

Rafferty was still wary of his new insights into the investigation, a wariness increased by the fact that his theories and the resolution towards which they pointed him were so perfectly formed, with each aspect dovetailed as if by a master craftsman, that he assumed he must have missed something vital. So worried was he by this suspicion that he decided to sleep on his theories for another night before he risked either confiding them to Llewellyn or taking any further action.

It was a decision he was to regret in the clearer light of mid-morning.

Rafferty did a double-take when he saw Llewellyn enter the police station. He recalled his cousin Nigel – he of the designer suits and estate agent spiel and his talk of 'mirror imaging' – just before the Made in Heaven nightmare had begun. Because, with his gleaming white shirt, black tie and a suit that had a midnight sheen to it, Llewellyn looked as if the idea of mirror-imaging was something he had also taken to heart.

'You thinking of joining the sisters and

taking your vows after all, Daff?' Rafferty enquired. 'Or are you just hoping to blend in and earwig on what the sisters have to say amongst themselves about our cadaver and how he found his way into their holy soil?'

'Joining the sisters?' Llewellyn repeated, with a face as straight as a ruler. 'Hardly. I know you think my preference for smart suits and fastidious attention to personal grooming are both somewhat suspect, especially in a policeman, but even you can't have failed to notice that I'm not only the wrong gender, but that I'm also a married man.'

Llewellyn paused before adding, in rather more intimate family tones, 'I know you indulged a little more than was wise at my wedding, but surely you can't have forgotten the small fact of my nuptials? You *were* my best man when I married your cousin Maureen.'

Rafferty smiled. But it was a smile that held very little humour. 'So I was,' he acknowledged. 'And if you're not thinking of taking your vows, would you like to tell me why you're done up like the spectre at the feast? Did you dream I died in the night? Are you thinking of returning the best man compliment at one of *my* major rites of passage, and practising being chief usher at my funeral?'

'No funeral. But when I awoke this morning, something told me this was the

297

most suitable garb.'

'Something *told* you?' Rafferty, wanting to check thoroughly for any flaws in the rest of his conclusions before he confided them to Llewellyn, had told him no more than the bare bones of his theories. At least, he *thought* it was only the bare bones he had confided. So why was Llewellyn dressed as if he too believed he was in at the kill? Surely he couldn't have confided in his sergeant and promptly forgotten all about it?

But with a mind so pulverized by religion and blackmail, he suspected anything was possible.

Rafferty gave Llewellyn a hesitant smile and decided he needed to put himself out of his misery. If his intellectual sergeant was about to launch into one of his logical criticisms of his theories he'd rather he got it over with. So he asked, 'Hearing voices now, are we? It'll be visions next, and then God help us!'

He didn't think he could bear it if, along with all his other virtues, his sergeant got religion too.

'I really don't know *what* spoke to me. But,' Llewellyn quietly observed, 'you look pretty sombrely suited yourself.'

Llewellyn's observation was spot on, because Rafferty too had chosen to dress in more solemn garb than usual that morning. He had even put aside his usual preference for gaudy ties. But that was, as he told his clever sergeant, because he too had been hearing voices.

Or rather *a* voice. His own. Providing him with a perfect solution to the crime. This perfection had made him doubt himself and his conclusions the previous night. But now, growing more confident as daylight banished his doubts, he felt certain that even Llewellyn wouldn't be able to find fault with the rest of his theories and the conclusion they had led him to.

As they made their way to the car park, he quietly explained his thoughts to Llewellyn: not only had the late elder sister of Sister Clare left a substantial legacy to the dead man, Peter Bodham, but, he suspected, she had also written to Bodham inviting him to come to see her just before she died. Rafferty suspected, too, that she then told him the rest of what her letter had presumably merely hinted at: that his mother, his *real* mother, hadn't been the late Sister Clare at all.

'Or rather,' Rafferty, still getting to grips with his conclusions, corrected himself, 'that she *had* been Sister Clare, but the original one – Mother Catherine, as she now claims to be – rather than the woman who's been dead these thirty years.'

He turned out of the rear Bacon Lane entrance to the police car park and took a right on to Abbots' Walk. 'My guess is that the woman we know as Mother Catherine adopted the dead nun's identity after the massacre in Africa. From the papers he left in his home, it seems Peter Bodham, her son, took the opportunity afforded him under the 1975 Adoptions Act to trace his natural mother when he reached the age of eighteen.

'Mother Catherine, as she now is, also took an opportunity. I believe she took the opportunity afforded her by the massacre in Africa to change identities with the dead nun, the *real* Sister Catherine. It was her intention to ensure that, should the illegitimate son she had borne as a young girl make use of the new Act to attempt to trace her, thereby revealing her long-concealed shame to the world, all he would discover was that she had died.'

Anticipating some objection to his theories, Rafferty was surprised when Llewellyn said nothing. His sergeant's silence encouraged him to continue more confidently, albeit with a shudder as they passed the stark ruins of the ancient priory before crossing the river at Tiffey Reach.

'As it turned out, she failed. Annemarie Jones' elder sister Sophia Ansell, although aware – unlike Rosalind Wilson – of the secretly borne baby, of their sister Annemarie's change of identity, *and* of the fact that she was still very much alive, found herself unable to keep up the deception on her deathbed.

'I presume Peter Bodham, not believing his

aunt's denials that Annemarie was his mother, had continued to write to her in the hope that she would acknowledge him as family, so she would have known his latest address when she finally decided to tell him the truth.

'You remember Mr Mitchelson said that his lodger cancelled his trip to Africa in September shortly after receiving a rare, handwritten letter?'

Llewellyn nodded.

'I think that letter was from Sophia Ansell. Peter Bodham's aunt. The aunt who was finally prepared to acknowledge the relationship.'

Rafferty slowed and changed gears as they approached the bridge over the river. 'Mr Mitchelson said Bodham seemed excited, in a way that he hadn't been by the thought of the trip to Africa. Understandable, I suppose, if you consider that he knew that all he would find in Africa was the place where the natural mother he had tried to trace had supposedly been killed so long ago.

'I think Sophia's letter hinted that his mother hadn't died. It would certainly explain why a lonely, solitary man with no family, no friends, would appear excited. He thought he was about to find his long lost mother.

'Instead, what he found was death. Previously, when he had learned of his "mother's" violent death at the hands of a mob in Africa, he believed that his quest to find her had ended before it had begun.

'Like the real Sister Clare, his natural mother, apparently did, he too disappeared into the grave. And, as we have since learned, Peter Bodham never took up his aunt's bequest.'

Again Llewellyn raised no objection to his theory. Instead, he voiced a question. 'So what put you on to her?'

'The dead man's watch. You might recall that Mother Catherine mentioned that, since it was expensive looking, it might help us to learn his identity.'

Llewellyn nodded.

Rafferty felt himself easing his foot off the accelerator as they got closer to the convent. 'I thought nothing of it at the time. But later – ' *Much* later, he reminded himself – 'I realized something wasn't quite right. I couldn't put my finger on it. But it finally hit me that Mother Catherine hadn't actually *seen* the body. She sent Sister Perpetua back to the grave with Sister Rita to act as another witness with the excuse that she had to tend to the hysterical Cecile.

'Of course, it was possible that Sister Rita or Sister Perpetua had mentioned the watch to the Prioress. But these nuns don't go in for idle gossip like other women. Anyway, I questioned both of them yesterday and both confirmed they hadn't mentioned the watch or even that the dead man was naked. Do you not remember her calling the other sisters away from his "nakedness"?'

Again Llewellyn nodded.

'And given the distance between the grave and where Mother Catherine was standing, with her poor eyesight – which her optician confirmed for me when I contacted him first thing – she could never have seen either the watch or that he was naked. Her knowledge was a pointer to guilt.'

'But by all accounts she's an intelligent woman, an accomplished woman. How could she have so foolishly given herself away?'

Recognizing that Llewellyn's words indicated his acceptance of his theories, Rafferty sighed as he slowed again to cross Northway, though whether his sigh was of relief or melancholy, he wasn't sure. 'Ah. There's the rub, Dafyd. You see, I think she *wanted* to be found out. I imagine that's why she didn't remove Bodham's expensive watch. She must have been in a very confused and distraught state of mind.'

'Poor lady.'

For a moment, Rafferty was inclined to rebuke Llewellyn. But then he nodded and realized that Llewellyn had spoken nothing but the truth. Annemarie Jones had made one mistake in her youth. But it was a mistake which the *mores* of the time regarded as a shameful sin. A mistake which, if it had occurred a generation or two later, would no longer be considered sinful or even shameful. Ironically, the sin which had caused both her and her son to pay such a heavy price would nowadays be rewarded with taxpayer's money and a council flat. Annemarie Jones' one mistake chased her through her life and brought her son to his grave. And now, with the walls of the convent appearing in the middle distance, Rafferty found himself echoing Llewellyn's 'Poor lady.'

Quietly, before they reached the convent, Rafferty explained the rest. 'Although she was certainly a professed nun – I rang the diocesan office first thing and they checked back with her original convent – I suspect our Prioress never actually had a vocation to be one. I think, for her, it was indeed a form of running away.'

'And taking on Sister Catherine's identity after the massacre in Africa was another form of running away?'

'Exactly. Think, man. Think when it was that the massacre happened, and what legislation was brought in around that time. The Adoptions Act, which allows adopted children, once they reach eighteen, to attempt to trace their natural parents. Peter Bodham was born in 1957, when Annemarie was almost eighteen. That meant he would turn eighteen the year the Adoptions Act became law. I think she must have been terrified that her shameful secret could become common knowledge. And I think that fear caused her to return to that impetuous behaviour her old neighbour told us was Annemarie's as a young girl. I think she acted first and thought later.'

'You mean, when she survived the massacre in Africa earlier that year, she saw it as an opportunity to make a far more telling escape from the shame her son represented, and become somebody else entirely?'

Rafferty nodded. 'How could Peter Bodham possibly trace her then, she must have thought, Adoption Act or no Adoption Act? And, to make doubly sure, and to further lessen the possibility that her change of identity might be questioned, I suspect she deliberately burned her own face and hands. I imagine, if we check back, we'll find that both nuns were of a similar height and build.'

'But what about their voices? She couldn't have adopted the voice of the dead nun. That alone would surely have revealed her deception.'

'True. I even recall noting, right at the beginning of the case, that she had no trace of a Yorkshire accent. But, as with the watch, I gave that no more thought till much later. I imagine that, right after the massacre, she pretended the trauma of it made her unable to speak. And then, while she was recuperating in hospital, she wrote to the Bishop asking permission to change to an enclosed order, ensuring she could avoid the nuns in the community that did know her. As we know, her request was granted. She must have believed that even the hierarchy of the Catholic Church would feel so dreadfully sorry for her after all she'd been through that they wouldn't refuse her request. So Annemarie was able to make her third and final escape – into an enclosed order where none of the sisters would be in a position to say she wasn't who she claimed to be.'

Rafferty pulled into the side of the road just past the convent. But, although he levered up the hand brake and turned off the engine, he made no attempt to get out of the car.

'Strangely, the danger came from the very son she thought she had escaped for ever. The son she must have believed was no longer a threat to her. Because, on learning the truth about his natural mother from his aunt after so many years, and realizing how his own mother had lied to him, he must have been traumatized. Not only by the second rejection of him when he came to see her at the convent, but by the fact that she had compounded that rejection with a dreadful deceit.

'He must also have been furious at the realization that he, her only natural child, had never had the opportunity to use the word "Mother" yet it was one freely used by the rest of the convent community.

'Bodham, now in his middle years, never

married, childless and without anyone in the world to call his own, furious and upset, must have contacted Mother Catherine demanding to see her a second time. Forewarned by a phone call from her dying sister of the reason for Bodham's insistence – that her thirty-year-old lies were about to come out – Mother Catherine probably specified a time for his visit while the other nuns were attending one of the more lengthy daily Offices. She must have intercepted him at the gate and let him secretly into the grounds to speak to him privately.'

Rafferty imagined she had hoped to dissuade her son from claiming her as his mother as it would reveal her double deceit to the world: that she wasn't pure in mind, body *or* spirit. And that she had, in fact, adopted for her own ends the identity of a holy nun who had died in harrowing circumstances in order to make her illegitimate son think she was dead.

But, as he quietly explained, her hastily put-together attempt at deception ultimately failed and her son knew all. He was a threat to her reputation, her holy life and her newly elevated position as Mother Superior. With turmoil threatening everything she had made of her life since her disastrous early pregnancy, she had reverted to the impetuous act-first-think-later person she had been in her youth.

'I think she must have distracted him in

some way, got him to turn away from her and, before she even knew what she was going to do, her son lay dead at her feet, his skull caved in by a handily placed rock.'

Rafferty knew he could no longer put off the dénouement. He tapped Llewellyn on the shoulder, said, 'Come on,' and climbed out of the car. They walked silently, side by side, to the main door of the convent. Sister Ursula must have seen their faces through the grille, for she hobbled towards them, more bent over than ever, and opened the door to their summons. She gazed sadly at them, but didn't speak.

It was the first indication that Rafferty's earlier feeling of unease was about to be validated. He glanced at Llewellyn. Both instinctively quickened their pace as they approached the corridor that led to Mother Catherine's office. As they turned the corner, Llewellyn nodded towards the office door and the crowd of brown-garbed nuns gathered at its entrance.

It was then that Rafferty acknowledged that his foreboding had been correct. He could only surmise that, after he had questioned them again, Sisters Rita and Perpetua had been sufficiently intrigued to repeat the question he had put to them to the rest of their community.

Certainly, to judge from the unseemly and unaccustomed noise pouring forth from the gaggle of nuns clustered outside Mother

Catherine's office as they approached, the 'something' that both Llewellyn's 'voices' and Rafferty's had anticipated had come to pass.

As was confirmed only a few seconds later. The letter clutched in Sister Rita's rough gardener's hand was pretty explicit. It had been addressed jointly to her and to Rafferty.

A second letter, addressed to the Bishop of the Diocese, was clutched in Sister Rita's other hand. She hadn't attempted to open that one. Sister Rita, not being one to stand on ceremony, hadn't waited to share the contents of the first letter with Rafferty. But when she saw him, Llewellyn hovering at his elbow, she handed it over without a word.

And as Rafferty swiftly scanned the hand-written sheets, with Llewellyn peering over his shoulder, he knew that his conclusions had been correct in every aspect.

*It's a terrible, grievous thing, to lose a child.* Rafferty's speed-reading slowed at this point.

And I was distraught at having to give up my baby. But times were so very different when I gave birth to my son. It was a shameful thing to bear an illegitimate child back in the fifties.

But, even more shaming than bearing an illegitimate child, is for that mother to know that she is responsible for her own child's death.

Whatever the times or the mores of society, that will always be an unforgivable act. I have begged God's forgiveness. Maybe, with his infinite mercy, He will forgive me. But I cannot forgive myself. I deserve eternal damnation. And I know the only way I can be certain of such a totally deserved punishment is to commit the sin of self murder. In this way, I hope to spend all eternity in atonement for my wickedness.

Rafferty gazed for a few moments through the open office door at Mother Catherine's body slumped across her desk, the remains of an empty bottle of powerful over-the-counter painkillers strewn on its surface.

She had removed her veil and habit and was wearing ordinary clothes. Presumably, as she faced death, she had been willing to acknowledge that she no longer had the right to wear the robes of a religious.

'Check for a pulse, Dafyd,' Rafferty instructed. Rafferty somehow knew this was pointless, but they had a routine to go through.

The pointlessness proved thirty seconds later when Llewellyn looked across and shook his head, he said, 'OK, let's get the scene locked up.' Rafferty turned to address the sisters, whose expressions exhibited varying degrees of shock. Even now, he wasn't sure whether their shock was caused by the deceit practised on them by the

'Mother' Catherine they had all looked up to so much, or by the unbearable thought that she would spend all eternity paying for her sins.

Strangely, or perhaps not so strangely, he found himself taking refuge in religion. And as he again adopted the role of priest to the sisters, he found not one of them questioned his authority.

'Sisters,' he said. 'May I suggest you take yourselves to the chapel to pray for her immortal soul?'

Quietly, led by Sister Rita, they trooped up the corridor, their sandals slap-slapping in a sadly muted harmony on the stone slabs of the floor.

# Nineteen

'I rather suspect she *wanted* to be caught,' Rafferty commented again several hours later as, the body of the Prioress having been removed to the mortuary, he and Llewellyn packed up the gear in their borrowed office at the convent before heading back to the station.

'Why else leave a clearly pricey watch on the dead man's wrist? Why mention it when she must have suspected I would find out she hadn't seen it? And why put him in a grave so shallow that it was inevitable some animal would disturb it? Why duck out of accompanying Sister Rita to the grave herself to confirm the facts when she could have deputed any of the older nuns to the task of calming the hysterical novice, Cecile? And why was the missing spare set of keys to the convent not replaced?

'If they had been taken by either Father Kelly or Dr Peterson, both men had ample opportunity to replace them. The fact that they remained missing from their hook so long after the murder encouraged me to speculate on the reason why. I could only

312

conclude that the killer wanted to be caught and was providing me with clues to their identity.

'And who more likely than a guilt-ridden religious to act in such a way? Now you know why I felt certain, down to my lapsed Catholic bones, that one of the sisters was the killer.' Rafferty was careful to keep to himself the fact that he had only found answers to all these questions long after his religious prejudices had already prompted him to latch on to one – any – of the sisters as the guilty party.

But at least this murder and the woman who had inflicted such a violent death had cured him of his brief flirtation with the Catholic faith. Never again would he allow it to tempt him back to the fold. He still hadn't told Llewellyn of his near-conversion and he didn't do so now. As Abra had advised him in what seemed a lifetime ago, there were some things a man should keep close to his chest.

'You want to know what I think, Dafyd?' Rafferty didn't wait for the Welshman's response, aware, even after his latest successful search for the truth, that his intellectual sergeant didn't always find his thoughts either impressive or admirable. 'I think that what she had done truly horrified her. How could it not? Her mind must have been in turmoil when her dying sister warned her that her son would be in contact and would turn up at the convent again. And that this time, he would not swallow the lies she had previously told him.

'If she did have some sort of religious vocation, which I have my doubts about, she must have suffered a crisis of faith. How could she not, after what she had done? And then there was her fear of exposure and the revelation of the many deceptions necessary after her hasty ill-thought-through adoption of Sister Catherine's identity.

'I suppose, too, before the murder, she had been worried about losing the position of Mother, which with the expected death of Mother Joseph had seemed as guaranteed as anything can be in this life.

'But after she killed her son, I think all these things were eclipsed by her distress at what she had done. I imagine, when her son raged at her for her dreadful deceit, she must have suffered some kind of brainstorm. After all, she had lived a lie for years. It must have been a dreadful strain. I think it was that final stress of her son's bitter accusations that made her forget her God, pick up that heavy rock, and bring it crashing down on his head.

'Almost as soon as she had hit him she must have been overcome by horror at what she had done, not able to believe that the man lying at her feet – her only child – was dead, and that she was responsible. Worse, that her killing of her own child was a sin that no amount of praying could ever put right.

'Hardly surprising that she should feel that taking her own life, although yet another sin under her Catholic faith, was the only suitable retribution. That old "eye for an eye" syndrome. She had taken another's life, so she had to sacrifice her own. It just took her a while to build up to it.'

'The Catholic faith is a harsh one, is it not?' Llewellyn observed quietly as they carried their final boxed-up statement forms and other police paraphernalia to the car and put them in the boot. 'With a harsh, demanding, unforgiving doctrine.'

Llewellyn clutched the handle to the vehicle's boot, but before he closed it, he told Rafferty, 'I have some insight now into why you have chosen to remain lapsed all these years.'

'Tell me about it,' Rafferty muttered. It wasn't an invitation.

Nor was it one that Llewellyn took up. Instead, he changed tack entirely.

'I've been meaning to ask you about those blackmail letters you received. Did you manage to find some resolution there, too?'

'Don't worry about them, Dafyd. They've been squared away. The letters and the blackmailer both.'

It was the second resolution. Fortunately, it was one that Llewellyn chose not to question him about further.

It occurred to Rafferty as they climbed in the car that a man would be a fool indeed not to also square away his and Abra's futures. He didn't want to risk her being enticed away by a man who was slightly less of a fool than himself.

But although he acknowledged that his ma had saved his bacon, his sanity and his career, he still found the thought of having *two* Mrs Raffertys in his life a traumatic one. Certainly, it was a decision not to be taken lightly.

But then again, he acknowledged as he turned the car and headed for the police station, and even though marriage lines had never stopped anyone straying, he wasn't a man to shy away from a challenge.